Praise for Sally Kilpatrick's Previous Novels

"Fans of Southern contemporary romance will be charmed."
—*Publishers Weekly*

"Witty, warm, and as complex and heart-wrenching
as only love and family can be."
—*Heroes and Heartbreakers*

"Readers will both laugh and cry as Declan and Presley face
loss, learn life lessons from ghosts, and realize life is much
easier to handle with someone by your side."
—*Booklist*

"Pleasantly engaging."
—*Library Journal*

"In short, this one is pretty much as close to perfect as
a reading experience can get."
—*Nashville Book Worm*

"A cute story with just the right blend of romance, sadness,
and humor. If you enjoy your books with quirky characters and
lots of heart . . . you should give this one a try."
—*Harlequin Junkie*

"Sweet, funny and charming . . . Absolutely lovely."
—*Bookish Devices*

"Kilpatrick mixes loss and devastation with hope and a little bit
of Southern charm. She will leave the reader laughing through
tears. This is an incred̶i̶b̶l̶e̶ ̶d̶e̶b̶u̶t̶ ̶f̶r̶o̶m̶ ̶a̶ ̶p̶r̶o̶mising storyteller."

D1004704

Books by Sally Kilpatrick

The Happy Hour Choir

Bittersweet Creek

Better Get to Livin'

Bless Her Heart

Orange Blossom Special (novella)

Published by Kensington Publishing Corp.

bless
her heart

sally kilpatrick

Kensington Books
www.kensingtonbooks.com

This book is a work of fiction. Names, characters, places, and incidents either are products of the author's imagination or are used fictitiously. Any resemblance to actual persons, living or dead, events, or locales is entirely coincidental.

KENSINGTON BOOKS are published by

Kensington Publishing Corp.
119 West 40th Street
New York, NY 10018

Copyright © 2017 by Sally Kilpatrick

All rights reserved. No part of this book may be reproduced in any form or by any means without the prior written consent of the Publisher, excepting brief quotes used in reviews.

All Kensington titles, imprints, and distributed lines are available at special quantity discounts for bulk purchases for sales promotion, premiums, fund-raising, educational, or institutional use.

Special book excerpts or customized printings can also be created to fit specific needs. For details, write or phone the office of the Kensington Sales Manager: Kensington Publishing Corp., 119 West 40th Street, New York, NY 10018. Attn. Sales Department. Phone: 1-800-221-2647.

Kensington and the K logo Reg. U.S. Pat. & TM Off.

eISBN-13: 978-1-4967-1074-1
eISBN-10: 1-4967-1074-6
First Kensington Electronic Edition: November 2017

ISBN-13: 978-1-4967-1073-4
ISBN-10: 1-4967-1073-8
First Kensington Trade Paperback Printing: November 2017

10 9 8 7 6 5 4 3 2 1

Printed in the United States of America

For Tanya, who has never once blessed my heart

acknowledgments

As always, thank you to my folks at Kensington: Editor Wendy McCurdy, copy editor Tracy Wilson, Paula, Lulu, my cover folks, and anyone else I may be missing. I love you guys and thank you for letting me be a part of the Kensington family.

Elisabeth, you answer all of my silly questions about Baptists because I can't remember all of my adventures with Julie and Polly. I gave John your and Colin's last name because y'all are a few of *my* favorite Baptists. It's a privilege to be your friend.

Tina Whittle, I couldn't have done the Tarot scene without you—thanks for your invaluable expertise. I regret to inform you that Julia kinda wants her own story, so I may be asking for more assistance in the future.

These folks helped me on all sorts of hypothetical situations: Kim Knight (also my Spiritual Advisor), Clayton Matthews, Sonia Labovitz, La-Tessa Montgomery, Julie Cothren Hudson, and Vicki Stout. Thank you so, so much for sharing your expertise and, in some cases, some really personal stories.

Shout-out to the Chamber Choir, my most dedicated, who answered questions, suggested recipes and names, and, in general, made the writing process a whole heckuva lot more fun.

Thanks to Jenni and Anna for taking a gander at my first attempts of this novel. Immense gratitude to Tanya Michaels who read the whole damn thing and didn't pull any punches when it came to making the story better. Finally, thanks to my mom— she reads all of my work and always makes it better.

This is my fourth novel, and I am still petrified that I will forget to name someone in the acknowledgments. Just know that I appreciate you but suffer from a very scattered brain. Also, any errors you find are mine and mine alone. Feel free to bless my heart.

Thanks to The Hobbit and Her Majesty for putting up with Mommy's crazy job, especially those last few weeks when things get frantic. Ryan, I couldn't do it without you. I love you, and I thank you for making life so awesome that I have to imagine all of the strife required for a proper conflict.

chapter 1

There were only three words in the English language that I hated with all of my being: *bless, your,* and *heart*—specifically in that order. One look through the glass door that led to Love Ministries, and I knew those words were winging my way. Miss Georgette wrestled with the door, pushing when she ought to pull. She came to the little brick building twice every week, but she still had trouble with that door. Today, the older lady wore a knit pantsuit with a cat appliqué on the front. Siamese cat earrings dangled from her ears.

"Why, Posey. Are you *still* working as a receptionist?"

"Yes, ma'am." Just as I had for the past five years.

"Well."

Don't say it. Don't say it. Don't say it.

"Bless your heart."

My entire body relaxed. I'd braced myself for her words as one would brace for bullets when standing in front of a firing squad. She'd said them. It was done.

"You know, I still say you would've made a right fine elementary teacher. I was so disappointed when you didn't take a job after you graduated."

"I am sorry about that," I said. Mainly sorry for myself, but sorry nonetheless.

She continued speaking as if she hadn't heard me. "You were one of my absolute best students when I taught elementary education at the college. I still have some of the games and projects that you made."

Miss Georgette reminded me of this every time she came through the doors. While flattered that she still had some of my school projects, I wished she wouldn't remind me that my life hadn't exactly gone as planned. At thirty-two years old, I was supposed to be almost ten years into a teaching career with at least two children. I had d) none of the above.

"I heard from Lisa who heard from Jackie that Heather Mickens has been put on bed rest so they have a supply position open in first grade. You should apply and see how you like it."

Here was a first: Miss Georgette actually pushing me in the direction of a teaching job instead of bemoaning the fact I didn't have one. "Oh, I don't know. I bet I've forgotten everything I once knew. The standards have probably changed, and—"

"Pish-posh. First graders are the same as they ever were." Miss Georgette waved away my concerns, and the Siamese cats hanging from her ears dangled in time to the motion. "You should apply for the job and at least see what happens. Ellery Elementary won't find a more upstanding lady than you."

I looked down at my floral dress with the lace collar. I spent a lot of time cultivating my image as "upstanding" because everyone knew my mother had a bit of a past. Sure, I might dress like an extra on *The Golden Girls* now, but I was the daughter of the legendary hippie girl who ran away from home and came back pregnant. I was the baby she bore, a girl who'd never known a father. Never mind the fact I had nothing to do with my mother's actions. They, of course, were all reasons to bless my heart.

I could still hear the voices, the whispered snatches of conversation from the teachers and professors as I made my way through Ellery Elementary, then Yessum High and finally the local college, always doing my best to be invisible.

Her mama makes her clothes out of hemp instead of getting them at the store.

Well, bless her heart.

No clue who her father is. Vonda over at the Health Department saw the birth certificate and said no father was listed.

That's awful. Bless her heart.

Did you hear her mama's got pregnant again? Still not married.

Mmm-hmm. Bless her heart.

Now she's married that Chad Love. He has to be at least ten years older than she is.

Oh, bless her heart.

They've been married forever now and still no kids. Think something's wrong with one of them?

Probably her. Poor thing, bless her heart.

Miss Georgette waved a beefy hand in front of my face. "Did you hear me, Posey?"

"No, ma'am. I'm sorry. I remembered some things I have to do." I made a show of making notes on my planner then looked up. "What were you saying?"

"I was saying you should apply for the supply position, and that I would be happy to put in a good word for you if you did."

"That's really kind of you, Miss Georgette."

The tips of her ears and the tops of her cheeks turned pink. "It would be nothing. My pleasure, really."

"Well, I appreciate it." Surprisingly, I did. Aside from the constant heart-blessing, Miss Georgette had always been very good to me.

"Don't you forget to turn in that application," she admonished as she started down the hall toward her weekly Bible study.

Unlikely that I would forget. Even more unlikely that I would turn in the application. Chad didn't want me to work outside the home. When we first married, the plan was for me to stay home and be mother to our children. He promised me at least two even though I wanted four. God, however, had other plans. After ten years of trying to get pregnant, I had nothing to show for the effort. We'd been to a few doctors even though Chad wanted to leave everything to God's will. The last doctor told me I would never conceive. I tried to mean it when I prayed "thy will be done," but I couldn't help but add a plea for motherhood. God had changed his mind once or twice, right?

After the doctor's pronouncement, I asked Chad about adoption. He said he didn't feel comfortable having some stranger's baby in his house. That hurt my heart. Then I asked about teaching again, but he always found a way to talk me out of it. Funny that I, the daughter of Ellery's most notorious single mom, would allow a man to talk me out of anything, but we'd left the Baptist Church about two years into our marriage to form a ministry that relied on the principle of men being the head of their respective households. Wives, of course, were to be cherished in addition to being submissive. I had to admit it was quite freeing not to have to make any decisions.

Even so, I chafed at having to wait for his blessing—or God's—to do what I wanted to do.

It can't hurt to look for an application.

I booted up my computer and searched for the Yessum County School System, the online application taunting me. Since I obviously wouldn't be having babies any time soon, I could at least teach them. This receptionist job was supposed to have been temporary. Not enough people came through the door to merit my existence anyway. Sometimes I wondered how Chad kept the doors open, but, as head of the household, he handled all of the finances so I took it on faith that he had everything under control. Submission and obedience, as he was fond of reminding me, were more difficult than his position of authority and responsibility.

Down the hall behind me Chad whistled as he approached. I quickly switched tabs to a document before he could see the application. He didn't like for me to be on the Internet. He said he was afraid I'd stumble upon something impure. To his point, it *was* the Internet.

"Posey, are all of my Bible study members here?" he asked, leaning over my desk with a smile that didn't quite reach his eyes.

"They're all here," I said.

Still he leaned, studying me, so I took a moment to study him. My husband looked more handsome now than he had before: dark hair and brown eyes with crinkles at the edges. Sometimes I wondered how he had ended up with a plain girl like me, but he could talk almost anyone into anything, and I was no exception. He'd sold me on the American dream: nice house and two and a half kids, even joking that he didn't know how we'd make that half. I suggested a dog instead, but he reminded me he was allergic.

Then he'd sold me on being a submissive wife, pointing out that, without a father, my home life had been less than ideal. He was right about that. Granny and Mom had argued. Often they had no extra money to go around. Thanks to Mom's less than disciplined behavior, I'd had my heart blessed more times than I could count. I couldn't argue with him that she would've benefited from the discipline that seemingly eluded her until she'd had her third child.

Chad was all about discipline. If I spent too much on groceries, then he took away some of my pin money to remind me to be more frugal. If I overindulged in sweets and my pants got too tight, he hid the cookies. If I got behind with clerical tasks or domestic chores, then he had me stay late an hour at work or had me get up an hour earlier on Saturday to make up for lost time. Sometimes I muttered under my breath at his "suggestions," but I did have to admit that we stayed on budget, I stayed in my pants, and everything ran smoothly at home and at work. In that way, he'd given me the stability I'd always craved.

At least he'd never actually raised his hand to me even though some of the ministers he communicated with did take the ideas of submissive wives and discipline quite literally.

Well, there was that one time, but I'd made him understand there were two things I wouldn't tolerate: infidelity and being hit. I'd given him one more chance on the second, but there were no extra chances on the first.

"Posey, dear?"

"Yes?"

"You were daydreaming again," he said as he chucked my

chin. "Would you be a dear and go to the Calais Café to get us lunch today?" He slid his glasses back up his nose.

"Of course," I said, "Do we have enough money in the checking account, though?"

"Always thinking, you," he said as he reached for his wallet and took out a couple of twenties. "You know what I like. Be sure to bring back the change, though."

"I'll have it by noon."

He kissed my cheek, then headed down the hall still whistling. How was it possible that he didn't seem to age at all, but I couldn't keep the ravages of time at bay? Today would be another day to skip dessert or anything fatty because my shapewear was cutting into me again. He had that dignified sprinkle of gray at his temple, but my dark brown hair threatened to go salt-and-pepper any day now. He still wore the same pant size as when we got married, but my hips kept spreading.

They looked like childbearing hips. Oh, the irony.

While Chad talked to the old ladies down the hall about Revelation for the umpteenth dozenth time, I created a new email address and then filled out the application to be a supply teacher. It felt sneaky to do so, but Chad insisted that we share an email address, and I wasn't ready to tell him yet. It was worth whatever lecture he might give me to be able to surprise him with something I'd done for the good of our family.

As penance, I determined I would get him dessert even though I wouldn't be having any. Once at the Calais Café, I knew he wanted the chicken potpie and a slice of pecan pie. Finding something healthy for myself would be more difficult. After looking over the menu, I settled on a chicken Caesar salad with light Italian dressing on the side. They had a pristine chocolate pie in the safe, uncut with mile-high meringue that had browned just so. My mouth watered, but I passed.

Once I returned I thought we might lunch together, but Chad told me he needed to take a working lunch. "Oh, you got me pie, too! How thoughtful of you."

This earned me a kiss on the lips and a covert pinch on the

butt once he was sure no one was looking. Then he took his lunch to the back, and I sat down at my lonely reception desk to convince myself that I did, indeed, like chicken Caesar salad.

My self wasn't having it that day.

When Amanda Kildare appeared on the other side of the door, teary-eyed and looking both ways, I wasn't sad about pushing the salad to the side. Amanda and I had gone to school together, but we hadn't moved in the same circles. She had been popular. Me? Not so much. Even so, she'd started coming to me for advice when she and her husband jumped ship from First Baptist to attend Love Ministries. I didn't like giving advice, but Chad had told me to say a quick prayer and offer up what words I could because he wasn't an expert on those things women discussed.

I suppose my staid *Golden Girls* aesthetic inspired confidence.

Next thing I knew, she stood over my desk wringing her hands. "Everything okay, Amanda?"

"No. Not really. I see you're eating lunch, but could I talk to you for a few minutes? I need some advice."

"Sure, but Chad's just down the hall."

She hesitated and looked toward his office, as though afraid he would appear. "Really, this is something that needs to be discussed woman-to-woman."

"It's not gossip, right?" I was so not in the mood to hear Chad recite the gossip passage from Romans later.

"No, no. This is about me."

"Well, I'll help you if I can," I said.

If I'd been hoping for something quickly discussed over the reception desk, I was destined for disappointment. Amanda went across the little lobby to drag an overstuffed chair behind the desk. It got hung up between the desk and the wall, so she stepped over and sat down, leaning over her knees. She smelled of Chanel Number Five, with every golden hair in place and her sweater set just so. Her tiny little boots tapped on the floor, the perfect shade of brown and the perfect style for her designer jeans. No matter how many times she came through the door, I couldn't help but marvel at what brought the former Homecoming Queen to me.

Finally, she whispered, "You know *that* book?"

Heavens. That again? I had a pretty good idea where this was going, but I cautiously asked, "Which book?"

Amanda reached behind her for what had to be a designer handbag and opened it enough for me to see. Sure enough, it was, indeed, *that* book, the gray one with the tie on the cover.

"I know of the book."

He eyes gleamed with hope. "Have you read it?"

"No, should I?"

Her shoulders slumped. "You're going to judge me, too."

"Amanda, you know I wouldn't do that. Judge not lest ye be judged."

She took a deep breath and launched into her story, a variation of which I'd been hearing for months. She'd been curious, wanting to see what all of the fuss was about. She'd asked her husband to try some new things in the bedroom. I mentally placed my bets for who'd upset her: Husband? Friend? Aunt? Sister?

"And then he told his mother!"

I did not see that one coming.

"As if I weren't already embarrassed enough that he was telling his mother about our sex life, she told me I was going to hell for reading such filth. Do you think I'm going to hell, Posey?"

Ah, the million-dollar question. At least ten different women had been in my office over the past few months, all wanting to know if I thought they were going to hell for reading a book. "Tell me, Amanda, have you killed anyone recently?"

"No," she said with a sniff.

"Stolen from anyone? Maybe disrespected your parents or coveted your neighbor's husband?"

"No! Ew."

"Did this book make you commit adultery?"

"You know it didn't."

"Maybe you made a graven image or took up Satanism?"

She gasped, "What has gotten into you?"

Even as she said it, all of my examples dawned on her. "Oh. I get it. You're saying that I haven't caused anyone harm so it's okay."

I shrugged. "There's a difference between 'okay' and 'good.' There's that whole passage about thinking on what's pure and lovely and admirable, but I don't think reading a book is going to send you to hell. Unless it has to do with devil worship."

She graced me with the Homecoming smile that had launched a thousand votes. "Thank you, Posey. You know, I would feel better, though, if you would read the book and then tell me it's okay."

"No, thank you. I don't really have much time for reading." Or, more accurately, I didn't make time for things I didn't want to read in the first place.

"Well, I'm done with this book, so I'll leave it here with you." She took the book in question and put it in my bottom drawer.

"Amanda—"

"No, I trust you to get rid of it," she said with that beaming smile. "Thank you so much for making me feel better."

"I didn't do that much," I said. "I still think you should've spoken with Chad. He's the preacher."

She dragged the chair back to where it belonged, and turned to look at me with her expression all scrunched up. "No. He would've given me the lecture about asking my husband permission for what I read or something like that. You give better advice because you help people figure things out for themselves rather than just telling them what to do."

I didn't have an answer for that, but I wished I had someone who'd help me figure things out without telling me what to do. I opened my mouth to say "You're welcome," but Amanda was already gone.

She hadn't closed the desk drawer all the way, and the book mocked me, tempted me even. I reached for the book just as I heard Chad whistling his way down the hall. I slammed the drawer shut so he wouldn't see it.

chapter 2

The next day I dressed with care and got up early to make mint brownies.

"Why did you make brownies?" Chad asked once we were seated in the car and on the way to work.

"Because John O'Brien is coming to tune the piano," I said. "He really likes brownies and he's tuning the piano at a discount, so it's the least that I could do."

"Well, I think you should prayerfully consider whether or not you should share those brownies with him," Chad said.

"Why?"

"Weren't you just complaining about how your clothes are getting too tight?"

Shapewear, actually, but ouch.

"Would you like me to save any for you?" I asked.

"You know I prefer blondies," he said.

It was true that my husband hated chocolate. Often, I'd thought that maybe—just maybe—if I'd hated chocolate, too, then I could've been more svelte.

We arrived at Love Ministries quickly, and I took my seat at the reception desk while Chad went down the hall. Even before the computer booted up, Naomi Rawls yanked open the door, wearing a perfectly matched tank top and fitted workout pants.

She had to be dressed for the Zumba class she taught down at First Baptist. "Is Chad in?"

"He just got here." I pointed down the tiny hallway, and she headed in that direction.

Chad had suggested I try Zumba, and I went to two classes, but dancing exercises weren't for me. I never could get the hang of having my arms do one thing while my legs did another. Either the dancing gene had skipped me or years of growing up in a school system that didn't allow proms had stunted my rhythmic growth.

I had to admit Naomi looked quite healthy and rosy. Maybe I should give Zumba another go.

No, her eyes had been red-rimmed from crying. I looked curiously down the hall, but I could only hear the soft murmur of voices. Usually, he called me into the office when a woman wanted to see him. He said it was for propriety, but I'd seen the article he read about avoiding law suits.

Oh, Posey, you don't know. Maybe it's a really personal matter she doesn't want to share with just anyone.

As long as she didn't come in to ask me if reading *that* book meant she was going to hell, I didn't care.

I typed up the newsletter that included the month's happenings as well as a prayer list. The format went out of whack, so I fussed and fiddled with the email until lunchtime. When I went into the break room for lunch, I found Chad's spaghetti container empty but unwashed in the sink. I rinsed it out while I waited for my spaghetti to heat in the microwave.

I eyed the bottles of Mexican Coke in the fridge. I could resist regular Coke, but the Mexican variety, made with real sugar, tasted better. Granny, in her more lucid moments, spoke with woe of the days of New Coke and how the old recipe simply wasn't the same as it had been before the Max Headroom fiasco. I'd thought she was crazy until I'd tasted the difference for myself. Granny, as it turned out, was crazy like a fox. Sure, she thought she was living in the fifties and carried a baby doll around with her, but she still knew things.

With a heavy sigh, I closed the fridge and got a glass of water from the sink instead. If only I could lose weight the Chad way: cutting out bread at supper.

I wasn't even eating real pasta, and still I hadn't lost a pound. No, my spaghetti sauce rested on spaghetti squash, which all of the Internet articles swore to me would taste exactly like noodles. Such articles reminded me that the Internet lied. Chad had hated the stuff so much, I'd had to boil him some pasta on the spot. I wanted real noodles, but I persevered through the spaghetti squash. It was the principle of the thing, really. After devoting an hour of my time to roasting the gourd, I was going to eat it.

Or at least some of it.

In the end, I scrapped half of the spaghetti-squash concoction into the trash and took up my post at the reception desk. The mint brownies called to me, but I ignored them. Twice I reached behind me to the shelf where I'd put them. Twice I turned around and concentrated on emails and voicemails and snail mail.

At two exactly, John O'Brien showed up. He had no trouble pulling open the door instead of pushing, and, as always, he looked effortlessly gorgeous with his ripped jeans and his blond hair pulled back into a ponytail. Chad didn't like for John to wear the ripped jeans into the church building, but John had worked as a roadie for a semi-famous rock band up until two years ago. I didn't think he had enough money to replace his wardrobe, not that he seemed inclined to do so.

"Working hard or hardly working?" he asked with a grin that revealed dimples. I'd spent many an eighth grade earth science class contemplating those dimples.

"The second one," I said, willing my heart to keep its beating rhythmic and normal. Completely normal.

So what if I'd had a crush on John O'Brien since eighth grade? I was a married woman, but I could appreciate the view. As my bestie Liza always said, she might've ordered but that didn't mean she couldn't look at the menu. Whatever menu he was on, John O'Brien was the best entrée. That much I knew.

"You're going to make me suffer, aren't you?"

"Hmm. What?"

"The brownies. Did you forget to make the brownies?" he asked.

Oh, the brownies. "Of course, I didn't forget. I reached behind me for the pan and lifted the tin foil. The smell of chocolate and mint wafted across the office area, and my stomach growled from not having finished my lunch. He closed his eyes and inhaled deeply, his eyelashes ridiculously dark and long.

"These are like Thin Mints only I don't have to wait for the Girl Scouts to bring them. Posey, you're the best." He took the plastic knife I offered and cut off a healthy slab of brownie, moaning as he took the first bite. My mouth salivated, my stomach growled in protest. Still I resisted the call of the brownies.

"One day you're going to get tired of these. Then what will I do?" I teased.

"You'll think of something." He tried to hand me the pan, but I held up my hands in surrender.

"You keep them. It's a disposable pan."

"Are you sure?"

I understood his confusion. Usually I kept the brownies, but I had weight to lose and Chad didn't like chocolate, so I had no reason to keep them. In fact, the sooner they got out of my general vicinity, the more likely I was to resist temptation. "I'm sure. I need to lose a little weight."

He chucked my chin. "That's crazy talk. You're pretty just the way you are."

I sucked in a deep breath, but he didn't seem to notice. Instead, he balanced the pan of brownies on one hand and headed off toward the sanctuary humming "How Great Thou Art."

John O'Brien thought I was pretty. The idea of it made tears prick my eyes because I'd spent my high school years attempting to achieve invisibility to everyone but him. Then I'd met Chad within two months of my freshman year of college, and we'd been together ever since. Come to think of it, I didn't think Chad had ever called me pretty or beautiful. Certainly not sexy.

The last person to call me pretty was probably my mother as she took my picture after college graduation.

Posey Love, you will not be starstruck over being called pretty. Pretty is ephemeral and not in the least important. You're supposed to be virtuous. You know, with a price far above rubies.

True, but I had yet to meet a girl who didn't appreciate being told she was beautiful. Or receiving rubies.

Chad cleared his throat, and I jumped sky high. "I didn't mean to scare you. Just wanted to know if you'd typed up the minutes from the last church council meeting yet?"

"Yes. I emailed them to you last week."

He lifted an eyebrow. "I don't see them in my mailbox. Maybe you're emailing them to your other husband."

Ha. As if I would ever want two husbands.

Even though I could've sworn I'd sent the minutes, I said, "I'll send them again."

That task quickly completed, I turned to face him. "Is Naomi okay? She looked really upset when she came through this morning."

He frowned, and I wondered how bad her situation was. "She's fine now. Don't worry your pretty little head over it."

That wasn't the kind of pretty I was looking for.

"I assume Mr. O'Brien is tuning the piano?"

"Yes," I said, even though we could both clearly hear the repeated tones as John tried a key and made adjustments, then tried the key again to make sure it was perfectly in tune. I couldn't hear the difference, but apparently he could.

"Did you give him the entire tray of brownies?" My husband asked nonchalantly.

"Well, yes, I didn't need the calories, and you don't like chocolate, so—"

"You didn't give him one of our good pans, did you?"

Since when did he care about *our* pans? He did none of the cooking and only washed the dishes once a month. "It's disposable."

"And how much did that cost you?"

"Four dollars for three of them, I think."

"Well, as long as it's in the budget." He shrugged and turned on his heel to leave. He often came and questioned me about silly things while John was tuning the piano. It was almost as though he intuited my crush, but he had nothing to fear. One of the reasons I'd gone along with our move to Love Ministries and the shift to Chad's philosophies is that the flipside of submission was to be loved as Jesus loved the church. To me, that meant faithfulness, and faithfulness meant that I wouldn't have to worry about being abandoned.

Mom claimed I had a fear of abandonment stemming from Daddy issues.

During one of our more memorable arguments, I'd told her I wouldn't have Daddy issues if I'd had a Daddy, that maybe she should've gotten married before she got pregnant.

We'd since called an uneasy truce.

To avoid thinking about my mother, I decided to check myself for early senility. I *knew* I'd emailed Chad those minutes. Sure enough I found them in my Sent folder. Why he couldn't admit he lost things was beyond me. In the end, it was easier to resend anything he couldn't find than to argue. Of course, part of the reason he came down the hall to ask me, rather than calling, was because he liked to keep an eye on John.

Chad hadn't wanted to hire John in the first place, but I'd sensed the piano tuner needed a job and had hired him out of instinct without asking Chad first. That hadn't gone over well, but he'd grudgingly kept John on because he took a sizable pay cut to tune our piano. He said it was because he enjoyed tuning the unusual model, but I suspected he appreciated the fact I was one of the first people to hire him after he came back to town.

He'd come back from the last tour broken, a skinny, haggard version of himself. People kept their distance, especially when word got out that he was attending AA meetings and was trying to get sober. Eventually he found himself and his charm, a trait he used to wear down the folks in Ellery, especially those at First Baptist. The Baptists loved a good redemption story, and John had a testimony both stellar and authentic. Now he tuned pianos and played guitar for the contemporary service. Parents, once assured he was once again on the straight and narrow, brought their kids to him for guitar and piano lessons. He also played for weddings and even worked with the high school drama club when they put on a musical.

In short, it made no sense for Chad to hate him.

"She's still a beauty," John said as he walked through the lobby. The piano he'd tuned had once belonged to Mrs. Morris and was some kind of weird one, which made sense since Mrs. Morris herself was a tad eccentric. John had done research to figure out how to tune her equally eccentric piano and had had to buy a different set of tools that Chad, of course, refused to reimburse him for.

"Well, we do thank you." I slid an envelope with a check across the top of the reception desk to him.

"And I thank you. For the check and for the brownies."

"Have a great week, John," I said as he left.

"You, too, Posey."

Chad cleared his throat. "If you're done flirting, I thought we might leave early this afternoon."

"Okay." I'd been planning to shred some documents and go by the bank to make a deposit. Of course, the documents weren't going anywhere. Since the cash had been intended for Chad's birthday, it was headed to our personal account and could also wait. I slipped the envelope full of last week's love offering into my purse. Getting to go home early was an unexpected boon. I even had a roast in the Crock-Pot. I might actually get to do some reading if we went home. I loved to read and had time to do so at work, but Chad said it looked unprofessional.

"Oh, what's this?"

In my haste to get my purse, I'd left the bottom drawer partially open, and Chad had spotted Amanda's errant book.

"I, uh, Amanda left it. Her mother-in-law told her she was going to hell for reading it."

He chuckled. "That depends. Did she use the book to kill someone?"

"That's what I asked her!"

"You should've sent her to me if she had questions of faith." My elation at having done something right immediately deflated.

"I'm sorry. I thought you didn't want to be a part of woman questions."

"Ah, but this—" he said, brandishing the book "—is a question of faith."

Again, so much easier to agree than to question or argue. "Next woman who comes in, I'll send her straight to you." Because I didn't want to have to talk to her about *that* book anyway.

"You know," Chad said. "Some women have said this book helped their marriage."

He had that gleam in his eye. I went through my mental calendar. My period was officially overdue. I didn't *have* to sleep with my husband. I wasn't really feeling it at that moment, but all of the books and articles I read about conceiving warned me not to discourage such behavior for fear that husbands would stop finding the fun in sex. "Did they now?"

He gave me his best salesman's grin, and I couldn't help but wonder if *he* had read the book. "Yes, ma'am. When we get home, why don't you put on something uncomfortable," he said. "I'm thinking the red."

Ugh. The red was quite literally uncomfortable. Downright scratchy, even.

"Maybe the black pumps, too."

Those caused blisters.

"Definitely the blond wig."

Itchy and hot and decidedly un-sexy.

The things I did for love.

chapter 3

Twenty-one minutes later—ten to get home, seven to get into the outfit requested, and four for Chad to exercise his husbandly rights—I lay on my back with my feet in the air. I took this position on the four-poster bed out of habit: holding your feet in the air was supposed to help conception. The good news was that the red lingerie had torn and one heel of the cheap black hooker shoes had broken off. Both of those could go in the trash now. The bad news was that the blond wig still had life and that Chad was calling me from the kitchen as if he didn't know how to operate the Crock-Pot.

"Just a minute." I shimmied out of the lingerie and tossed both it and the pumps in the trash before wrapping myself in a terry cloth robe to pad down the hall.

Our marriage hadn't always been this way. I couldn't help but remember the week after our honeymoon. Chad had skipped supper entirely one night. He'd brought home poseys for his Posey, and we made love until midnight before retreating to the kitchen for a snack and giggling over the cold lasagna I'd made earlier. Those days he was voracious, but sweet. That was before he started studying the letters of Paul and became more concerned with what I wore and where I went. That was before I'd taken a bajillion pregnancy tests that turned up negative and well before he decided being intimate with me was such a chore.

What would he do if I yelled down the hall that he could get his own roast?

That smidge of rebellion brought a smile to my face. Paul never said that man couldn't get his own pot roast.

"Posey? I'm starving!"

I opened my mouth to tell him to do something about it, but I didn't feel like a fight. Besides, if tomorrow's pregnancy test came back negative, then it would take me a full two weeks to butter him back up. Arguing wasn't worth it. Ten times easier to pad down the hall and fix his plate, and that is what I did.

Chad sat at his spot at the kitchen table, perusing the *Ellery Gazette* and waiting for me to serve him as June once served Ward. There was a time when I desired this tableau. Now I dreamed about a husband who knew the intricacies of a Crock-Pot, those being that you turned the knob counterclockwise from Low to Off and then removed the lid and used the handy ladle to the side.

"No salad?" he asked.

And when would I have been fixing the salad considering he was in such a hurry to get me into lingerie? "No salad. If you'd really like one, the ingredients are in the fridge, though."

First, he looked at me as if I'd lost my mind. Then he sighed the forlorn sigh of a man who'd been wronged but would nobly plod on. "No, that's okay. Too late now."

I piled his plate with roast, potatoes, and carrots. I spooned out green beans from the smaller Crock-Pot I also had going. Before I could fix a plate of my own, he said, "Have a seat so I can say grace."

I sat, annoyed he couldn't at least wait for me to get my plate.

"Father God, we thank you for another day of your blessings. Please help us to remember obedience to Your word. Bless this food to the nourishment of our bodies and our bodies to thy service. Amen."

Not getting a perfectly capable man a salad was not being disobedient. I thought about telling my husband that, but, again, not worth it. He often included "obedience" in any prayer after I didn't do something he wanted. I fixed a plate of roast, carrots, and potatoes, and sat down to enjoy the meal.

"Could you get me some tea?" he asked, just as I held my fork poised over the plate.

This was his second test. If I didn't get his tea, then we would have a fight. The past few years he'd been researching this thing called Christian Domestic Discipline. It took wifely submission too far for my tastes, saying husbands could send their wives to the corner or wash their mouths out with soap or even spank them. I had no desire for a lecture on the subject, so I went to get his tea.

Reaching into the fridge, I saw we only had enough sweet tea for one. Oh, well. I didn't need the calories anyway.

By the time I sat down to eat, he was almost finished, lapping up his food as if afraid someone might take it away from him.

"What's the rush?" I asked.

"New Bible study starts tonight," he said as he lay his napkin beside his plate. He didn't make a move to put his plate into the sink, but, then again, I knew he wouldn't.

"Oh. Is this one for the men?"

He chuckled. "You could say that."

Good. If he left then I could do the dishes at my own pace and then soak in a bubble bath with a completely frivolous book while he was gone. Only he wasn't leaving. Instead, he stared at me with a look I knew only too well.

He rocked back and forth on the balls of his feet, and I put my napkin down gently beside my plate because I knew what he was going to say next.

"How about one for the road?"

Twelve minutes later—eight for a panting Chad to finally exercise his husbandly rights, four to clear the table then decide not to do the dishes—I soaked in the tub with *that* book. Heaven help me but curiosity had gotten the better part of me, and I wanted to see what the fuss was all about. So far I'd only come across a naïve college girl who reminded me a lot of myself at that age. I, too, hadn't had a computer. I, too, was still a virgin in my early twenties. Unlike the protagonist of this story, though, I'd heard plenty of snickers if I admitted to either of those things, so I didn't.

Honestly, the book wasn't holding my attention so I tossed it out into the bedroom and sank deeply in the tub, smiling at the thought I might finally be pregnant.

Tomorrow marked three days.

I had never been three days late before—well, not since marrying anyway. Three days early? All the time, but never three days late which mean this *had* to finally be the moment I was pregnant. Underneath the warm water, I lightly pressed both hands over my stomach. Somewhere in there was life, and I would be a mother. I would finally get to do all of the things my mother didn't do. I'd already married a good, stable man to be the father of my children, hadn't I? He made enough money that I would be able to stay at home and concentrate on being a wife and mother. I would finally have an excuse to hang out with my best friend, Liza, again. Her new baby, a three-month-old, would be the right age for playdates in a few years. I'd be the mother who came up with all of those themed birthday party ideas. I'd be the mother who set distinct boundaries with a firm, but gentle, hand. Unlike my mother, I would pack lunches with encouraging notes and make every preschool and elementary school party.

Wait. The elementary school.

What if I got called back for an interview?

No matter. It was a supply position, so I could try out teaching to see if I really liked it and then wait until the kiddo was old enough for kindergarten before staring a full-time job.

Unless we had more than one child.

Well, in that case I would wait until the youngest was ready for kindergarten and then I would take a look at the job market. I could always take classes to stay current with my certification. Chad couldn't make me work the reception desk forever, now could he?

He could, and I'd probably let him. Unless . . .

Would he send our child to the corner for tiny infractions? I already knew how he felt about sparing the rod, since he wanted me to buy into his ridiculous ideas of discipline. For the first time ever, probably because this was the first time pregnancy seemed imminent, I worried about what kind of father Chad would be. Before we got married he seemed eager to have children, but that eagerness quickly faded. At this point I was afraid of what he'd say when I told him. But if the child were part his, he would have to love it, wouldn't he?

At least I'd finally be able to stay home as we'd originally agreed, and that would free me of the reception desk if nothing else. I might have to get into more fights with him for our child, but it would be such a small price to pay.

The water had gone cold, and I didn't feel like reading more even if I could reach the book I'd flung, so I stepped out of the tub and got dressed for bed. I told myself I'd leave the dirty dishes for him in the morning since, technically, it was supposed to be his job to wash them, but in the end I couldn't stand it. I threw back the covers and padded down the hall to scrape clean the dishes then finally fell asleep to the whirring sounds of the dishwasher.

chapter 4

The whirr of the dishwasher had turned into the sounds of a heavy engine and the obnoxious beeps of a large truck backing up. Was it trash day? My not-quite-awake brain scrambled for an answer. No, trash pickup wasn't for another two days. What was that horrendous beeping then? I rolled over to ask Chad, but he wasn't there. His pillow didn't even have an indentation. It did, however, have a note:

Had to go to Nashville for a conference—be back in a week.

What the heck did that mean?

I jumped out of bed and crammed my feet into the bunny slippers Liza had given me last Christmas while I pulled a plaid flannel robe around me. Running down the hall, I stubbed my toe on the curio cabinet that had once belonged to Chad's grandmother. I hissed rather than cursed—a lady of my stature shouldn't say such words—and hobbled to the front door where I fumbled with the lock and dead bolt, flinging open the door just in time to see a tow truck hauling off our elderly Toyota.

I slammed the door behind me and limped down the driveway, almost tripping because bunny slippers weren't good running shoes. "Hey! Come back here! There has to be some kind of mistake."

As the tow truck rounded the corner I got a glimpse of a name so long that it had to be Winkenhoffer. The fact that they were one of only two towing companies in town didn't hurt my deductions. I ran my hands through my hair. Where was my husband? How did he get to Nashville without our lone car? Who left for a conference in the middle of the night?

And why hadn't he spent the night? Only one other night in our marriage had he not come home, but that was before he saw the light and dropped his career in real estate to become founder and pastor of Love Ministries. He'd been playing poker with the boys and had too much to drink that night, deciding to crash on someone's couch rather than drive drunk or awaken me at two in the morning to come get him. He hadn't conveyed any of this to me, though, so I'd called the police on him.

That was the only time he'd ever slapped me.

I could almost taste the memory of blood from where his slap had made my teeth cut my inner cheek. I'd have to call him first. I wouldn't call the police on him again, that was for sure. I trudged up the driveway, almost stumbling as I lost my balance stepping on a large rock with the paper-thin soles of the bunny slippers. A little bit of coffee, and I'd be able to sort all of this out.

I should probably have decaf, though—just in case.

When I tried the front door, it didn't budge.

Locked.

In my fumbling, I'd managed to lock myself out. Of course, I had. Around the house I went, testing windows and doors, but all were locked securely. I checked the fake rock I'd put in the shrubbery, but the hidden panel was empty. Of course, it was. Chad often forgot his key, but he was never the one to put it back. I was.

He'd forgotten his key a few days before. In my mind's eye, I could see the silver key sitting on the edge of the kitchen counter, and I cursed myself for not putting it back in its place. At the time I'd thought it would serve Chad right not to find the key where it ought to be and thus remind him to put it back himself, but here I was getting bitten in the butt by my own pettiness.

With nothing left to do but find someone at home so I could borrow their phone to call Liza, I started walking. Obviously the Winkenhoffers were awake. Maybe I should walk around the corner to their offices and see if I could get my car back as well as make a phone call to Liza for the spare key. None of the houses around me showed signs of life and the sky had begun to pinken, so I walked on. Maybe everyone would be too asleep to notice how my teal plaid robe clashed with my red polka-dotted pajamas. Maybe no one would be awake to see the hot pink bunny slippers—their ears flopping with each step. Maybe—nope, there was Mr. James out picking up his newspaper and scratching his head at why Chad Love's wife was wandering about town in her sleepwear.

I sighed deeply. I had a long lecture in my future about how I needed to be above reproach since Love Ministries was new and small and thus I needed to mind my appearance in public. If he thought for one minute that I wasn't going to call him out for leaving in the middle of the night, he was sadly mistaken.

Fifteen minutes later, I entered the Winkenhoffer Towing Offices with aching feet and a bit of a pant. Did the shortness of breath associated with pregnancy come on so soon? No, more than likely, I was out of shape and/or walking in house slippers simply took more out of a person than walking in proper shoes. Mrs. Winkenhoffer, matriarch of the establishment, stood behind the desk, her steel gray hair piled high on her head. She wore cat-eye glasses with a beaded string attached to either side so she could wear them around her neck when she didn't need them. As I explained my situation, she peered over the rims of her glasses. Her right eye glared through me, but her left showed the filmy possibility of a cataract.

"So, let me get this straight," she said finally. "Your car got repossessed and you locked yourself out of your house and had to walk almost a mile to get here?"

Don't say it. Don't say it. Don't say it.

"Why, bless your heart, honey."

I had gritted my teeth so hard something popped in my jaw. At least now the moment had passed, the pity party over. "Yes, ma'am. If you could just tell me what I need to do to get my car back, I would greatly appreciate it."

Mrs. Winkenhoffer pushed her glasses back up her nose and turned to the computer. She typed and typed, her mouth pursed in concentration. Finally she spoke. "Says here that First Farmer's put in the call to get your car. You'll have to take it up with them."

"This has to be some kind of mistake. I know Chad has missed a water bill or a phone bill from time to time, but I've never known him to miss a car payment."

"Happens to more people than you'd think." Mrs. Winkenhoffer patted my hand a little too hard. "Now you go on up to the First Farmer's later today. I bet they'll let you have the car back if you can pay enough to get current."

Taking deep jagged breaths, I willed my tears to stay put. Soon I'd be a mother, and I would have to learn to handle situations like this without losing my cool. I could do this. I *would* do this. First, I'd call Chad. If he didn't answer, I'd call Liza. "Do you mind if I borrow your phone?"

"Not at all," Mrs. Winkenhoffer said as she handed me a grimy cordless one.

I dialed Chad's number twice, misdialing the first time since I didn't have the number memorized. My old antique flip phone didn't do much, but it could easily store the few numbers I used regularly. My call went to voicemail, so I left a message, keeping my tone light and breezy even as I told him the car had been repossessed and that I had been locked out of the house and could he please come get me.

Next I called Liza's number. It rang and rang and then cut off. This puzzled me, so I kept dialing until, on the fourth ring, she picked up the phone. "Look, I don't know who you are or why you keep calling, but cut it out. I just got the baby to sleep."

"Liza, it's me."

The long pause didn't bode well.

"Posey?"

"Yes."

Rustling on the other end told me she was sitting up in bed. "What the hell are you doing at Winkenhoffer's?"

"Um, my car got repossessed, and I accidentally locked myself out of the house." Again, I almost cried—something expectant mothers were famous for—but I wasn't about to shed a tear. No, I would have to set an example for my children about staying calm in the midst of unpleasant circumstances, and I might as well start now.

"Where's Chad?"

"At a conference in Nashville."

Another long pause, and then Liza muttered under her breath for a few minutes accompanied my more rustling and the creak of box springs. "I'll be there in ten."

Liza pulled up in her minivan, a Cardinals cap pulled low over her strawberry blonde hair. I swallowed a lump of guilt. I hadn't seen her or Nathaniel in a month. She probably thought I hadn't been by because Chad didn't like her—she didn't like him any more than he liked her—but the truth of the matter was that jealousy had been eating me alive. She'd gotten pregnant by accident, and I had been trying for so very long. My right hand traveled to my stomach. Since I might finally be pregnant, it was easier, even exciting to see how much Liza's little one had grown.

"You know, you didn't have to lock yourself out of the house just to see me."

"I know. I'm a horrible friend."

"You're a horrible honorary aunt, you mean. I hope you're studying up on ways to spoil this child because you know I don't have any brothers or sisters."

I climbed into the passenger seat and looked back, but I couldn't see the baby because the car seat faced backward so I turned around and studied my toes. "I am a terrible aunt. I'm sorry."

Liza squeezed my hand and I looked up to her freckled face. She smiled in spite of her awful best friend and the bags under her eyes. "Posey, I'm teasing. Although I would like to see more of you."

"I never wanted to wake up the baby or get in the way."

Liza arched an eyebrow. "Well, you woke up the baby this morning with your bajillion calls. Fortunately, he fell asleep again on the way over here. That child is going to be the death of me if he doesn't start sleeping through the night again."

"He's not four months old yet, is he?"

"No, but he slept through the night all of last week and then quit, so I'd say he's definitely a tease," she said as she eased the minivan out into the road.

"Not a speed demon anymore, huh?"

Liza snorted. "I won't so much as risk taking a speed bump too fast if that boy is sleeping."

True to her word, Liza eased into the driveway and then opened the van door carefully before contorting herself to get the baby's bucket seat out without slamming it into the door frame. "Oh, I forgot. Key's in the side pocket of the diaper bag," she whispered.

It took me a minute to find which side pocket contained the house key, but I rummaged around until I did and then closed the side door of the van. The door slammed harder than intended, and Liza shot me a dirty look even though she was already on the front stoop. Sorting through her keys carefully so they wouldn't jingle, I finally found the one that fit my front door and pushed it open so Liza could enter first. She set the bucket seat down gently, and I knelt to take a look at my pseudonephew.

"Oh, Liza, he's perfect." I drank in his peaceful face, so chubby with roly-poly arms and legs to match. His hair seemed thinner than before and maybe darker? He clenched his hands in fists as though determined to wring every last bit of rest from his nap.

When I finally looked up at Liza, she had a misty look in her eyes. "He's pretty damn cute, isn't he?"

While she looked at her son, I studied my best friend. No

makeup, dark circles under her eyes, and a suspicious stain on her yoga pants—this wasn't the Liza I'd gone to high school with. That Liza had once spent fifteen minutes fixing her hair before we went outside to play badminton using a water hose as the perfect indication of an invisible net. High School Liza would've never been caught outside the house in such a state of disarray.

Of course, High School Posey would've never envisioned locking herself out of her house or having her car repossessed, so clearly teenagers had no idea what was to come.

"Why don't you let me make you some coffee?"

Liza looked around warily. "Is Chad coming back soon?"

"He left a note last night about being gone to a conference for a week. First I'd heard of it."

Liza snorted. "That doesn't sound suspicious at all."

"Well, I'm not calling the police again."

Her expression sobered. That time Chad had slapped me, she paid him a visit at work. Since it was before Love Ministries, I had no idea what she said, but I did know he never slapped me again. He also told me never to invite Liza over again, but I ignored that edict.

Come to think of it, the receptionist job came about not long after he came home early and found Liza and me giggling over tea. That's also about the time he started researching "put your wife in a corner" and the like. Well, I wanted to put him in a corner for getting the car repossessed. We'd see how *he* liked it.

"Didn't you say something about coffee?" Liza asked.

I nodded and headed for the kitchen. Surely, he hadn't made me work the receptionist job just so I wouldn't have any free time away from him. Surely, not.

You know he would do something like that.

I ignored my thoughts and concentrated on making coffee. While it slowly dripped, I searched the pantry for something to eat, but I came up short since I was not supposed to have anything sweet. After my second fruitless search through the pantry, it hit me: the drawer in the coffee table. Chad thought he was hiding his cookies from me, but I knew they were there. I also knew he knew exactly how many were in the container. I usually didn't risk taking one because it wasn't worth the lecture or possibly being sent to the corner.

Yeah, well, if you got the car repossessed because you hadn't been paying the note, the least you could do was share your cookies.

So, I went to the living room and opened that drawer to find a brand new package of Oreos.

"Breakfast of champions?" I asked as I slid the cookies on the table.

"Ooo, feeling rebellious today, are we? I like it." Liza rocked the bucket seat when Nathaniel fretted.

"Get my car repossessed, and I will eat your cookies. Make a note," I said as I got two mugs, creamer, and the sugar bowl.

About the time we started the second cup, we seemed to find ourselves.

"Posey, what in heaven's name happened in college that you would marry a man who doesn't share his cookies?"

I shrugged and studied my new cup of coffee, the one I was needlessly stirring. "He's the head of the household."

Liza waited. Her eyes bored through me until I had no choice but to look up and meet her gaze. "If he can't pay the bills on time, then maybe *you* need to be the head of the household."

It sounded good in theory, but I didn't even know how to do such things anymore. Chad had been paying all of the bills—supposedly by computer—and I didn't even know what all we paid. Water, electricity, and the house and car payments obviously, but we didn't have cable since Chad had given away our television several years ago because he claimed it was distracting me from doing the laundry. He gave me cash to buy groceries, and I had to find a way to stretch what he gave me to the end of the month.

"I'm still waiting for you to move in next door," she said.

I grinned. When we were little girls, we'd talked about buying houses that were side by side so we could live next to each other. We would be able to talk every day, and our kids would play together. That future had been so rosy and so devoid of the realities of life.

Liza sighed, "Chickadee, you know I don't want to get into your business, but you do have some money set aside, right? You know, just in case?"

"The Oatmeal Reserve is alive and well." I looked to the pantry where I knew the two Quaker Oats canisters sat, one with money and the other with oats. Only once had I listened to my mother, and it galled to think she might be right. She'd told me to keep a rainy day fund of cash for myself, and to put it somewhere my husband would never think to look. The measly fund had mainly grown as a dollar or two here and there, but over the years I'd started putting any Christmas and birthday money in there because money couldn't buy the one thing I wanted.

"And Chad still has no idea?" Liza asked.

I shook my head and twisted open another Oreo. One morning as the honeymoon dimmed, Chad blessed me out for making oatmeal and made his opinions on the stuff clear. In retrospect, I'd started the Oatmeal Reserve by shoving that first five dollars into the canister as a sort of rebellion against his rant. He only tolerated having oats in the kitchen now because, as a health food, they were supposed to make me skinnier.

"I have money," I finally said. I didn't know how much, but I did have money. "But I'm sure there's a logical explanation for all of this."

Liza gave me a heart-blessing look of pity. I wanted to smack her.

"Posey, are you happy?"

"Of course, I'm happy." My answer came too quickly, and we both knew it. "I mean, what adult is really happy? You mean to tell me everything is peachy keen with Owen right now?"

"No," she said, "but this child will someday sleep through the night. We will emerge from the fog and look at each other and say, 'Oh, there you are.' I know this because sometimes I look at him and feel the love even if I fall asleep because I'm too tired to do anything about it."

When was the last time I'd looked at my husband and *felt* love?

Did it matter if I felt love? We were married now. Till death did us part.

"I worry about you, Posey. None of this feels like . . . you."

She didn't even know about how extreme Chad had been with his more intense insistence on wifely submission. My fists closed underneath the table, and I opened my mouth to protest. She held out a hand.

"Let me finish. We used to be inseparable, and now I only see you when you lock yourself out of your house. I know I had the baby, but you could still come over for a movie or some gin rummy. You hate the color blue, and yet that's the color of almost every single wall in your house. And what's up with the freaky angel collection? I got you that first one almost as a joke. You're not a teacher like you wanted to be. I haven't seen you take pictures since . . . college."

True. Once I'd taken great joy in photography. Chad didn't share my aesthetic.

"Maybe, well, maybe Chad's not the best man for you. I have a hard time believing he left in the middle of the night—the same night when your car got repossessed—to go to a conference you didn't know anything about."

"Liza," I said, in warning. My blood pressure didn't like her ideas at all. When Chad and I had married, I'd had the two conditions: no hitting and no adultery. If he ever hit me again or left me for another woman, then I would end our marriage.

"You are my best friend. I want to see you happy. That's all."

"Easy for you to say," I snapped. "We can't all get what we want."

Liza sat back. "Well. Okay. I've been missing my friend Posey for a really long time, but I'm not sure she lives here anymore."

"Maybe she doesn't."

Liza stood slowly with that regal dignity she'd always been able to muster. "Thanks for the coffee."

Even as I watched her go, I knew I should go after her. I knew I should apologize, but what she'd said had punched me in the gut. To suggest Chad had left me for dubious reasons was irresponsible. And what did happy have to do with anything? What adult was actually happy? She wasn't even happy—complaining about not being able to sleep through the night when she at least had a baby. Where did she get off lecturing me as if I had somehow let her down? I'd gotten married. That was all.

The front door clicked softly behind her, and that made me even madder. The girl couldn't even slam the door anymore because she was so worried about waking up the baby. The baby this and the baby that. Couldn't she see that I couldn't do any of those things with her because I hadn't been able to have a child?

But maybe . . .

I banged my head on the table harder than I meant to.

Posey, you are an awful human being. Your best friend got out of bed at the butt crack of dawn to let you into your house. She expressed her concern over your happiness and demonstrated that she missed you and wanted to spend more time with you, and you were a jerk.

Great. My hormones had to be out of whack.

I would make all of this up to Liza just as soon as I got the car back and talked to Chad and knew that everything would be okay.

First, I had to see what was in the Oatmeal Reserve.

chapter 5

Five hundred twelve dollars and eighty-three cents.

I looked at the money strewn all over the kitchen table, ten years' worth of saving for this day even if I didn't know it at the time. If I were lucky—something I hadn't been all day—I would have enough in the Oatmeal Reserve to rescue my Camry. Hastily I shoved the money back into the Oats container and placed it beside its twin. Even with the change, the cash canister felt lighter just as an almost empty one would. Twin Quakers looked at me with sly smiles as if assuring me they would protect my secret stash.

Somewhere in the other room my phone buzzed.

It might be Chad! I jumped up from the table and ran for the living room, this time stubbing my toe on the coffee table. I didn't cuss it because it had yielded Oreos in my time of need.

When I couldn't immediately put fingers on my phone, I dumped the contents of my purse into the overstuffed chair where I used to sit to watch television. I flipped it open then had to figure out how to scroll through the messages because my little sister, Rain, could text more in two minutes than my little screen would hold.

Posey you have to come get me now it's urgent
And then:

Look I know you're there and I know Mom told you not to pick me up from school ever again even though you are my emergency contact but it's really impt

As I was attempting to text a reply—a slow endeavor since I had to hit each number a certain amount of times to get the exact letter I needed—she texted again:

Come get me now!!!!!!!!!! It's about Chad!!!!!!!!!!

I sighed and backspaced on my original message about how I wasn't about to get involved in her hooky problem. Instead I texted:

Against my better judgment I am coming to get you, but I have no car so you have at least twenty minutes to fake an illness.

Halfway down the hall, I thought to check my voicemail, but I had no new messages. Quickly, I changed into my favorite dress, a black one with no collar and a minimal amount of flowers. I'd have to go by the bank as soon as I picked up Rain. Goodness knew, I needed to try to figure out what was going on with the car. In addition to Oreo consumption, Chad was going to have to forgive me for breaking into his rolltop desk where he kept all of the financial information.

Eating the Oreos alone was enough to warrant "discipline," but, to my way of thinking, he owed me several good explanations as to his sudden departure and why our car had been towed in the middle of the night. If he wasn't paying the bills, then Liza was right. That was a job I needed to take over.

My phone buzzed again, and I dug around in my purse in expectation.

It wasn't him; it was Rain.

Hurry up!!!

It took me a minute so I knew what I was talking about when I responded:

Patience is a virtue

Yessum County High School was almost the same as when Liza and I had roamed its halls.

The ancient floors had been waxed to a shine, but the whole

place smelled of institutional nostalgia. I checked in at the front office only to be directed to the attendance office. Well, that was new. Back in my day, we'd only needed one office for all of our shenanigans, thank you very much.

When I reached the attendance office/clinic, a small room that had once held textbooks, Rain lay on a cot with a washcloth over her forehead, her face contorted in pain. If there were awards given to students for faking illness, then Rain would've been the shoo-in every year. Her crazy high IQ meant school bored her. To make matters worse, she didn't play well with others, and so didn't want to attend for social reasons.

"Migraine?" I whispered.

Nurse Radford, who had been at Yessum County long before my high school years, snorted. "Maybe. She says she gets them with her cycle, but who knows? She was in here almost a month ago to the day, though. Where's Miss Lark?"

"She, ah, couldn't come." I hated to lie, but this statement was, in fact, true. My mother couldn't come to get Rain because she didn't know Rain was fake-sick. I was having a banner day when it came to breaking rules.

The nurse narrowed her eyes. "Miss Lark told me not to let that child leave unless she was missing an appendage."

"I know, I know," I said softly. "She's a bit of a handful."

"You, on the other hand. I think I saw you once in the four years you attended high school."

I smiled, remembering that day well. I'd been walking from lunch to the band room. Instead of watching where I was going, my eyes were glued to John O'Brien playing Frisbee in the courtyard. My toe hit an uneven patch of sidewalk and down I went. My knee was a bloody mess, but the whole thing had been worth it to look up into John's concerned eyes and to have him help me to the nurse's office.

"I guess I can trust you," Nurse Radford said as she looked up from the information card. "You are listed as an emergency contact."

Another teen girl appeared in the door with a hangdog expression, and the nurse sighed. "You go over there to the checkout station, and I'll be with you in a moment." Nurse Radford moved from checkout area to nursing area, and I watched her examine her latest patient, the pale girl who was either a really good actress or who needed the cot more than Rain.

The nurse shuffled back to the desk that served as the attendance office portion of the room.

"Are you having to pull double duty?"

She sighed. "Budget cuts. They figured that I could handle attendance and nursing since so many of the people checking out are sick. Of course, I have to deal with all of the orthodontist and doctor appointments, too. I think I've lost five pounds from the trotting back and forth."

"I'm sorry."

"It is what it is." She shrugged. "Everything going well between you and Chadwick?"

I nodded even though, no, no it was not going well.

"Never pegged him for a preacher," she said. "Goes to show you never know. Of course, he is new to the whole thing, isn't he?"

"Fairly." New was a relative term. Chad had started Love Ministries over five years ago. Of course, in a town where most churches dated back to the late eighteen hundreds, I suppose his little fledgling congregation was new. He and a few members of First Baptist had splintered from the main congregation over a couple of points about marriage. After a bitter dispute, the church had made the unorthodox—but not unprecedented—decision to allow a deacon to retain his position despite the fact his wife had divorced him. Chad took that opportunity to double down on the importance of not divorcing and of the man's responsibilities as the head of the household. He also emphasized giving support to widows and widowers so they wouldn't feel compelled to remarry and to Paul's passage about remaining celibate if you could. Hence Love Ministries consisted of mostly widows and widowers, a few spinsters, and a handful of devoted couples.

"Well," Nurse Radford said as she passed the clipboard for me to sign. "Just remember that you are always welcome back at First Baptist should something happen."

Blood ran icy cold in my veins. "What would possibly happen?"

"Nothing," she said a little too quickly. I looked down at the clipboard and saw Courtney Rawls's name toward the top. Maybe Naomi had been upset about her daughter when she went to see Chad. The nurse shrugged and turned her attention back to her newest charge. I walked over to Rain and gently touched her shoulder. "Come on, and I'll take you home."

"Can you guide me?" she asked in a small voice. "The light really hurts my eyes."

And so I led my little sister out of the high school while she held a damp washcloth over her eyes. She kept up the charade for at least a block before she remembered. "You don't have a car, do you?"

"Nope."

Down went the hand with the washcloth, and she tossed her long, glossy black hair over her shoulder. "Well. That really puts a crimp in my style."

"You had news for me?" I had to almost shout over the roar of the passing cars.

"Take me to McDonald's, and I'll tell you over a sausage biscuit."

"You're supposed to be sick."

She slapped the cloth back over her forehead. "Trust me. A sausage biscuit will miraculously heal this migraine. I'm sure Mom's vegetarian meal plan is one of my triggers."

I guided her in the direction of the McDonald's. "Have you heard the one about the little boy who cried wolf?"

"He's a rank amateur."

And I had to be an easy mark because not only had I picked up my sister from school, but I somehow also ended up buying her breakfast. I opted for hash browns and another coffee for myself—decaf this time.

"Thanks, sis," she said as she crumpled up the wrapper. "I really was hungry. Cereal doesn't go that far."

"Rain, would you just tell me what's so urgent?"

She looked over each shoulder, but the only other people there were a group of older men sitting in the back corner talking politics.

"Okay, so when I got to school today, Courtney Rawls was having a sobfest in the hall, and I couldn't miss it because I have to pass her locker to get to mine. So many people were crowded around her, I almost couldn't get through. It was ridiculous. I mean, why are there all these sheeple who can't watch what they're doing and—"

"Rain."

"Sorry. So, anyhow, as I was passing by, Courtney busts over and says, 'Tell your sister I said thanks for nothing!' "

"Me?"

"Duh. You're the only sister I have."

Rain chose that moment to take a long sip from her Dr. Pepper. Sun streamed through the window highlighting her olive skin, huge brown eyes, and dark hair—she looked exactly like her father, but she acted like no one else in the family. Well, maybe Granny. She, too, had a flair for the dramatic.

"And?"

"Okay, so then I'm all, 'What did my sister ever do to you?' and she's all 'Maybe if she'd kept her husband happy then he wouldn't have run off with my mom.' "

I put a hand over my mouth to keep my breakfast from making a return appearance. Finally, I managed to ask, "What?"

"Your husband ran off with Courtney's mom. I think I heard her telling her friends they went to Nashville."

The restaurant spun around me. "That's impossible."

Even as I said the words, I remembered the note. A conference in Nashville? More like a tryst.

"Well, she was mad enough to take a swing at me. I'll tell you that."

"Rain!"

My little sister held up both hands. "She missed, and I didn't hit back. This time."

Fingers shaking, I took my phone from my purse. Still no message from Chad. I hit redial, but found myself in voicemail once again. "Do you have Courtney's number?"

"Ew, no."

I thought of the small card the nurse had pulled from her files to make sure I was authorized to pick up Rain. "You're going back to school. I bet Courtney's mom's number is in the attendance office."

Rain wrinkled her nose. "Uh-uh."

"Oh, yes, you are. That sausage biscuit has miraculously healed you, and you are going to distract the nurse while signing back in so I can get a phone number for Courtney's mother."

"Are you insane?" Rain asked, putting her hand over my forehead as if checking for fever. "I'll get in trouble for faking and you'll get in trouble for helping me."

"Do you have a better idea?"

"Don't you have her number somewhere in the church?"

I thought of Naomi running and sniffling through Love Ministries the day before. I didn't have her number, but I might be able to find it in Chad's office. Anger, buoyed by purpose, simmered just under the surface of disbelief.

"Does this mean I don't have to go back to school?" Rain asked.

I hesitated. She should go back to school, but, should he suddenly return, Chad wouldn't say a word as long as I had someone with me. Hating myself for giving in to her, I said, "No. You can help me search Chad's office."

Rain clapped her hands. "Oh, that'll be fun."

We walked behind First Baptist and traipsed through a lawn or two to come to the little brick building that served as Love Ministries. Once upon a time, the building had been an office for vacuum cleaner sales and repairs. Then it had briefly served as a pawn shop. Now it housed Chad's tiny little congregation, hiding behind one set of the buildings on Main Street.

When the door didn't open, I fished through my purse for my

keys. Some secret part of me I hadn't been listening to for quite some time felt lighter at his absence. Then there was another part of me that wanted to look over my shoulder and make sure he hadn't just driven up.

Remember the car. Remember Naomi. Remember that you're the one who's been wronged.

The door finally opened. I stopped just inside, but Rain walked down the hall to Chad's office. I stared at the reception desk with something akin to loathing.

"It's locked," she said.

"I don't have a key for his office," I said.

"Got a screwdriver?"

"A what?"

"A screwdriver, you crazy woman. Mom and I had to take off a doorknob last week when Granny locked herself in the bathroom."

Once upon a time I had been a smart woman. What had happened to me? Now a teenager was thinking circles around me. "Um, I think there's a tool set in the maintenance closet."

Rain met me at the tiny closet, and we found a little box. She took it and sifted through the tools until she came to a Phillips head screwdriver of the appropriate size. With a bit of work and some foul words upon chipping her manicure, my little sister wrestled the door knob off and jimmied the mechanism until the door opened.

"I really hope this works," I said.

Rain shrugged. "He's not the brightest crayon in the box. I bet we'll find her number on his desk blotter."

The same desk blotter where he'd been known to exercise his husbandly rights on occasion? Bile rose up in my throat. "I can't look. Will you search for me?"

"Oh, I got this," she said with a beautiful grin born of mischief.

I paced the hall while Rain rifled through Chad's things. Twice I walked up to his office door, but I couldn't bring myself to walk in there. Something also made me stand between the front door and the office as if guarding my sister. If my intense desire to toss my Oreos were any indication, I had to be pregnant. I couldn't even think about that. There had to be a logical explanation for all of this.

"Found it!"

Paper ripped, and Rain dashed down the hall. Sure enough, she held a piece of the desk calendar. Chad had scrawled "Naomi" and a number. I looked at it. Could I dial this number? What if the whole thing was a big misunderstanding and Chad wasn't the one who'd run off with Courtney's mom? What was the etiquette in such a situation?

Posey, there is no etiquette in calling the woman who ran off with your husband. She's waived all rights to etiquette.

With a deep breath I started punching in the number, dropping my little flip phone when it started ringing. I was still kneeling on the floor when I answered with a hesitant, "Hello?"

"Ah, Posey."

Chad's smooth voice made me stand up straight. I swallowed a couple of times to find my voice. "Where have you been?"

"You got my note. I'm going to be out of town for a week. You might want to get your things from the house and the car."

"Too late for that," I growled. "The car got towed this morning."

"Temper, temper. I needed some money, and the ministry hasn't been doing too well. I'm sure you'll manage while I collect on some debts."

Someone giggled in the background, and my blood boiled. "Don't come back."

"What?" He had the audacity to sound confused and wounded, as if he were the wronged party.

"You heard me. Don't come back. I know you ran off with Naomi Rawls, and there's no need for you to come back."

"Now, Posey." His voice took on that stern timbre that usually had me backing away from him, but I took a deep breath and forged ahead. No need to back away from a phone.

"No. Adultery is my limit. You are no longer welcome in my home."

He chuckled. "About that. I sold *my* house—you'll recall it was in *my* name—so you need to get whatever you want to take before the end of the month."

I sank to the floor. "Why are you doing this?"

"I told you. I need the money. I made a few bad investments. It's true that Naomi is here, but she's helping me straighten some financial things out. You can go to your mother's house until I come back."

"I want a divorce."

My words surprised him into silence. Truth be told, they'd shocked me, too. Rain, on the other hand, was jumping up and down and silently clapping in glee.

Chad cleared his throat, and I could imagine him rolling back and forth on the balls of his feet. No, he couldn't be rocking because it sounded as though he were walking, as if he wanted to be out of hearing range of the giggling woman I presumed to be Naomi Rawls. Hate washed over me, and I thought for a minute I might throw up right there in the hall.

"Posey, don't be ridiculous. You know I don't believe in divorce. If I tell you there's nothing to worry about and that Naomi and I are here for business reasons only, then it is your job to believe me, to trust me, and to wait for me. I'm sure losing the car and the house has been a shock, but I am in charge, and I will handle things. When I get home, we're going to have a discussion about your attitude, too."

I swallowed hard. A part of me wanted to believe he would take care of me. I told that part of me to take a long walk off a short pier because the stability he'd once given me wasn't worth what I'd given up for him.

"You made me a promise. You vowed to be faithful."

"I am being faithful in all matters of the heart." His voice came out muffled, but his condescension had melted into charm just to keep me off base.

My temper spiked. Matters of the heart left a lot of room for sins of the flesh.

"You're right," I said in a jagged breath. "I should trust you."

Rain face-palmed, but I held out an index finger.

"That's more like it. You'll wait for me then?"

I slowly counted to five. "I'll wait."

"That's a good girl. He practically purred, and my skin crawled by how pleased with himself he was. Little did he know I was taking a page from my mother's playbook: get someone cozy and then ask them an innocent question.

"I missed you this morning. I didn't know what to do when they took the car," I said. Rain mimed ramming a finger down her throat in disgust.

"That must've been stressful, and I've missed you, too." I could almost hear the preening on the other end of the line, so pleased with himself for having his cake and eating it, too.

"How was Bible study last night?"

"What Bible study?"

"That's what I thought. So you had sex with me twice and then left to . . . run off with another woman. Does she know what you did before you left?"

His silence spoke volumes. I tried not to look at Rain who was, unfortunately, hanging on my every word.

Tears flooded my vision, but I managed to speak over the lump in my throat. "Do not come crawling back to me. I want a divorce by the end of the month or . . . or . . . or—"

"Or what?" he asked in an eerily calm voice, the one that told me I'd gone too far. He was thinking about praying for obedience again. For the barest of seconds, terror raced up my spine, but then I remembered Naomi's giggle in the background. I thought about my worry this morning when I couldn't find him, about how he'd embarrassed me by allowing the car to be towed off and that was before anyone found out he'd left me.

"Something bad. I'll think of something."

He laughed, and my face burned with shame. I couldn't even threaten my husband properly.

"Oh, Posey. Don't try to be someone you're not. Be a good girl and go to your mother's house. I'll be back in a week to straighten everything out—including you."

My mother's house? Of all of the places I could go he wanted to send me there? "Screw you, Chadwick Paul Love. You don't know me at all. You never have, and now you never will."

My fingers shook as I tried to hit the button that would disconnect the call. I kept missing the button, but I could still hear him yelling for me so I hurled the phone down the hall. It broke into two pieces as it hit the reception desk.

I bolted for the bathroom and heaved up my breakfast.

chapter 6

When I emerged from the bathroom, Rain leaned against the wall in the hall. She looked up from her phone, a shiny iPhone. "I have good news and bad news."

"Tell me the bad news, first," I said. Might as well add on to the day.

"Your phone is dead."

Of course it was. I had no way to get a new phone. I might not even still have a job. Chad signed the checks. How was I supposed to get paid if he wasn't here? And I still had to get all of my things out of the house and—

Posey, stop. Breathe.

"What's the good news?"

Rain grinned and held a hand up high. "You found your spine and told that asshole off for once!"

I numbly high-fived her. "I did? I mean, I have?"

"Girl, it was epic. You really had me going there for a minute, but you were just doing that thing Mom does when she's trying to get one of us to incriminate ourselves. It was badass!"

I should be getting on to my sister for cussing, but being a badass sounded so much better than whatever I actually was.

Liza's question about whether or not I was happy came to mind. I needed to apologize to her. I needed to go to the bank to see about the car. I needed to check on that application with the school system since that job might end up being my saving grace. I needed—

I wanted to go back to bed and pull the covers over my head.

"Posey, earth to Posey!" Rain had been waving her hand in front of my face.

"I'm sorry, what?"

"Want me to call Mom to give you a ride back to your house? Maybe if you talk to her she won't lose her mind over the fact I missed a little school."

Not that I would have a house to go home to much longer. "Maybe. I'm going to need to talk to her anyway."

Rain paused, immediately suspicious. "About what?"

"Chad sold the house out from under me. I'll be homeless in a month."

My jaded teenaged sister drew in a breath of shock. "That was . . . cold."

I could only nod. "I hope I'm doing the right thing."

"By what?"

"By telling him I want a divorce. I mean, I don't even have a job and I don't know how to get a divorce and—"

There I stopped because I didn't want to say the words aloud, I didn't want to jinx anything. While I was vomiting in the bathroom earlier, remorse had snuck into the room. After growing up without a father, could I do the same to my child? Even if the father in question was awful? Would I be able to get a divorce once Chad found out? Would he leave Naomi then? Would I want him to?

Rain's eyes narrowed. "And what?"

I took a deep jagged breath. "I may be pregnant. Finally."

Rain squealed and hugged me tightly. "I'm going to be an auntie!"

I held up both hands to stave off her enthusiasm, but I couldn't hold back the smile. "I don't know for sure."

"Well, then we need to get a pregnancy test and find out." Rain grabbed my hand for the first time since she was seven, and she dragged me toward the door. "The drugstore is just across the parking lot. Let's go!"

"Rain, I don't want everyone to be in my business!"

"Then I'll buy it!"

I just looked at her until she realized what would happen if one of the clerks sold a pregnancy test to a teen girl. News would canvas the town in less than twelve hours, and our mother worked just a block away so she'd hear it quicker.

"Fine, fine. I'll go with you, though. Moral support."

Usually, I bought pregnancy tests in bulk in Jefferson where no one paid any attention to me, but I'd run out some time back and had refused to buy more in disgust at my inability to procreate. At this point my period was later than it had ever been. This had to be it, didn't it? I mean, finding out I was pregnant on the very day I asked for a divorce would have to be an important codicil to Murphy's Law and thus the only logical outcome, right? "I'll get my purse."

Rain squeed. "Yay! This is so much more fun than going to school."

I shot her a dirty look for her schadenfreude, but my own heart leapt with excitement at the possibilities. I hadn't thought about Rain as an aunt. There was such an age gap between us, we'd never really been that close—other than wiping her butt when she was a baby. Harder to get much closer than that. She'd been only a child when I married Chad. I still remembered the uncertainty in her eyes as she prepared to walk down the aisle, an ungainly overage flower girl at seven or eight. She knew me as the older sister who made her go to bed on time but who also snuck her Happy Meals when Mom wasn't looking. She hadn't figured me out yet, which was fair since I had yet to figure her out.

Heck, I wasn't too sure about myself, but that little flower girl was now a teenager—almost a college student—and she was dragging me across the parking lot to the back entrance of the drugstore. I stopped in the middle. "I don't know if I want to know."

"Come on, Pose, doesn't this day deserve at least one good thing?"

Heck, yeah, it did! I started walking but stopped again. Could I handle a negative test? Just one more *bad* thing in an already horrific day?

"Posey. Stop being a chicken."

My feet began moving before my brain caught up. Liza had used those words hundreds of times to get me to do stupid stuff. There was the time we took toilet paper and rolled the principal's lawn because he'd made the dress code more restrictive right after we'd done our back-to-school shopping. Or the time she talked me into helping her "borrow" a goat to let loose on the football field. I'd drawn the line at climbing the water tower, but she'd gone to the top and then waved at me so hard, I was afraid she'd topple over.

Somehow, I found myself on the drugstore aisle that held feminine plumbing products and pregnancy tests. They didn't have my preferred brand and, of course, they charged more than the stores in Jefferson, but I picked out a box with three tests and proceeded to the cash register. Rain's hand still held mine, her once impeccably manicured nails digging into my palm ever so slightly.

Mrs. Hunter didn't say a word as she rang me up. She didn't crack so much as a smile, and for that I was grateful.

My breath came in short gulps as we walked back to Love Ministries. It was lunchtime, and I knew that morning pee was the best pee.

And the fact I thought things like "morning pee is the best pee" was a sad testimony to how long I'd been trying to get pregnant.

Rain followed me to the bathroom door.

"I may have it down to an art form, but you are not going to watch me pee on a stick."

She nodded, and backed against the wall, taking her phone from her back pocket. I entered the bathroom, locking the door even though Love Ministries held no one other than my sister and me. Carefully, I undid the packaging, all the time saying a prayer. After more pregnancy tests than I could count, my prayer had come down to one word, repeated over and over: *please*.

I sat on the toilet arranging my legs in such a way that I could accomplish my task with little muss or fuss. Once done I gingerly set the stick on top of the little metal box generally reserved for used sanitary products. I forced myself to get up and wash my hands in the sink. At this point I could guess what three minutes felt like. Even so I looked down at my watch and began to time just so I would have something to do. The tiny bathroom didn't offer me room to pace as I did at home.

Once, I'd told myself to be busy with other things and then come back to the test. That day I'd changed out the laundry and loaded the dishwasher, then fielded a phone call. I forgot about the test all too well. I still remembered the joy of the positive reading, then the agony of going to the OB only to have him tell me that I wasn't pregnant and that you could get a false positive if you left the test out too long.

I wouldn't leave this test out too long.

I washed my hands again so I could chew on my nails, but then I didn't want to chew my nails so I paced: two steps toward the toilet, and two steps back. The bathroom felt as though it were closing in on me. I checked my watch, but only a minute and a half had passed. My eyes darted in the direction of the test, but I willed them to look away. Instead, I looked into the mirror, checking my face for clogged pores. I found a few, but the search didn't take a full minute and a half.

Now my mind wandered back to what in the heck I was going to do about Chad and this baby, but I couldn't allow myself to think any more about the baby until I knew there was a baby to think about. A nasty inner voice told me I needed to call him back right then and beg his forgiveness because there was no way I'd be able to make it without him. Flawed as my husband was, hadn't Jesus said to let those without guilt cast the first stone?

That nasty voice sounded a lot like Chad himself.

For the first time in ten years of going through the motions like a robot, I came to a very important realization: I didn't want Chad to be involved in raising my child. I had been so focused on becoming a mother that I hadn't thought too much about the father, but today had certainly brought that issue to the fore. A glance at my watch told me the moment of truth was at hand. I took a deep breath and reach for the test.

Negative.

Slumping against the wall, I allowed myself a moment of despair before I began the pep talk portion of the pregnancy test process.

Posey, remember your mantra about early morning pee? Also, you're totally dehydrated. You can try again first thing in the morning. Tomorrow really is another day.

I wrapped the test in toilet paper and washed my hands yet again in water so hot my hands hurt. I steeled myself for Rain's eager eyes as I reached for the doorknob. Sure enough she stood up straight when I opened the door, her large brown eyes full of question and hope. "And?"

I shook my head, the tears pricking at my eyelids. She deflated like a pricked balloon, and I realized having someone with me meant she would need a pep talk, too. "Look, Rain. It's still early, and the tests are most effective first thing in the morning."

"So you can try again?" she asked, already bolstered because her young life hadn't brought her anywhere near as many negative tests.

"Yes, I can try again."

She reached for my hand and squeezed it. "Whatever happens, it'll be okay, Posey. I know you think you don't have anyone but Chad, but that's a lie he's been telling you. You have me and Mom and Granny and Henny and Liza."

"Liza's mad at me."

"She'll get over it."

"Granny's senile."

Rain shrugged. "I think she's actually getting mellow in her old age."

"And Mom . . ."

"Mom loves you. I know she's, well, her, but she loves you. Promise."

Good thing my mother loved me since I would be begging her

for a place to stay by the end of the month—especially now that I'd managed to alienate Liza.

"We need some lunch," Rain said. "Let's close this place up and get some lunch."

As we walked toward the front door, a tall black man in a flawless gray suit entered the building. He took one look at me and grinned, "Ring around the Rosie!"

"Malik," I said with a weak smile. Malik Foster and I had gone to school together. He refused to let go of the nursery rhyme nickname. "What brings you here?"

He frowned. "Well, I'm afraid I have a bit of bad news."

I laughed, but the sound came out hollow and humorless. "Why not? Everyone else has bad news today. Why not you?"

"Is Chad here?"

"No." I bit back any thoughts I had on Chad or his whereabouts.

Malik had the decency to look sheepish as he scratched his head. "Well, Chad's behind on the payments, and I'm afraid we're going to have to foreclose."

That answered my question about whether or not I still had the receptionist job I hated. "Of course, you are."

"I'm really sorry, Posey, but it's business. I work for the bank, and I don't even have to come here to tell you guys, but I thought that was the least I could do since I helped Chad get the loan."

"That's kind of you. Chad isn't here. I don't know when he's coming back. As long as my name doesn't appear anywhere on those papers, you do what you need to do. All I ask is that you give me a little notice to get a few things out of here."

"I'm afraid I can't let you do that."

"What?"

"We need to auction off anything that belongs to the church to help offset the amount owed."

"In that case, all I need is my purse," I said.

"I really am sorry," Malik said.

"Thanks for letting me know," I said as I brushed past him

with Rain behind me. I wrestled the key from the ring and tossed it at him. "Lock up when you leave."

He sputtered something about how that wasn't the way to do things, but I was already on my way to have pie for lunch. And a huge juicy cheeseburger. With fries.

Or a grilled cheese sandwich since I'd already spent most of my cash to buy breakfast for my little sister.

The love offering! I still had the offering the church had given as a birthday gift to Chad.

"Know what?" I asked my sister. "We're having lunch. On Chad."

Maybe, after lunch, I'd feel like visiting the bank to see about rescuing my Camry.

chapter 7

It took almost all of the money in the Oatmeal Reserve, four hours, three pitying looks, two hand pats with an "Are you okay?" and one heart blessing to get my car back. Mrs. Winkenhoffer, who was at the bank making a deposit, was the worst hand pat offender. Her twin sister, Imogene Dale, completely blindsided me with a "Bless your heart" as she led me back to her office, where she worked as a loan officer. I should've seen that one coming—twins, after all.

Home again finally, I knew I needed to start packing, but I couldn't make myself get up from the couch even if I did hate it. Chad had picked out the leather monstrosity that stuck to my legs in the summer and chilled me in the winter. Before we married, he'd shown me the little brick house and told me I could decorate it in any way I liked. Then he'd put me on an "allowance" and proceeded to pick out several pieces of furniture himself. There was probably a metaphor for our relationship in there somewhere.

Looking around the room I didn't see much of anything I wanted to save. Certainly, I didn't want to save the ugly old curio that had belonged to Chad's grandmother. It would serve him right if I sold it in a yard sale, and my frequently stubbed toes would thank me. Come to think of it, I didn't want any of the angel collection it housed, either. The figurines with their blank faces creeped me out. Liza had given me the best friend angel about the time Chad took up the ministry. Not long after, I'd dropped the figurine and broken off both wings. Superglue had put them back together, but the epoxy could only do so much. Meanwhile, Chad decided angels were the perfect things for his wife to collect, so they had poured in from friends and congregation members.

They looked like an army of faceless assassins.

I stood, finally, and took the one angel Liza had given me— that one I would keep—and I closed the door on the other ones. In the guest bedroom, I took some photo albums from my childhood and teenage years out from under the bed and stacked them into a low rocking chair. I would take the chair, one that had belonged to my grandmother, the one I'd put so hopefully in the corner when I mentally made plans to make this room into a nursery. The closet held a few of my dresses and Chad's summer wardrobe. I'd sell all of it.

Something niggled at the back of my mind as I turned to go, something I couldn't quite remember. . . .

My camera.

Liza had mentioned how much I used to love photography. What I'd never told her—or anyone, really—was that my love of photography waned as Chad's interest grew. Unfortunately, his favorite pictures to take were those of me in compromising positions. I'd finally hidden my camera, telling him it was broken.

I felt around on the top shelf of the closet, yanking down old blankets in the process. Sure enough, my old digital camera fell to the floor but landed on one of the blankets. It needed batteries now, but blessedly the special battery hadn't corroded. If memory served, a pair of double-As would work long enough for me to see if the pictures were still there. The junk drawer in the kitchen yielded two batteries, and I took a deep breath as I turned the camera on and went to the saved photos.

I had deleted nothing.

Looking at the photos made me sick, and I itched to delete them.

No.

Those photos could come in handy as an example of Chad's sadistic side.

I put the camera in my purse and then trudged to the master bedroom, looking at the four-poster bed with disgust. As long as I lived I would never sleep in another four-poster bed.

The drawers full of thongs taunted me. I would burn them. Never could I understand why Chad wanted me to wear dresses that made me look like an extra on *The Golden Girls* while wearing scraps of lace underneath. Nope. I would be wearing jeans and T-shirts as soon as I found a job and earned enough money to buy what I wanted. In the closet I had an entire chest of drawers full of lingerie. Obscenely high-heeled pumps lined up around my closet floor. I'd burn those and the lingerie along with the thongs. The wigs would have to go, too.

All of this had been Chad's idea—he told me my constant harping on "ovulation" and "conception" were making him lose interest. He wanted me to "spice things up." I didn't have a problem with any of his plans in the abstract; I didn't like the person he became when I wore what he wanted me to wear. He became mean and cruel and selfish, but up until this point I'd convinced myself that I was imagining things, that I needed to cut him some slack because I'd put him under too much pressure.

Nope. He really was mean and cruel and selfish.

Somewhat in a daze, I went to the laundry room for the largest basket I had, and I filled it to the brim with lingerie and wigs. Outside I went with a box of matches, and I made a pile of the lingerie and thongs and set the whole thing on fire. Only as I watched them burn did I realize I now had no underwear aside from the pair I was wearing and whatever might be in the hamper waiting to be washed. To make matters worse some of the synthetic fibers gave off an awful odor as they burned.

Then I heard the police siren.

I stomped at the fire but then caught the hem of my dress on fire and had to stop, drop, and roll. Len Rogers, stalwart sheriff of Yessum County, found me rolling on the ground.

"Posey Love, what in God's name are you doing?" he asked, his arms akimbo.

"Um, I, uh. I felt the need to burn some trash," I said as I stood and dusted myself off.

"At ten at night?" He leaned forward and used a stick to pick up a charred bustier by a strap. When the strap broke and the bustier fell back into the fire, he fished out a wig that had burned to the point that it looked like a medieval monk's haircut.

I blushed to my core but dared him to say anything. He sighed deeply. "I suppose that this is a pile of leaves, then?"

"What?" But then my brain caught up with my mouth. Technically, no one was supposed to burn anything inside the city limits except leaves and grass. "I mean, yes. Yes, it's, um, a pile of leaves I never got around to burning." Even though it's March and the trees are budding out rather than shedding leaves.

"I'm going to leave you with a warning," he said. "But please don't burn anything again. Mrs. Dale across the street got worried about you when she saw the smoke, said she was afraid you might be doing harm to yourself."

Oh. I hadn't thought anyone would be worrying about me.

"I won't burn anything else, Len. I promise."

He nodded. "Good to hear. I'm heading home. You make sure that fire is good and out."

I should offer him something, but all I had was half a pack of Oreos. Maybe I'd make some brownies and drop them off at the sheriff's department to say thanks for not adding a ticket to my day. He'd made it to the corner of the house when I yelled, "Hey, Len?"

He turned around.

"Thank you."

"You're welcome," he said with a smile and a nod.

I surveyed my failed fire as the last of it smoked. I stomped on the ashes and then doused them in water.

What had I been thinking? I hadn't even had a bucket of water handy. I'd burned the whole pile instead of adding a little bit at a time. I could've burned the whole household down. The whole neighborhood, even.

Posey, at one point you used to be smart.

Once I was sure the fire was completely out, I put the wet remains in a trash bag and took it to the huge trash can. Inspired, I took one of the big bags usually reserved for lawn refuse and filled it with the high-heeled shoes I hated so much. Then I wheeled the can to the curb in the hopes that Chad had at least paid for the trash service.

Maybe the best thing for me to do would be to go to bed. Surely, the next day couldn't be worse. Surely.

I thought of the pregnancy tests and my missing period. Yes, I would drink a glass of water and go to bed.

I woke up at three, four, and five before convincing myself to just get up and get it over with.

Groggily, I trudged to the bathroom. The wrapper around the pregnancy test didn't want to tear, but I persevered. A few minutes later, I paced up and down the hall where I couldn't see the test while I waited for the three minutes to pass.

Oddly, I remembered the day my mother, her eyes red-rimmed from crying, told me she was pregnant with Rain. As a freshman in high school, I thought my mother truly hated me. I blamed her for getting pregnant. Why couldn't she be like other mothers and marry a nice man and stay home and bake cookies? Or, heck, she could work as a teacher or a secretary or maybe a dental hygienist. I didn't care if she became a pilot like Amelia Earhart, whose biography we'd once read together. All I knew was that I didn't want her to be pregnant again when my classmates had just calmed down about her.

Henny was finally getting to the point I could stand him now that all-day school tired him out. I did *not* want another baby in the house. No more free babysitting. No weird stares from people. No whispers about how my mom was such a slut.

No matter what I wanted, Mom was pregnant. She sat Henny and me down and told us in a faux-cheerful voice that we were going to have a little sister. Henny thought it was the greatest thing ever, not realizing that by the time his little sister was old enough to play Legos with him, he'd be through with them. I stared through my mom. That day I made myself a promise: no more flights of fancy with Amelia Earhart. I would concentrate on getting a good education and finding a good man who would never leave me.

About that.

Maybe Granny was right. Maybe the Adams Girls truly were cursed in matters of the heart.

My watch indicated the proper amount of time had passed, and I walked to the bathroom. This was my moment of truth.

Negative.

Considering the events of the past twenty-four hours, I should've felt relief. Instead agony ripped through me. Not again. At the first signs of hyperventilating, I willed my breath to come in even inhales and exhales. Time for the other pep talk.

Posey, you are only thirty-two. There's still time for you to be a mother.

I decided to add a new piece of inspiration to otherwise well-worn thoughts:

Now you can even look into adoption since it doesn't matter what Chad believes about only wanting to raise his own flesh and blood.

My breath even, I stood up straight and disposed of the test, washing my hands in scalding hot water. In the mirror, I saw an older version of myself, a makeupless scarecrow with a grim expression. I didn't look a thing like my petite and blond mother. Was this what my father looked like? Did he have those same fine lines around his eyes? Maybe his genetics were the ones to blame for my inability to get pregnant.

Of course, that hadn't stopped him from impregnating my mother, not that I knew anything about how my conception came about other than the fact it took place on some kind of commune south of Nashville.

Intentional community, the voice of my mother inwardly corrected.

"Oh." Something moved between my legs. I grabbed at my last pair of clean underwear in such a hurry that I scratched my thigh. Sure enough, there was that telltale brown spot, proof that

I wasn't pregnant after all. The room spun around me, my vision misted with tears.

I sat down on the toilet. My fist traveled to my mouth to keep from sobbing aloud, a habit from all those years of not wanting Chad to hear me cry.

No reason to worry about that anymore.

So I cried out loud, a keening wail. I let my sobs shake the walls of the empty house, ten years' worth of them, until I lay on the floor, gasping for breath.

Not even this one thing, God?

My answer came in the form of cramps, and I went searching the hampers for a pair of underwear to wear to Jefferson long enough to get supplies and new panties that actually covered my backside.

New underwear and then I would have to take charge of several things: apologizing to Liza, seeing Ben about a divorce, and asking my mother if I could move in with her. The whole plan felt as though my life were skidding backward, as if another pawn had bumped me back to Start in a game of Sorry!

No, it wasn't a game of Sorry!

It was the Game of Life, and my peg had fallen out of the car. No, it was a biblical version of the Game of Life, and I was the prodigal daughter.

All my life I'd empathized with the older child, the one who stayed put and did everything right but couldn't seem to merit a party. Now, I saw I was the youngest, the child who'd been in a hurry to run away from home. Maybe I hadn't squandered an inheritance or been reduced to feeding pigs, but I was about to head home with nothing to show for my thirty-two years on this earth.

One thing I knew: Mom would never cook the fatted calf—she was a vegetarian—but, if I were lucky, she might meet me on the path with the modern-day equivalent of a ring and robe.

chapter 8

No two ways about it, I dillydallied in Jefferson. I didn't want to admit defeat to my mother. The night before my wedding she'd lectured me about how marrying Chad would be a mistake. I had stalked off after shouting "You never cared before. Why do you suddenly care now?" Our most recent blowout about "daddy issues" hadn't helped. Holidays and chance meetings in town had been civil, but it was safe to say my mother and I weren't in a good place.

At the edge of one row of store fronts in Ellery sat a building she had renovated and claimed as her own.

I had never been there.

Today, however, I would darken the door of Au Naturel, a health food store/yoga studio and the cause of many snickers when I was in high school. As I opened the door, I heard mystical pan flute instead of modern chimes. Despite the warmth of the building with its hardwood floors, breezy interior, and soft lighting, I wanted to run. Chad had called this store a den of iniquity, a haven for New Agers who loved crystals and chakras.

Yeah, well, Chad has shown his true colors, now hasn't he?

I took a step forward, but didn't see anyone.

"Lark's upstairs finishing up."

In the corner, a cozy nook with two overstuffed chairs, a coffee table, and shelves full of books, sat a woman I didn't recognize. She had wild dark hair and olive skin. As if she knew I was trying to place her, she looked up from the cards she'd lain out on the table to smile at me. "Can I help you?"

"No, I'm, um, I'm looking for my mother."

The lady in the corner studied me intently then her features brightened. "You must be Posey! Your mother talks about you all the time."

"She does?"

"Oh, yes. She talks about you and Rain and Henny. I'm Julia, by the way. I've only been here for a few weeks." She walked forward with outstretched hand. "Your mother was kind enough to let me do tarot readings here for a while until I can afford a place of my own."

I shook her hand. Of course, my "kind" mother, the woman who took in every sort of stray but never seemed to have time for her oldest child. Sounded just like her.

"Whoa. You have some strong energy," Julia said with a frown. "Could I do a reading for you? First one's free."

I bit my tongue to keep from saying something about how drug pushers used that line and I wasn't about to go anywhere near tarot cards or crystals or any of that other nonsense. "No thank you."

"Well, I'll be here if you change your mind."

I opened my mouth to speak, but my mother came down the stairs before I could. "Posey!"

Lark Adams was just a little over fifty, but she easily looked forty. Petite and blond with a body trim from years of doing yoga, she didn't look genetically related to me in the least. I'd often wondered if I were her first stray after all, maybe a baby on the side of the road she'd found. She had once shown me stretch marks on her hip, pointing out an almost faded set that belonged to me, more defined white ropy ones that belonged to Henny, and the last set, still purple, that belonged to Rain. Her battle scars, as she liked to call them, were her proof that I was hers.

Of course, we both knew Granny had raised me.

"Mom. There are some things I need to ask you."

She drew on a coat, probably more to cover her workout gear than for the weather. "I was just heading out to the Ash Wednesday service. Come with me."

"I don't think—"

"I can't be late. I promised Mrs. Dale that I would sit with her. You can talk to me on the way there and on the way back."

Before I knew it, I was walking outside with my mother. She'd swept me up into her plans as she always seemed to do, one of the reasons I avoided her when I could. I huffed as I tried to keep up with her brisk pace, but now I knew I was out of shape rather than pregnant. Tears pricked once again, but I tamped them down. "Mom, I'm just going to come out and say it: I need a place to stay."

"Of course! Your room is pretty much as you left it. Your brother has been sleeping in there, but I'm sure he'll be a gentleman and sleep on the couch. He needs to get out and find a place of his own anyway. This might be just the push he needs."

There she went again, deflecting interest from me to someone else.

Or did her chatter mean she was nervous?

"Thank you. I suppose you heard about Chad."

"Well, I'm a proponent of believing none of what you hear and only half of what you see, but Rain did tell me that, at least according to her friend, he'd left town with another woman."

Calling Courtney Rawls a friend of Rain's was probably a stretch.

"Is this the point where you say 'I told you so'?"

My mother stopped and turned to face me, gripping both of my shoulders. "Honey, I wouldn't dream of it. I can't afford to toss stones at those particular glass houses."

She squeezed my upper arms and rubbed them awkwardly before turning to face the church.

Stunned that she'd quoted scripture, I paused a second longer than she did and had to jog a few steps to keep up. "Where are we going again?"

"First Methodist. Today's Ash Wednesday."

She said all of this as though it made perfect sense. "Since when have you attended First Methodist or participated in Ash Wednesday?"

"Since about five years ago."

I'd really been out of touch if I didn't know my mother was attending church. Neither Ash Wednesday nor Lent were recognized by First Baptist or Love Ministries. For one thing, neither was mentioned in the Bible and Jesus had that whole passage about not letting people know you were fasting. Then there was the fact that setting aside only forty days to avoid sin meant you had another three hundred and twenty-five or so to contend with, and, of course, that Lent was so Catholic. Baptists didn't tend to truck with high church rituals.

In spite of all of that, I stood on the front steps of First Methodist. I wished I could bottle whatever it was that made people—even me, especially me—follow my mother wherever she went. Now I was following her into First Methodist where Imogene Dale could harass me about the fire I'd started the night before.

"We're running a little late," my mother whispered. She grabbed my hand to drag me inside and down the aisle, and I looked down at her hand. Her hands were warm and capable, as always. Would my life have gone differently, if she'd taken my hand more when I was a kid? I thought of how Rain had taken my hand the day before. Both mother and sister supported me in ways that didn't make any sense. Chad had often pointed out how they'd abandoned me, how he'd been there to pick up the pieces and take care of me.

But had he really?

It didn't matter. If I were going to follow through and get a divorce—and I had no reason not to now that I knew I wasn't pregnant—then I was going to have to stop thinking about him.

Yes, Posey, but you were *married to the man for ten years. He was your constant companion. These things may take time.*

An intense feeling of not having time, of being in a hurry smothered me. What if I didn't have time? Here I'd wasted at least ten years of my life. I had nothing to show for it but an angel with broken wings, an obsolete camera, and a whole host of regrets.

My mother squeezed my hand then let it go as the minister took the pulpit. Sure enough, Miss Imogene sat on her other side and smiled at me. She reached over my mother to pat my hand, and I thanked the organist for preventing her from saying *those* words. I had to look away from her pitying expression, so I drank in the sanctuary with its elegant chandelier, polished wooden altar and pews, and colorful stained glass. I was so used to a small room and Chad at a lectern that I'd forgotten what it was like to sit in a large, airy sanctuary. I'd never gone to a church with stained glass windows, either. In addition to the rich colors of the windows, First Methodist housed mahogany pews with velvet seats, and plush carpet. A spring sun brightened the stained glass—everything felt so . . . opulent. And wrong.

Then again, I'd spent my whole life trying to do everything right and look where that had landed me: jilted, jobless, and childless. Maybe I should try something different. Maybe I should try doing everything wrong for once.

"The grace of the Lord Jesus Christ be with you," boomed the minister, and I jumped out of my skin, properly chastised.

"And also with you," everyone but me responded. I put my hands on the pew in front of me, ready to bolt as the responsive reading continued. The whole thing sounded like a cult. Fortunately, we went into a hymn, even if it wasn't one I knew. Hymns were, at the very least, familiar territory. From there the minister read a Psalm.

I swayed from foot to foot, my night of fitful sleep catching up to me. The last place I wanted to be was church. Why was I here with the woman who wouldn't take me to church back when I begged? One summer, just after the second grade, I begged to be taken to Vacation Bible School. Sure, my intentions weren't entirely noble—I wanted to join my classmates and to hopefully prove to them that I wasn't a weirdo—but I was open to the idea of church.

My mother, who still looked like a teenager, peered down at

me as she was preparing to go out on a date, "But why do you really want to go, Posey? Are you wanting to go to church or are you wanting to see your friends?"

I wasn't a dumb child, but I also couldn't lie, so I said, "Both."

She'd said, "I think it's just for your friends, and I'm not sure I want you subjected to hellfire and brimstone at such a young age. When you're older, you can go to church if you want to. Then you can decide what you believe."

I believed that I wanted to go to Vacation Bible School because I'd heard it was going to be fun.

So I'd gone to Granny. She'd been delighted at my showing an interest in church and had walked me the three blocks herself on the days Mom took the car. Stubborn as I was, I decided I was grown up enough to make my decision about the church right then and there. Vacation Bible School started off innocently enough. We learned about Jonah in the whale and Noah's Ark. We played on the playground and drank red Kool-Aid and ate Nutter Butters. All of us learned to sing "Mine Eyes Have Seen the Glory," and the music leader taught us to slow down for the third verse that started "In the beauty of the lilies" but to then ramp it up and sing dramatically the last verse about how Christ was "coming like the glory of the morning on the wave."

That music burned through my tiny body straight to my heart. When the preacher spoke of eternal damnation if I didn't recognize Jesus Christ as my personal savior, then I and several of my classmates walked to the front of the sanctuary with the confidence of the children we were. Later, my mother and my grandmother argued late into the night about whether or not I would go back to the church and be baptized. They spoke in low, harsh whispers, but I could still hear them.

"She is a child! They used scare tactics," my mother said.

"And if she really did have a religious experience?" my grandmother asked. "Are you one hundred percent sure that our Posey didn't *mean* what she did? Are you willing to stake your life on it?"

"I didn't know what I was doing when I was her age and had almost the exact same experience."

"And disavowing that experience and running off to San Francisco? How did that work out for you?"

"Well, we got Posey out of the deal," my mother had finally grumbled.

"Yes, but at what price?"

"Mother. If both you and the church hadn't clamped down so hard on me, maybe I wouldn't have run away."

"Here we go again. Let's blame me for all of your problems. Yes, it was all *my* fault."

They remained silent for so long I'd almost fallen asleep. At last my mother said softly, "Fine. Let her go."

In another couple of Sundays I'd worn a white robe over a shorts set, and Brother Lewis submerged me in a glass tank behind the altar. I hadn't even known the tank was back there since it usually sat hidden behind curtains. I hadn't known that I would be completely submerged, and I certainly hadn't known the entire congregation would be watching. Standing in a see-through tub with the once scary but now mellow preacher holding my hand, I feared drowning even as I answered his questions in a small voice. When it was time to submerge me in the name of the Father and the Son and the Holy Ghost, I flailed, making a splash and striking his thigh.

Just as suddenly I stood again, water streaming into my eyes. Would I go to hell for striking a minister? I looked up into kind, smiling eyes. "Welcome to the church, Little Sister," he said.

I'd been going to church ever since.

My mother's presence in the institution she once despised puzzled me, but I'd long since learned to let Lark be Lark.

By this point in the Ash Wednesday service the minister had moved on to Matthew. He droned on about "not looking somber as the hypocrites do" while we fasted. Finally, we got to sit down, and the sermon began. Dour-faced Reverend Ford spoke about the traditions of Lent, the excesses of Fat Tuesday as exemplified by Mardi Gras—that actually sounded fun. He admonished his flock to make sacrifices that would bring them closer to God but pointed out that sometimes it was better to add something to your routine rather than to just give something up. He talked about his preteen daughter giving up soft drinks and how his wife vowed to get up fifteen minutes earlier each day for a devotion.

In essence, we were to find something that hampered us from being the best person we could be and to either add something to address it or to give something up if it held us back. If you drank too much, then give up alcohol. If television kept you from your family, then give that up. If you were unhappy about your physical health, add an exercise regime. The sky was the limit, he said, as long as we examined ourselves and looked at what was holding us back and keeping us from being the person God intended us to be.

Maybe Chad should look into giving up profligate spending and adultery.

No, I needed to think about myself. Not Chad. Chad would mean nothing to me just as soon as I could figure out how to divorce him. I needed to think on myself and what I needed to do because Liza was right: I wasn't happy.

What could I give up—or add—for Lent? My husband? Nah, he'd taken himself away. Having a baby? That had been taken from me, too. Chocolate? Too trivial in comparison to the other two. What was something I had too much of, something that made me unhappy because it wasn't good for me. Something—

Church.

The word came to me as if the Lord himself had whispered it, but I knew that couldn't be the case. Why would God tell me to give up church? That made absolutely no sense. Of course, church did remind me of Chad, and I needed to stop thinking about him so it made sense in a crazy, weird sort of way.

Come to think of it, Chad hadn't believed in Lent or giving things up. He said that was something Catholics did.

Heck, if Chad thought it was a bad idea, then maybe it was the absolute best idea for me.

If I still missed God after forty days, I could always come back to the fold. Maybe I could even find a different fold, one that better suited me. Having the bank foreclose on Love Ministries might end up being one of the best things to ever happen to me because now I was forced to look for another job and, goodness knew, I hadn't been doing anything more than stumble through life the past few years.

But giving up church? That's so . . . wrong.

And what has doing all of the right things done for you?

Oh, that devil on my shoulder had a very valid point. I'd gone to church only to have my self-professed minister husband leave me. I'd made excellent grades in school and completed my degree but never worked a day in my chosen profession. For heaven's sake, I'd held on to my virginity until my wedding night, and my reward had been infertility. Doing things right hadn't turned out so well. Maybe I should try doing things wrong for a while, see if that helped.

The minister called for people to come forward, and I watched the pews empty in an orderly fashion. At the altar, the minister dabbed something gray on the forehead of each person. This really was a cult, wasn't it? Well, getting dirt on my head was different than anything I'd ever done until this point, so why not? I followed my mother down the side of the church, inching forward toward the minister. He wore robes, something else Chad liked to make fun of and call too "high church." My mother, head bowed, looked up just in time to get her ashes. The minister turned to someone on his other side and then it was my turn.

He daubed ashes in a cross pattern on my forehead and softly said, "You are dust, and to dust you will return."

Cheery thought, that.

He cupped my cheek for the merest of seconds before sending me on my way. Was this what it was like to have a father? Did daddies remind their children of life's limitations even as they patted them on the cheek to remind them they weren't alone? Mom grabbed my hand, and I realized I had stood there in front of the minister for a second too long.

Finally, the last of the congregation received their ashes and returned to their seats.

Funny, I felt lighter, almost giddy, at the thought I wouldn't have to go to church again for at least forty days.

Maybe not ever.

It felt . . . wicked.

But I could also breathe again, almost smile, and so I decided I would observe Lent for the first time ever—by not going to church.

chapter 9

We walked back to Au Naturel in silence.

"Are you sure it's okay if I move in, Mom?" I said as we reached the door.

"Of course," she said. We entered the store and she looked at the counter with a frown. "Could you possibly watch the cash register for me this afternoon? Your brother is supposed to be here, but he didn't show. Again."

We'd spoken more sentences in a couple of hours than we had the previous five years, and she was going to let me sit behind the cash register? At least she trusted me.

"Mom, I don't know how the register works or what anything costs. I don't think this is a good idea."

"You're a smart girl. You'll figure out the cash register and everything has a price tag. Julia can help you if you have a problem. Now I've got to get ready for my afternoon classes."

Without waiting for a yes, she climbed the stairs.

"How does she do that?" I muttered, not expecting an answer.

Julia chuckled. "She's a Leo."

Whatever that meant. I walked behind the scarred counter, admiring its age. The ceiling had the old elaborate tin tiles, too. Mom had renovated, but she'd stayed true to original spirit of the building.

"It used to be a feed store," Julia said.

"Last I remember it was a discount furniture store."

"No, back when the building was first built. That's why the back dock is raised and there's such a large door. People could back up their wagons for supplies."

And thank you for that scintillating history lesson, strange lady.

I shuffled through the papers by the register and stacked them neatly. Nothing left to do there I walked around to see what a natural foods store might carry. Mom carried organic foods—especially foods without GMOs or gluten and lots of things made out of nuts—but nothing perishable. Supplements, a few makeup products, clothing for yoga, and the books in the corner rounded out her inventory. I hadn't thought out my tour of the store because I ended up in the very corner full of books where Julia sat with a table and several weird cards laid out in front of her.

"Posey. Please let me do a reading. You're practically vibrating."

Out of reflex, I shied away from the idea of any kind of divination. Chad had once called me the Witch of Endor just because I ate a fortune cookie and smiled at the prediction inside. That was the last of Chinese food in our house. Come to think of it, some hot and sour soup sounded really nice. Doing yet another thing that would tick off my soon-to-be ex-husband would be a pleasant bonus. "The first one's free, right?"

She grinned. "Absolutely, but I warn you: one reading may leave you wanting more."

"Pretty sure that's your strategy," I grumbled as I sank into one of the overstuffed chairs in the corner.

"Sometimes, but, in your case, I really want to know. That, and I'm bored. Not as much call for tarot here as there was back in—"

She stopped, and I didn't press her for more details. She could keep her secrets. Goodness knew, I wanted to keep mine.

Julia collected the cards that had been on the table and put them in the stack. Then she handed me the deck.

"What am I doing?"

"I'd like for you to shuffle the cards and let them pick up some of your energy. Don't worry. There's no wrong way to do it."

I fumbled with the deck of larger cards. In high school, I'd been a crack Spades player, but I'd given up cards once I married Chad. Technically, I wasn't supposed to be playing cards before, but we'd never gambled and justified it to ourselves in that way. The larger cards wouldn't yield to my whims. They butted into each other and didn't want to shuffle.

Julia chuckled, a sound I was beginning to heartily dislike. "That's enough. They're ready. You're trying to force it, and they've shuffled as much as they want."

I was glad to give up the cards.

"Now cut the deck with your left hand," Julia said softly. "I'm going to use something called a truncated Celtic cross."

A cross? In Tarot? Nevertheless, Julia gently lay down the cards ending in a circular pattern with a card in the middle. It had another card laid horizontally on top of it.

Julia considered me, her head tilted to one side. Then she looked down at the cards and back up at me. She pointed to the card in the middle, the one underneath a scary looking—

"Is that the devil?"

I hadn't even finished day one of Lent, and the Lord was going to smite me for giving up church and engaging in divination. My fingers dug into the upholstered arms of the chair. For the second time that day, I was ready to bolt.

"Calm down," Julia said. "It is the devil card, but it's not as bad as it seems. We'll get to it."

"Not as bad as it seems?"

"Patience is a virtue."

The words I'd recently texted to Rain resonated in a way they shouldn't have since the expression was cliché, but they still gave me pause. What had I gotten myself into? Forget about Chad and Love Ministries. Granny would have a flying duck fit that I was looking at tarot cards. I frowned. Did she know Mom was doing such things in her store?

"Let's start with your central card," Julia said as she removed the devil long enough to show me a beautiful woman. "You have the Empress. Think about fertility and abundance, creativity and intuition."

I laughed bitterly. Oh, yes. I was the poster child for fertility. "That's impossible."

"What do you mean?"

"I can't get pregnant. I've been trying for ten years."

Julia's brow furrowed. She looked at the deck and back at me. "Well, there are other kinds of fertility. Maybe of the imagination or of getting in touch with your intuition or an abundance of something."

I held my tongue, but this whole thing was a bunch of malarkey. I didn't have an abundance of anything except stripper shoes, and I'd tossed those in the trash. My intuition was obviously lacking since I didn't see my husband's betrayal coming, and I hadn't done anything creative in years. Still, I nodded for her to continue.

"Ah, maybe the Empress is about getting in touch with the feminine."

I snorted. Lucky guess since I was about to move in with my mother, my sister, my grandmother, and my brother. The house would be so full of femininity it might explode. At the very least, Henny would run screaming.

Julia's expression hardened, and I knew better than to laugh or snort again. "You need to claim that part of you that's holy and blessed."

"I don't feel either of those things."

"That's why you need to *claim* it." Julia looked down at the cards again. "That Which Crosses is the Devil Card. "You will have to deal with your dark side. Sometimes we have to step off the path to figure out where the path really is. Maybe you give in to indulgences or something taboo. You may have secrets or have committed transgressions—"

Ridiculous. I hadn't done anything wrong in ages. Other than give up church just a few minutes ago. Somehow that didn't seem to be on par with murder or theft or, I don't know, adultery.

"The illusion is that you are the things you have done, but look at how loose the chains are on both man and woman on this card. You can slip out if you wish because the bondage is of your own making. Beware bad decisions and foolish choices that limit you—"

Bondage? That reminded me of Amanda's crazy book.

And my even crazier husband.

"Don't be afraid of the devils on your shoulder, but you will have to deal with them or they will deal with you. Harshly."

I swallowed hard thinking back to that Vacation Bible School sermon that had impelled me to walk down the aisle to the altar. I couldn't remember the words of that sermon, but I felt the same fear today. The crazy idea that I was at a crossroads and taking the wrong path would be the death of me. I wanted to get up from the reading, but I remained frozen in fear. Why was I here? So far I had a card for fertility even though I was barren, and a card that told me not to make bad choices. Surely the reading couldn't get worse.

"Your card below is Death—"

"Death?"

"As I was saying, don't panic. Think of it more as a transformation and, yes, such change often involves loss. When you combine it with the Devil Card, though, it tells me the loss has been hard. Have you lost some things that matter?"

I laughed again even though I'd told myself I wouldn't. "My husband, my house, my car." Yet another hope for pregnancy. "But you probably could've found that out from Rain or just about any random stranger in the grocery store."

Julia smiled. "Yes, but you shuffled the cards. I'm just telling you what they mean."

I didn't have an answer for that. Rationally, I felt her interpretation might still be biased, but everything she said made so much sense. Well, except for the fertility part. And the bad choices I most certainly was not going to make.

"Maybe some of the things you lost weren't worth keeping. It may be rough going for a while, but death is part of a natural cycle, and it will give way to rebirth."

Rebirth sounded nice.

"Over here you have the Six of Cups, Reversed. The card is about looking back, but the reversal means looking back isn't a pleasant memory and that the past may be haunting you here in the present. Now this card along with the Empress and Devil? I'm guessing Mommy issues—"

"Come on! Everyone knows that. You know that just from the few minutes you've watched the two of us together."

Julia stared through me. "Do you want me to finish the reading or not? Believe me, my personal curiosity has been satisfied."

Oddly enough, my curiosity had not. "Please continue."

"I was about to say there might be some acting out, but I think we've seen that. Just know that you need to resolve this conflicted energy if you want to move forward, and there's a sense of urgency, which I'll get to in a minute. Now above you have the Two of Cups which suggests you have a new romantic relationship."

"I'm about to get divorced, and I'm not sure I ever want to date again much less marry!"

"So." Julia picked up the deck. "I take it the idea is surprising."

"To say the least."

"Pick a card for clarification."

I picked another card even though I didn't want a love interest. I just wanted to get rid of my old one.

"Interesting! You drew the Knight of Cups which suggests your new love interest is a sweet and ardent lover."

Sweet and ardent? Well those were two words that didn't describe Chad in the least. Selfish, efficient, and ruthless would be better words for him.

Ruthless? Is that what I really thought about my husband?

Soon-to-be ex-husband. And yes. As well as manipulative, bossy, and selfish.

"Your Before Card tells what is to come, and you have the Eight of Wands which indicates sudden, unexpected news. This is the card of urgency I was telling you about earlier. You need to fix things with your mother and quick because something unexpected is coming. Often the Eight of Wands paired with the Empress means a baby is on the way since they are both symbols of fertility."

"Impossible," I said.

"Nothing is impossible with God," Julia said.

Had she just quoted the Bible in the middle of a tarot reading? On the day I'd decided to take a sabbatical from all things religious?

"I'm telling you. It's impossible." I heard the anguish in my own voice, an emotion I'd been tamping down since the car ride to Walmart for more underwear.

Julia shrugged. "I can only tell you what the cards say. I feel compelled to point out, too, that there are no Pentacles in this reading. That means a lack of stability, especially since even your positive cards suggest flux and change. You also don't have any Swords. Maybe your thinking is a little muddy right now?"

I could only nod at how accurate her last interpretation was.

"This doesn't mean you can't have stability and clarity," Julia said gently, "It just means that your choices impact your ability to achieve them."

"Okay," I mumbled. I wanted to curl up in the corner and have a good cry. Until Julia had started talking about stability and clarity, I hadn't realized how much I still wanted those two very things. Any time I'd been unhappy in my marriage, I'd comforted myself with the idea that I had stability.

In a daze, I stood and took my position behind the cash register. Whether or not I agreed with her reading, I owed Julia something. "Thank you," I said, surprised a bit at how much I'd meant it.

"You're welcome," she said as she returned the cards to a single stack.

My thoughts jumbled around Julia's words. I reminded myself that it was all bunch of hogwash, but my mind parsed her words even as my heart hoped against hope that she might be right about a few things.

* * *

That evening I drove what belongings I'd collected to my grandmother's house.

The white frame house that sat catty-cornered from the funeral home had been built around the turn of the century, and my grandmother had lived there most of that time. My mother had only left the house for her lost years. When she returned, she'd been pregnant with me. As I stood on the gravel drive looking up at the old house where I'd been raised, I wondered if prodigality ran in the family.

One step inside and I could tell a new regime had taken over. Lavender wafted through the air instead of the mulberry potpourri that my grandmother had always preferred. The walls of the living room had been painted a cheery yellow, and colorful afghans were stacked on top of each couch. My grandmother sat in her favorite recliner, crocheting and humming.

"Hi, Granny," I said.

"Who are you calling Granny? And hush or you'll wake the baby."

Sure enough, at her feet sat a doll's cradle with a swaddled bundle inside. Since last I'd seen her, Granny's "baby" had progressed from a cheap dollar store doll to a Cabbage Patch whose cutesy expression unnerved me.

A lady in pink scrubs entered from the kitchen. "Oh, hello. I'm Miranda. You must be Posey."

Huh. People in Chez Adams still talk about me.

I shook her hand.

"I'm the nurse. Or," she said as she winked, "I'm your grandmother's cousin Mabel. In fact, you should probably call me that. I don't mind."

"Thanks, Mabel."

"Everyone else is in the kitchen," Miranda/Mabel said. I headed in that direction, wondering what I'd see next. As I left the room, Granny shouted, "Mabel, come quick—and bring the castor oil!"

I looked over my shoulder, but Mabel, as I'd decided I would call her, was nonplussed as she explained to my grandmother why she didn't really need what she'd requested.

When I entered the kitchen, Rain sat at the table working on her nails. A textbook sat open beyond her. Mom stood at the stove stirring something in a big pot.

"Smells good," I said.

"Vegetable soup." She didn't even turn around to hug me, but I got the sense that she wanted it to seem as though I'd never left rather than I was moving in.

Taking a seat across from Rain, I asked, "How's Granny?"

"The same," Mom said.

"She's crazier by the day." Rain held out her nails and blew on them.

"She's suffering from dementia. She's not crazy," Mom said.

"Upgrade on the doll?"

"The other one lost her head, but she has to have one to keep her calm and grounded." Mom turned away from the stove and reached for the bowls. "Did you decide to give up anything for Lent?"

Ah, the classic conversation change. "Actually I did."

Both Mom and Rain looked at me in eager anticipation. I let them sweat it for a few extra seconds, entirely too satisfied with myself. "I decided to give up church for Lent."

Rain laughed out loud as Mom cried, "What?"

"After being married to a preacher and working in a church for over five years with only two weeks of vacation, I need a break. I even went to church on my off days. I need space."

"Okay, then," Mom said in that strained tone that suggested she had so much she wanted to say but she refused to influence me one way or another.

"Respect!" Rain said, offering her open palm for a high five. "Next you're going to tell me you want to try out the Seven Deadly Sins just to see what they're all about!"

"What?"

Rain rolled her eyes then gestured for my hand. She clipped fingernails as she spoke. "I forget you don't go to the Catholic Church. So there are, like these seven virtues but also seven main sins: Lust, Gluttony, Greed, Sloth, Envy, Wrath, and what is that last one?"

"Pride," Lark answered.

"Yes, that's it!"

"I know what the Seven Deadly Sins are. You just surprised me," I said as she put down my right hand and gestured for my left. I hadn't wanted a manicure, but I supposed the price was right, and Rain apparently wasn't going to take no for an answer. My nails were so short she'd already moved on to cuticles and buffing.

"Where did you learn all of this?" Mom asked.

"Ha, you think I chose Dad's church just to be a contrarian, but I like the Catholic Church. It's not perfect, but then again no church is. Besides, I like to see Abuelita every week."

"And here I thought we were more concerned with the Ten Commandments than a set of specific sins," I said.

"Tomato, tomahto." Rain inspected her handiwork and began applying a clear coat. If she ever wanted to make extra money, she could definitely work in a nail salon with her speed and accuracy.

"How do you think one would go about sampling the Seven Deadly Sins?" I asked.

"Posey! Don't even joke about such things," Mom said. "Sins hurt others as well as yourself. Think about your karma."

"I will be your spirit guide," Rain said with an impish smile. "Except for lust. I can't help you there. I guess I could point you in the right direction, though."

"You've both lost your minds," Mom said. "If you put bad into the universe, it will find you."

"Fine, karma. I've got it," I said with a wink to my little sister.

Rain favored me with a radiantly devilish grin.

chapter 10

I decided to take the next day off and I would've dearly loved to have slept in, but I woke up long before dawn and couldn't go back to sleep.

For some reason, I picked up the book Amanda Kildare had left behind. If people thought you could go to hell for reading it, then why not? I was about twenty pages from the end when Rain breezed through with a Pop-Tart in one hand and her backpack slung over one shoulder. "Where's Granny?"

"Mabel took her for a walk."

"What are you reading?" Rain crinkled her nose. "Oh, you're reading that book."

Her prudish behavior surprised me. "You didn't like it?"

"No. I wanted to throttle what's-her-head's inner goddess, and he was so . . . ugh."

"At least he let her look over a contract first," I said.

"Wait. What?"

"I said at least she had some choice in the whole thing," I said without looking up from the page where the heroine finally walks out the door. *I hear you, sister.* "Hard limits and safe words aren't bad."

"You're joking, right?"

"Well, it's not that different from my experience with Chad, to tell the truth. He held control of the finances and told me what to wear and where to work. He even bought the Camry without consulting me." He also obviously wanted to spank me, but I wasn't about to discuss that similarity between my life and *that book* with my sister.

"Posey, that's not normal."

"Maybe not, but Paul does tell wives to submit to their husbands."

"I don't think that's what Paul meant." My cynical little sister's face radiated pity. So help me, if she blessed my heart, I would leave the house and never return.

She shook it off, and I silently thanked her for it. "That's not how relationships work. Don't you read books? Watch television? Something?"

"Chad got rid of the television a year after we got married. Said the cable bill was a waste of money. He picked out all of the books in the house."

Rain held up one finger then dropped her backpack and trotted down the hall. A few minutes later, she returned with a stack of romance novels.

It was my turn to crinkle my nose. "Really?"

"Hey, these books have men who know how to treat a woman. You'll see."

"I've got to go job hunting tomorrow."

"So? I wasn't saying you had to read them right now." Rain plopped on the love seat across from me and put her feet on the coffee table.

Eighteen. How could she know anything about anything at the age of eighteen? Did she really think a few books—fiction at that—could teach me anything? "What makes you the expert on love?"

She waggled her eyebrows. "I know things."

"How many things? Does Mom know you know things?"

She sat up and leaned forward over her knees. "Mom only knows what she wants to know. She made Dad give me the birds and the bees talk. Because that's something you want to hear from your father. I overheard her telling him that she didn't think she was a good example to me so he should do it."

"At least you got a talk, and, hey, she did run off and come back pregnant with me. For all I know my father is an axe murderer."

"Yeah, but she raised you and she loves you," Rain said softly. "If you want to be mad at anyone, it needs to be Chad."

Out of the mouths of babes.

"You know," Rain said as she stood, "I know I said you didn't have to read any of those books right now, but I'm thinking we need to ease you into these sins with some good, old-fashioned sloth. Be lazy and read today."

"I've been reading all morning," I said.

She shrugged. "For it to be sloth, you need to go to extremes."

Outside someone laid on a horn. Rain rolled her eyes, but jumped to her feet. "Even the bus driver wants me to go to school. Mom told him not to let me miss the bus."

"They're both right," I said. "Now go get edumacated."

She made a funny face to hide the fact she found me at least slightly amusing and then ran out the door.

I spent the rest of the day gobbling up one of Rain's romances and then another. The first was a historical with an arranged marriage and a wife who pressed for her *wifely* rights. The second took place in modern times with an abused heroine who learned to love again. Chad had told me romance novels would give me unrealistic expectations, but the afterglow from two hard-won happily-ever-afters left me wondering if *he* were the problem instead of my supposedly high expectations.

Maybe someday I'd find that sweet and ardent lover Julia had talked about. I lay back and basked in the ending of the second story, closing my eyes to rest them. Warm afternoon sun washed over me. Having sore eyes, the beginning of a headache, and tight muscles felt positively decadent.

One thing I did know: I wasn't about to get hitched any time soon. Chad had almost killed my sense of self, but I would find it again. I should clean up and head over to Ben Little's office to find out how to get rid of my husband, but it was late so I picked up a third romance novel instead. Rain hadn't even cracked the spine on this one. I lifted it to my nose, enjoying the new book smell and then sighed happily as I flipped to Chapter One.

Sloth was my favorite.

After supper I thought I should do at least one productive thing since I'd have to spend the next one looking for a job. As the sun set, I rang Liza's doorbell. She came to the door in her ubiquitous yoga pants with her hair standing up and a fussy baby on her hip.

"You have got to quit waking this child up."

"It's seven o'clock at night. I thought this would be the one time I wouldn't wake up the baby," I said as I stepped inside. Liza's tiny house looked as though a tornado had been through. It had to be eating her alive.

"Up is down. I thought we had a routine going, but now I can't get him to sleep through the night anymore." She paused to yawn. "To top it all off, I think he's trying to start teething."

"Hand me the baby."

She relinquished the child, and I took him gratefully.

"Why don't you go take a nap."

"Posey—"

"I won't take no for an answer," I said, dancing with my honorary nephew. His fussing had already abated—probably because he wanted to know why the crazy lady was bouncing him so.

"I only have an hour before he'll want to eat."

"Go," I said.

She trudged down the hall, and I sat with Nathaniel in the recliner. "Little man, you need a nap, too. I'm sorry I woke you up."

We rocked for so long I almost went back to sleep. I could hold Liza's little boy forever, starting at his sweet expression, those sooty eyelashes, those delicate and expressive tiny hands. For half a second I considered taking my best friend's child and bolting. We could find a little town out west, maybe a cottage that looked on a lake. I would raise him as my own, and he would call me mother. God, I wanted my own child with a visceral need I couldn't explain. Maybe that's what women referred to when they spoke of their "biological clocks." All I knew is that I needed a baby, wanted one with every fiber of my being no matter how irrational it made me sound.

Nathaniel sighed in his sleep, and the pain of longing intermingled with the joy of holding such an exquisite creature.

Envy.

I had envied my best friend ever since she'd so excitedly told me she was expecting. Shame washed over me in heat and then chills as I thought about how brusque I had been with her, how I hadn't properly expressed joy and excitement with her. I'd been so selfish, so caught up in how unfair it was for her to accidentally get pregnant when I'd been trying so hard. I'd been a bad friend long before the other morning when I'd bristled at her well-meaning suggestions.

Envy was *not* my favorite.

I needed to atone.

Carefully, I slid the baby into the bassinet in the corner. Based on the pile of blankets by the recliner, it looked as though Liza had been sleeping out in the living room—probably in the hopes that Owen could get some sleep before his long work shifts. Liza needed to understand that she needed sleep, too. Quietly, I moved around the living room picking up papers and stacking the mail. Empty diaper and wipes boxes went to the kitchen. While in the kitchen, a glance into the laundry room revealed a load of dirty clothes so I started a load. With an eye to the baby, I cleared the table and loaded the dishwasher. When Liza entered the living room an hour and a half later, Nathaniel still slept, but all surfaces were clear, and dishwasher and washer hummed in the background.

Liza looked from baby to clean room to me then to the kitchen beyond before whispering, "Am I in the right house?"

I stood and opened my arms out to her. "I'm sorry, Liza. You were right, and—"

"You do not want to hug me. I don't think I've showered since the Reagan administration."

"Pretty sure you've had a shower since kindergarten."

"Whatever. It's bad."

"I don't care," I said as I hugged her.

"You are so forgiven after all of this," she said. "How'd you like to babysit sometime?"

It was on the tip of my tongue to mention that Chad liked for me to spend nights at home, but it didn't matter what Chad liked anymore. "I'd love to."

"We can have a sleepover like old times! You can sleep on the couch."

I frowned. "Your couch is stuffed with pebbles and loathing."

She sighed. "I know. I hate it, too. It came from my Aunt Hyacinth. If you knew her, you'd understand."

"How would you feel about leather?"

"That sounds fancy," she said.

"As it so happens I have a sofa that needs a home. It's yours if you'll help me out at the garage sale I'm having on Saturday."

"You're on."

"As for babysitting, you should drop Nathaniel off with me at the house one night. Go out on a date with Owen."

She flopped down on the couch of hatred, wincing because it really was the hardest one I'd ever encountered. "That would be great. I've forgotten what he looks like."

"How about tomorrow night? Then we'll yard sale it up on Saturday."

"Don't you need to tag things?" Liza asked, her brow furrowed. At least she was getting some of her perfectionism back.

"Nope. It's a fire sale. Everything must go. I'll negotiate. I'll give things away after noon. I'm ready to be done with all of this."

"Any word?"

How I loved her for not saying his name. "No. I think he's under the false impression that I'm going to do as he's requested. He's destined for disappointment."

Liza smiled. "Looks like my friend Posey has returned. Welcome back."

chapter 11

Today was not the day to sin with pride. I'd called the Board of Education since it'd occurred to me that they couldn't call me about the supply position because I had smashed my phone. They "had nothing to tell me at this time." A cursory glance at newspapers from both Ellery and Jefferson yielded few jobs with my lacking skill set. I found a few receptionist positions, but they were all either on the other side of Jefferson or they required me to know software programs I hadn't yet learned.

Ellery had nothing.

Nothing except for the fact my mother had left the house with a Help Wanted sign.

That's how I came to find myself standing in front of Au Naturel ready to ask my mother for a job after she'd already offered me a home. Most people would probably rejoice at how easily their problems had been solved, but pride pricked at me. I'd had everything so together. I'd been the child who didn't make waves or cause trouble, the one who never even needed help with homework. Now I needed to ask my mother for a job.

I took a deep breath and opened the door, wondering how long it would take the sound of the pan flute to drive me nutty.

Mom stood behind the counter, her hair in a high ponytail. She looked up with a dazzling smile that always effectively hid whatever she was really thinking. "Posey, what a surprise!"

"Hi, yes. I saw your sign, and I would like to apply for the job."
Her smile disappeared. "I'm not sure it's a good idea."

Knowing that her refusal was a possibility and hearing it were
two different things. Why had I thought I could count on her? Getting a roof over my head was more than I'd expected. "I understand."

I turned to go, willing my tears not to come until I'd closed the
door.

"Posey?"

Why did she have to make everything so difficult? Couldn't
she just let me leave in peace? "Yes?"

"How long would you need this job?"

I turned around to face her. "I don't know. I put in an application for a temporary position with the school system. I looked at
other receptionist jobs, but most wanted someone who could act
as an administrative assistant also, and I don't know all of the
computer programs they want me to know. I think they're hiring
at the Co-op, but they're looking for someone who can do heavy
lifting."

Mom chuckled. "I told myself I wouldn't ever hire another
family member after what your brother has put me through, but I
can't have you lifting those heavy feed sacks, now can I?"

"You can count on me to show up on time."

"I'm well aware of how annoyingly punctual you are. You did
demonstrate the other day that you could mind the shop and
most of my business comes from the studio anyway. You can
work here temporarily."

I took my place behind the register as Mom scampered off to
teach her first class of the morning.

"Hey, Mom, what does this job pay?"

"Not nearly enough," she sang over her shoulder.

Julia chuckled from her post in the corner.

"What are you laughing about?"

"Oh, nothing," she said as she studied the cards laid out before her.

I walked over to look at a more elaborate pattern than what she'd
lain down for me. "You're not getting much business, are you?"

When Julia looked up, her hazel eyes bored through me. "According to the cards, I should see a spike in business shortly. It always takes a while for people to come around. The advantage of small towns is that I'm not competing with those psychics who have neon signs. The downside is, well, most people here mistakenly think I'm doing something wrong."

"They're scared of divination."

Julia smiled down at the cards. "Humans have always searched for what's to come, and they've also always feared it. At least tarot helps them see what came before and what's happening in their lives in the present. If they're willing to listen, that is."

I still didn't feel particularly fertile or abundant. So far, I didn't think I'd made any bad choices, either. "We'll see."

"Also, I've almost talked your mother into letting me open a smoothie bar in the back. I think we could do some brisk business with the yoga students and other people in town. I have a weight loss supplement that works—"

"Really?"

"If you commit to exercise and understand it's not a quick process."

Of course. So much easier to put on weight rather than take it off. "I'm still interested."

"Excellent! You can be my guinea pig when I get started."

"And Mom's on board with this?"

"Not yet. But she will be."

At that moment Amanda Kildare walked in, stopping short. "Posey."

"Good morning. I read your book. Still don't think you're headed to hell."

"Oh, thank goodness," she said, her eyes nervously darting to Julia and back to me.

"Do you have an appointment with Julia?" I asked. "Please don't let me keep you."

She sagged with relief and walked purposely to Julia's nook.

I retreated to the cash register standing as far away from the women as possible and training my eyes on the street beyond the window.

John O'Brien crossed the street, and I wondered if he would be more like the heroes in the books Rain had loaned me. Surely he was a "sweet and ardent lover," even if he wasn't meant for me. I stared unabashedly until I realized he was heading to Au Naturel. I took a step back.

"Posey, I've been looking for you."

"Really?"

He laughed. "Well, I needed two things. First, I wanted to see if you were okay. I heard something about Chad and saw the notice on the church door."

"I'm okay." I didn't sound convincing even to myself.

"Okay's probably the best we can hope for now, huh? The second thing is that Mrs. Morris wants her piano back. She says she only loaned it to the church, and the bank had better not auction it off."

"Oh. Well. I don't have the keys anymore," I admitted. "I kinda gave them to Malik Foster."

"Good to know." John crammed his hands in his pocket. "Are you sure you're okay?"

"No, but I'm going to be."

He grinned. "That's what I like to hear. I'll see you around, huh?"

"Yeah, see you around," I echoed as I enjoyed watching John walk away.

That night my feet ached. At some point I would need to buy better shoes if I were going to keep working at Au Naturel. I could ignore the ache in my heels if I concentrated on the baby I held, though. Nathaniel was so fussy, but I couldn't fault him. Liza told me it was the first time they'd left him with someone else. She'd been so nervous as she explained everything in the diaper bag and then handed me a typed sheet of paper with his nighttime routine.

"Liza. Go have fun," I said. "I can handle this."

An hour later I wondered if I'd spoken too soon. My pseudo-nephew would not take his bottle, scrunching up his eyes as if to tell me, "That is not my mom, and you know it."

He only quit fussing when I walked him around the house in a colic hold, and my arms ached from the position of one hand under his little butt and the other over his stomach. Who knew that someone so small could weigh so much? Blessedly, Liza rang the doorbell a full thirty minutes before I expected her.

"Hand me the baby," she said.

"Gladly. I think he's missed you almost as much as you've missed him."

"Possibly," she said as she plopped down on the love seat and fiddled with her bra. "My boobs are killing me. The La Leche League video didn't say a thing about this. It was supposed to be all puppies and rainbows and happily nursing babies."

Granny snorted from where she sat in her recliner, crocheting. Her foot rocked her little crib, and I couldn't help but notice this afghan was misshapen. She'd lost the precision that was the hallmark of the other pieces around the room.

Nathaniel latched on, and both mother and child sighed with relief.

"Boy like that needs some Pablum."

Both Liza and I looked over to Granny who continued crocheting without even looking up.

"Some what?" I asked.

"Pablum. He was sleeping through the night but now he ain't, am I right?"

Liza looked from me to Granny. "Yes, how'd you know?"

"Had enough kids of my own, didn't I? That's a big boy and he's hungry." She looked over at her baby doll in the crib and smiled. She stayed quiet for so long I thought she'd retreated to that place she sometimes went.

"But, ma'am, the doctors say it's best to exclusively breastfeed until six months."

"Six months?" The idea offended her so much she slammed her work down into her lap. "That's ridiculous. We've all got better things to do than that. I'm not saying you ought to wean a baby too soon, and I'm not saying you should put them on formula exclusively, either. My little sister weaned her babies too early and you've never seen such a sickly lot."

Having met my Aunt Pauline, I thought the sickness of her

kids probably had more to do with her drafty house and the alcoholic husband who drank away half the grocery budget. I held my tongue on that subject, though. "And you don't think this . . . Pablum will hurt the baby?"

"Of course not! I gave it to my youngest and she gave it to hers. Stuff is a lifesaver. Just mix it with some breast milk, and you'll be back to thank me. I guarantee it."

I tried to imagine the logistics of putting a little breast milk into cereal, but all I could think of were Cheerios, and that wasn't an image I wanted in my head. Liza's head tilted to one side; she was considering it.

"The cereal comes in tiny flakes." My mother said from the doorway. Her amused expression suggested she'd heard the whole exchange and that I'd been wearing a look that conveyed my disgust and confusion.

"So this Pablum thing is okay?" I asked my mother quietly. She was the guru of all things natural, after all.

"Well, it worked for you, your brother, and your sister," she said with a shrug. "The doctor is probably right about keeping things as natural as you can for as long as you can, but there's a lot to be said for a mother's sanity, too."

Even dressed in her date night clothing, Liza looked bedraggled. The pants she wore looked suspiciously like a maternity pair, and I knew that had to bother her, too. She'd lain back against the love seat and closed her eyes which only emphasized the dark circles.

"Where can I find this Pablum?" she asked as she closed one side of her bra and burped the baby before putting him on her other side.

"Oh, they don't sell it anymore," Mom said.

I sighed in frustration. Just another one of Granny's wild goose chases, another thing from the good ol' days that someone had determined was no longer good for us. "Then why bother getting Liza's hopes up?"

"Pablum's just an old brand," she said. "They make the same kind of cereal under different names. The stuff comes in a box, and it's on the baby food aisle."

"And you're sure this is okay, Mrs. Adams?"

"Well, like I said, I used cereal, and Mom did before me. I didn't need it as much with Rain because she was so tiny, but for Posey and Henny, it was a lifesaver."

Nathaniel had been clenching his fist, sometimes beating Liza's breast as if to make more milk come. His tiny hand relaxed and his arm fell slowly as he succumbed to a full belly. God how I wanted that: a baby I could comfort and hold close.

Owen walked over from the front door where he'd been standing, awkwardly trying to decide if he should put his hands in his pockets, leave, or come sit down. Now that the baby had finished nursing, he knew his job: He took his son and burped him while Liza put her wardrobe to rights. His smile to child and then to mother made my heart ache. His large hands hardly fumbled with the little straps on the carrier as he gently nestled the sleeping baby inside.

When I looked up, Granny's hawk eyes stared through me.

"Posey, thank you so much for this date night. You have no idea what this has meant for me and Owen," Liza said as she stood. "Let me hug you while I smell decent."

"Yeah, thanks, Posey," Owen said. I'd always liked him. He didn't say much, but, then again, whoever was married to Liza wasn't destined to get many words in edgewise.

I clasped Liza tightly then walked both her and Owen to the door. "It was my pleasure. You'll have to let me watch him again one day."

"Oh, you're on," Liza said with a grin.

Owen effortlessly carried the baby carrier with one hand and took Liza's hand with the other. They leaned close enough to touch noses.

I tried to think of a time when Chad had leaned in like that, his nose touching mine for a second of contentment. Deep in the recesses of my fuzzy mind I could think of maybe one instance when we were first dating. We'd never had the opportunity to bond over a child. Now, we never would, and I was surprisingly okay with that. I couldn't see a man with limited Crock-Pot skills as the kind of father who would burp the baby or change a diaper.

"You, girl," Granny said as I closed the front door.

"Ma'am?"

"Have a seat."

I did, and she didn't speak for so long that I started to get up and head to the kitchen where I could hear the tea kettle's struggles to reach a boil.

When Granny looked up, skin hooded her eyes, enhancing her agony. "I can't remember who you are, but I know you're important so I have something to say to you: You think you want what she has, but it's not for you. It's a sin to covet."

My blood ran cold. I hadn't seen that one coming.

Granny's expression softened. "I know what it's like to want something you can't have, and the wanting will eat you alive if you let it. You'll get yours in God's own time."

In God's time. That's what Chad always said. I'd given up church so I didn't have to hear such things.

Besides, if God took any longer, I'd be Sarah's age by the time I had a child, and I didn't think current women had Biblical miracles like that anymore.

No, I'd continue to stay out of church, and I'd mark my own time, thank you very much.

chapter 12

The next morning I woke up at five even though I'd slept one last night in my old home so I wouldn't have to get up quite as early for the yard sale. Between Granny's words and my unwanted memories of Chad, I hadn't slept well, so I got up and walked through the house, hating all of the blue walls that Liza had pointed out not long ago. Funny how you could live so long and not notice a thing, but, once it was brought to your attention, you couldn't think of anything else.

Though it was still dark, I laid blankets on the dewy lawn. Even though I knew my car was safe, I still looked over my shoulder for the repo man. Over the past week, I'd learned that betrayals often happened in the darker hours. Once my lawn was almost hidden by quilts and blankets, I started cleaning out closets, taking out armload after armload of Chad's clothes, then mine, and dumping them on blankets. I tossed out drawers and brought out appliances. Laundry basket after laundry basket containing kitchen supplies landed on the ground. I put out one box with all of my angels and another with old dusty albums. Lamps, smaller pieces of furniture, appliances. I toted items out until my back ached and I panted from the exertion. Then I left the front door open as an invitation to anyone who wanted the old four-poster bed or that damned curio that had it out for my toes.

Once I was satisfied I'd put as many of my earthly possessions outside as I could, I sneaked inside for a cup of coffee as the sun finally peeked above the horizon. Rain had put yard sale signs all over town for me since I'd missed the deadline for the paper to print the information. All of her signs said the sale started at seven thirty which meant people would start showing up at six thirty, maybe even six. And three minutes 'til, I went out to the garage and sat in an old lawn chair with coffee cup in hand.

Sure enough, the first car arrived at six minutes after six. Others followed closely. At one point an elderly couple "helped" me spread out some housewares so they could pick through my pots and pans and take the best ones. By seven thirty, the sun had finally made her appearance. I'd already made quite a few sales when Liza showed up with a bounce in her step. Was she whistling?

"Who are you and what have you done with my friend Liza?" I asked.

"Your friend Liza made the grocery store two minutes before it closed. She tried that cereal thing, and everyone slept through the night. It was glorious!"

I couldn't help but smile. "I'm glad it worked out."

"You watch the baby. I have coffee and sausage biscuits in the car. Then I'll get the pack-and-play."

"This keeps getting better," I said, as I took Nathaniel from the carrier. Even he looked more alert. "That cereal treat you right, big man?"

"My Lucky Charms were awesome, thanks for asking!"

John O'Brien. And, of course, he'd eaten Lucky Charms for breakfast. Of course.

His dimples took my breath away.

"Uh, hi, John."

"Mind if I take a look at that weight bench?"

"Go right ahead." I stepped aside so he could walk into the garage and study the dusty weight bench Chad had used maybe twice. I'd left it in the garage because it was too heavy to drag out on the driveway. Goodness knew Chad had never let it see the light of day, so why start now, I figured.

John dusted off the bench with his hand and lay down. He tested the barbell. I watched the contours of his chest and the definition of his arms as he did a few bench presses. His T-shirt rode up ever so slightly, captivating me with a sliver of abs.

"Enjoying the view?" Liza asked.

I jumped out of my skin, and the baby fussed.

"You are so edgy," she said. "Put the baby down before you drop him."

"I would never—"

"I know, I know, but you can't hold him and have breakfast, and I'm scared you'll accidentally squeeze him to death if you keep holding him while watching John lift weights."

"That obvious?"

She arched an eyebrow and took the baby.

My eyes had traveled back to John, who was adding different weights to the barbell, when Mr. Ledbetter hollered, "How much for this hunk of junk?"

We haggled over the push mower, which was *not* a hunk of junk. I knew this because I had learned how to sharpen the blades and change the oil after our first mower had died from lack of maintenance. Mr. Ledbetter probably didn't need another lawn mower, but he was a staple of local yard sales. He liked to bargain.

In the end, I got almost what I wanted just by setting the first price so high. Mr. Ledbetter left, satisfied he'd bargained me down. We were both pleased. From there I had to scare a young mother away from the pack-and-play where Nathaniel slept, telling her neither playpen nor baby were for sale. She laughed at the second one and told me she had no need for another baby.

Meanwhile, Liza had put on her charm to sell my custom drapes to Imogene Dale, whose house was almost exactly like mine and thus had very similar windows. An older lady in nurse's scrubs bought almost all of *The Golden Girl* dress collection, and for that I was extremely grateful. Furniture flew out of the driveway as people showed up in trucks, ready to haul off larger items.

"Hey, Posey."

I turned to find John thumbing through some old LPs I'd found in the spare bedroom closet when Chad and I first moved in. I'd never owned a record player, so I knew nothing about them. "I want the weight bench, and I'm probably going to buy a bunch of these. How much were you thinking?"

"I don't know," I said. "What? Twenty for the weight bench and fifty cents each for the records?"

He frowned at me then pulled an album from the stack reverently. "This is an original Miles Davis. I see Queen and Jimi Hendrix. No way am I going to allow you to sell these for fifty cents each."

"Can I have that Hendrix back? Mom named my brother for him."

John handed over the record but looked sad to see it go. I took it to the garage and put it on top of the freezer under the old cigar box I was using to keep the money. When I returned, John said, "This box is worth at least a hundred dollars."

"Are you talking me *up* on a yard sale price? You do know that's not how any of this works, right?"

He rewarded me with those dimples and nodded slightly to the left before talking out of the corner of his mouth. "See that man over there?"

He could only be referring to the middle-aged man flipping through my books then pausing to eye the box John held. "Yeah?"

"I've been going to a lot of yard sales over the past few months because I'm still trying to get what I need for the old house I bought."

"The old Busbee farmhouse?"

"Yeah. Thank goodness that guy over there isn't looking for furniture, or I wouldn't have any. He's worse than Mr. Ledbetter, going to sales and talking people into selling for cheap things that he then sells on eBay for a fortune. I don't think that would be fair to you."

Someone cared about what was fair to me?

"Are you sure they're worth that much?"

"At least."

"Okay, then." Goodness knew, I could use the money. But did John have much more than I did?

As he brought out his wallet, he continued, "That guy bragged about it to me one day when he stiffed Mrs. Morris on some antique dishes. Watch out for people like him. If someone's insistent about lowering the price or how worthless something is, stand your ground and see if you can sell it online."

I swallowed hard and nodded. John handed me a stack of twenties.

"But, John—"

"They're worth it. Promise. Who's the rock and roll expert here?"

He walked off with his box of records, and the man standing among my books shook his head in disgust and headed out across the yard. Guess I didn't have anything else he was interested in buying.

I was looking forward to watching John load the weights when someone tapped my shoulder and I turned around to see Miss Georgette and her constant companion, Miss Lottie. The latter sniffed as she thumbed through my CDs, but Miss Georgette had something to say.

"I got a call from the Board of Education yesterday," she said, her enthusiasm infectious. "I was happy to tell them that you would be the best little first grade teacher they could find. I mentioned that no-good Chad Love had up and left you—I still can't believe he had us all fooled like that, the nerve!—and that you could really use the job. Imogene told me that her sister told her that you had the car repossessed. I saw the sign outside Love Ministries, and then I come over here and you are having to hold a rummage sale just to make some money, and it is a crying shame, I tell you."

She had to pause for more oxygen even while I held my breath because I was afraid of what might come next.

"Just bless your heart."

Yes, bless it indeed.

"You need to brush up on your methodology because I think

they are going to call you on Monday. I know it's just a supply position until the end of school, but you never know when they're going to need someone for the next year, and supply positions are such a great way to get your feet in the door. Have you thought about being a substitute teacher? That's another good way to get some experience while you wait for something over at the elementary school to open up. And this new principal is a real go-getter. She told me she's ready to fill that position because there's only so much a substitute can teach them, and—"

"Miss Georgette, I thank you so much for all of your help and—"

"How much for this?" Miss Lottie interrupted.

It was an Alan Jackson CD full of hymns. Great songs, but I didn't have a CD player anymore. "Fifty cents."

Without a word, the other lady dug into her coin purse and brought out two quarters then clutched Alan Jackson to her ample bosom as though she'd found the holy grail.

"Lottie, I thought we'd agreed that we didn't need to buy anything else at rummage sales," Miss Georgette chided.

"But look at that bedspread over there. Wouldn't that go well in your guest bedroom?"

Both ladies ambled off to take a look at the blue duvet, and I sighed in relief. If Miss Georgette had already received a call, then I needed to get a phone pronto just in case the go-getter principal called. Goodness knew I couldn't afford to miss the opportunity.

"Here, take the boy."

I opened my arms just in time to take Nathaniel. Judging by his heavy eyelids, Liza had just fed him.

"Washing my hands, and I'll be right back," Liza called out.

"Okay, I've loaded up the bench and weights. How much?"

I looked straight up into John's baby blues, and my mouth went dry. It ought to be a sin for a man to be so pretty. "I thought I told you twenty."

"Posey, please. That bench ain't from Walmart."

"Fine. You negotiated so well for me last time, you tell me."

He bent over his phone, one strand of hair escaping from his ponytail. Thank goodness I was holding the baby because the urge to push that strand of hair back was strong.

"Says here that bench probably cost about a hundred, another two for that set of weights—"

"I'll give you twenty if you'll just take it off for me." My eyes grew wide at the Freudian slip. "I mean, if you'll carry off the heavy weights."

His grin widened as my voice trailed off. "I'm thinking fifty is fairer."

Heck, I'll give you fifty dollars if you'll let me watch while you work out.

I shook my head. Where had that thought come from? I had to be losing my mind. Had my mother's wild genes caught up with me? Heat surged through my body, followed by a chill. Maybe I had a fever. Maybe I had an ague of insanity.

"You would know better than I do," I managed.

"Then sold," he said as he held out a crisp fifty. "Don't suppose you have a couch, do you?"

"Sorry, I gave the couch to Liza."

"Although you can have mine if you'd like," Liza said as she took her son from me. Now I didn't know what to do with my hands. I needed to always be holding a baby when talking to John. That way I wouldn't fidget so much.

"Don't do it," I said. "It's filled with rocks and hatred."

"I thought it was pebbles and loathing?"

"Upon reflection, I've upgraded its contents."

John laughed out loud and rewarded me with dimples. My stomach bottomed out, and a blush crept into my cheeks.

"Rocks and hatred might still be better than sitting on the floor. You serious, Liza?"

"Yep, I will *give* it to you if you will take it off my hands."

John started backing up, but pointed as he said. "You're on. Hey, I've got an appointment to tune the Frasiers' piano, and I'll see you ladies around."

"Bye," Liza and I said together.

He stopped and turned around. "I'm really going to miss those brownies."

"Maybe I'll make you some anyway. Even if I don't have a piano anymore."

"I'd like that." With a wave, he was off, making long strides toward his truck, which now held all of the components of the weight bench. I allowed myself a minute to mourn the fact I'd been talking to Miss Georgette and had missed the heavy lifting that had required.

"Still have a crush on O'Brien, eh?" Liza asked.

"Come on!"

"Maybe I'll make you some brownies anyway," Liza mimicked with exaggerated eyelash batting.

"Oh, shut up!"

"Man, I wish Owen and I could get more brownies. Wanna watch the baby tonight?"

"Oh, my gosh, would you please stop?" Great. Now I sounded like my little sister. I walked into the garage for some shade and a quick search for wherever I'd left my composure.

Liza followed me and lay a now sleeping Nathaniel in the pack-and-play. "I'm just saying you could do worse."

"I'm not even divorced yet, and I don't think I ever want to get married again."

"Who said anything about dating or getting married? I was talking about hooking up."

Well, anyone who cared about not taking advantage of me when buying a record collection at a yard sale would have to be a far better lover than Chad—not that I had much experience in that area, having gone to my wedding night a virgin. Of course, there was no way John O'Brien would ever want to slum it with a frump like me.

Although he had told me that I was pretty just the way I was.

He was just being nice.

Whatever. I might be laying off the church, but that didn't mean I needed to get wrapped up in fornication.

It's not like you'd get pregnant.

"Oh, for crying out loud!"

"What?" Liza asked.

Apparently, I was thinking out loud again. "Just arguing with myself."

"Yeah, you were," Liza said with a wicked grin. "You were arguing over whether or not you should make a move on John the Baptist. I vote yes."

"You got some last night, didn't you?"

"Yes. Finally, but who knows when this next drought may end, so please let me live vicariously through you."

Blessedly, Abigail Bolton motioned for me to come over. No way did I want to talk about sex with Liza. We were best friends and all, but she didn't need to know about the wigs and ridiculous shoes and corner time. She wouldn't understand how much I'd wanted to be pregnant or what I'd been willing to do to make it happen. She'd bless me out for kowtowing to Chad for all of those years—and she wouldn't be wrong. I just wasn't ready to hear it.

I knew I was attracted to John, but I couldn't go there, could I? I had more baggage than an airport carousel. And yet . . .

I couldn't help but wonder what it would be like to make love, to be intimate with a man who wouldn't ever send me to the corner, the kind of man who talked me up on yard sale prices because he was concerned about what was fair and just. It didn't hurt that he was quite easy on the eyeballs, and I hadn't been attracted to my husband for quite some time. Oh, I'd gone along with his shenanigans, and he'd made at least a little effort to take care of me, but, at the end of the day, sex was always about getting pregnant for me. For Chad, it was always about Chad.

By this point, Mrs. Bolton had taken out every plate, bowl, tea cup, and saucer to inspect each piece for cracks. After a fair amount of haggling, I managed to unload my entire set of china for a tidy sum. As I was stacking it up to count the pieces, I noticed an LP at the bottom of a box. Considering how much John had paid, the only decent thing to do would be to take him the LP, right?

Sure, and having an excuse to see him didn't hurt, either.

As I mindlessly wrapped china in newspaper, I thought of

what it would be like to bring the album to him. He would toss it over his shoulder and kiss me and—

"Posey? Don't you have a gravy boat, too?"

"No, ma'am. I'm afraid it got dropped early on in the marriage." More like thrown at a wall because Chad said I'd been flirting with the sack boy at the grocery store, but no need to tell the whole truth and nothing but. After all, it had been dropped. On the floor after it hit the wall. With force. While full of gravy. I thought I'd never find the last of the gravy splatters.

Such violence was a good reason to rein in my imagination. John O'Brien was not interested in me like that and, even if he was, I obviously wasn't a good judge of male character. Besides, I wouldn't do anyone any favors jumping into one relationship before I managed to get out of the other. We would have to be brownie buddies.

Of course, thanks to Liza, even "brownie" had a suggestive connotation.

Great. Now I was craving brownies.

Looked like my Saturday night would be spent with a pan of brownies and another one of Rain's romance novels, and I was okay with that. Looking forward to it, even. I could be relatively sure neither the brownies nor the book would let me down, and there was something to be said for that.

Rain showed up as we were packing the last of the things to take to Goodwill. We'd sold more than I had hoped, and Liza had kindly offered to take a load since she had the van. Rain poked around the boxes of what was left, her expression suggesting she saw nothing that interested her.

"Hey, Rain, think you could help me pick out a new phone?"

"Sure," she said. "Want to go tonight?"

It was either that or my plan of books and brownies. The more I thought about it, the more appealing brownies and a book sounded, but I really needed to get a new phone since Miss Georgette had already been called to give a reference for me. "Sure."

"Yay! Maybe we can get you some new clothes."

"With what? Do I have a money tree in the backyard that I somehow missed?"

"No, but I did find this in a box I was breaking down—it'd slipped under a flap." Rain held up a credit card.

I walked closer, recognizing it almost immediately. "I can't use Chad's credit card. He's probably already canceled it anyway."

Actually, he probably hadn't. That was his special credit card, the one he used for "adult" purchases that he made sure would be sent to the house in plain brown wrapping.

"I really think the least he owes you is a little shopping," Rain said as she dangled the card in front of me the way Eve probably offered Adam the ill-fated apple.

I took the card and put it in my back pocket.

"So what's the deal with these angels?" Rain asked as she kicked the box.

"Hey! Those are fragile," I said.

She took out her phone and started looking things up. "Do you have all of the figurines that go in the nativity set?"

"I think so?"

She sighed in exasperation. "Just let me sell these on eBay, okay? I'll give you the money when it's done."

"Sure," I said. Miss Georgette had bought one angel of the collection of seventy or more, but no one else had shown any interest in them. Not even the guy John pointed out as someone who liked to sell things for a profit. Of course, I didn't take him for the kind of person who was interested in faceless angels.

Rain hoisted the large box on one hip. "I'm taking these to the house. You make sure you're showered and ready to go by six thirty. Put some makeup on and do your hair, while you're at it."

"Why? I'm just going to get a phone."

She grinned. "No, no. I have a surprise for you."

"Rain, you know how I feel about surprises—especially after the week I've had."

"You'll like mine," she called without even looking back.

chapter 13

Rain's big surprise was that she had decided it was time for me to take on gluttony in the form of bottomless nachos and a margarita. Once we'd gone through the exhausting process of getting the best deal on a smartphone, Rain dragged me to a Mexican restaurant on the far side of Jefferson.

"I can't drink this."

"Of course you can," she said. "One margarita isn't going to hurt you."

"What if I'm allergic to tequila?"

"You aren't." Rain dragged her tortilla chip through the mixture of chicken, beans, and the good Lord only knew what else. At least she'd wisely ordered the chips on the side. The waiter had looked at her as though she were nutty, but her genius showed in the fact the chips never got soggy when served her way.

"I'm not drinking it." I carefully pushed the drink away from me.

"Fine." She pulled the drink closer and took a sip from the straw.

"You can't do that! You're underage!"

She rolled her eyes. "Way to tell everyone in the restaurant, Posey. Gosh. Look, the drinking age in Mexico is eighteen. I am an eighteen-year-old half-Mexican in a Mexican restaurant, I think that counts."

I took the drink from her. At the very least, I was legal. "Have you been drinking?"

She slow-blinked at me. "I go to a Catholic Church. I have Catholic friends. What do you think?"

"Fine. Don't tell me any more." Before I could think about it further, I put my lips to the straw and sucked up way too much margarita. The sweet and salt and fire caught in my throat and caused me to cough.

"Way to go," Rain said while I hacked. "My big sister is brave."

Brave? No one had ever called me brave. Cautious? Sure. Pragmatic? All the time. But no one had ever called me brave.

"Just sip it," my sister said. "Nurse it."

When I sipped the margarita, I found I liked it. I really liked the warm glow that began to emanate from the inside out despite the fact the drink itself was frozen. "This is really good!"

"Would I lie to you?"

"No. Not unless I was a school nurse."

Rain laughed, a golden sound similar to her laughter as a child. Gluttony might be my favorite.

My little sister wiped away a tear of laugher. "I think we need to get you a new wardrobe after this."

"No, I can't use Chad's credit card like that. It would be wrong."

She held up index finger over thumb. "Not even a little bit?"

Well, I did need new underwear. One of the pairs from Walmart already had a hole in it. I was half tempted to take it back, but who wanted to take holey underwear to the service desk? Not I. My week had provided more than enough opportunities for embarrassment, thank you very much.

"You know what you need? Cowboy boots."

"What? Have you been in the tequila?"

"Nope, but you have."

A cursory glance at my margarita showed I'd almost drained it. "That's entirely too easy to drink," I said before carefully navigating a chip full of chicken and beans to my mouth.

"She'll have another," Rain said to the waiter who'd appeared out of nowhere. I waved my arms and tried to tell him no, but only succeeded in choking a little bit on the too large bite of nacho I'd just eaten.

"And maybe a glass of water," Rain added.

Once I'd managed to get my nachos down the right pipe, I turned on my little sister. "What do you think you're doing?"

"One margarita does not gluttony make. Nor does the paltry amount of chips you've eaten. So, get to work."

Paltry? No wonder she'd scored so well on the SAT. I blinked and a new margarita had been slid in front of me. That second margarita somehow turned into a sampler of shots.

"No," I said, rubbing my belly. "I can neither eat nor drink anymore. Clothing shopping will be a disaster after this."

Rain reached for one of the shots.

"Fine!"

She instructed me on how to take my shot: salt on my hand, lick the salt, toss the shot, suck on the lime. I giggled. "This seems pornographic not to mention . . . unsanitary. You mean to tell me you've done this?"

"I may or may not have attended some parties where tequila was shot."

I snort-giggled at her wording. "Have you considered a career in law?"

She grinned, "Actually, I have."

She motioned for the check.

"Rain, you don't need to pay for this," I said. The restaurant spun around me, my words thick in my mouth.

"I have a job," she said. "Besides, you're eventually paying for it. I put all of those figurines on eBay and some of them are already selling."

"That's great!" I had no idea what she was talking about.

Once we'd paid, Rain took my arm. At first I thought she was being really sweet. Then I realized I needed help walking.

"I think I've achieved gluttony," I groaned.

"Good! Two down and five to go," she said.

"Three down," I said.

"Three?" she asked as we walked down the sidewalk.

"Envy."

"Wanna talk about it?"

"Not really." I stopped when we passed a tanning salon I knew I hadn't seen before. "Isn't the car in the other direction?"

"The car is in the other direction, but my new place of employment is two more shops down, and I want you to see it. Now tell me about envy anyway."

"I want to have a baby and a husband like Liza's. Even Granny saw it and told me not to covet."

"Oh, Granny." Rain shook her head. "I need to have you hang out with Abuelita more. She's not so judgy. And she buys the good tequila."

"There's better tequila?" At the moment I couldn't think of anything more wonderful than the warm, fuzzy, dizzy euphoria that enveloped me.

"Uh, yeah. The stuff they gave you for shots is all right, but I'm guessing they put the rotgut in the margaritas."

I stumbled over an uneven place in the sidewalk. At least I thought the sidewalk was uneven. I could've tripped over my own feet.

"Maybe we overdid it," she said.

"D'ya think?"

"Just a little bit farther," she said.

I didn't want to see Rain's new job. I didn't want to see it in a boat or with a goat or on a train or in the rain. "I think home would be better."

"We'll be quick," she said.

Next thing I knew, we were standing under a sign that said The Pole Cat.

"Rain."

"I'm just working the reception desk!"

No. No more reception desks. Ever.

"Tell me you're not a stripper."

"No. Not yet, anyway."

"Not yet?"

"Look, college is expensive and neither Mom nor Papi have the money for undergrad much less law school. Know what they have near college campuses? Strip clubs. Vanderbilt ain't cheap, big sis."

"But—"

"But nothing. I'm going to be a lawyer, and that's a lot of tuition."

I didn't have an answer for that, so inside we went. "You do know *Pole Cat* is another name for skunk, right?"

"Don't be judgy," she said through gritted teeth.

"I'm not judgy!"

"Yes, you are!"

"No, I'm not. I'm worried."

She fixed me with a skeptical look that was Granny made over. "Don't look at me like that. Big sisters have the right to worry."

"Whatever. Tonight's a free mini-class, and you're going." Rain put her hands on her hips, her dark eyes daring me to disagree.

"Not a good idea. I don't have rhythm even when I'm sober."

"You're coming or I'll tell Granny you're the one who broke her Jimmy Carter commemorative plate."

"You wouldn't!"

"Oh, I would. I want you to come in here and see everything so you'll know it's all okay."

"Fine."

We walked in and Rain asked if we could join the free class. The lady behind the reception desk greeted us with a big smile and a clipboard for our contact information. I gave her Chad's email address.

As we walked past her, I noticed she wore at least three-inch heels. "You going to have wear shoes like that?"

"Only if I become an instructor," Rain said.

Shame I'd thrown away my collection since Rain and I shared a shoe size despite our differences in height. Then again, I never wanted my little sister to have to take a walk in my shoes.

We entered a dark room with hardwood floors, a mirrored wall and, of course, several poles. "Have mercy."

Rain scored a flute of champagne from a lady walking around with a tray. She handed it to me. "Would you loosen up, please?"

I drank the stuff mainly because it was in my hand but also because I was in a room with poles. And women wearing lingerie. And it was uncomfortable.

The instructor taught choreography, getting very intimate with the pole. Each student took a turn, even my sister. Rain, as much as I hated to admit it, had a natural gift that probably came from all of those years of gymnastics. But then she turned to me. "Okay, Pose, show me what you've got."

"Oh, no. I am observing."

I must've been too loud because the instructor came over, her ample bosom spilling over the top of a tightly hooked corset. "In this room there are no observers, only participants. You do not watch a dance class. You *dance* a dance class." She looked down at my name tag. "Looks like Posey here needs some encouragement, y'all."

The class began to chant, "Po-sey, Po-sey, Po-sey, Po-sey!"

Rain took my flute, and I somehow found myself acting out the moves I remembered to thunderous applause and whistles. Apparently, the members of the class had taken the admonition to encourage each other to heart because they were definitely applauding effort and grit rather than talent. Or even basic coordination, really.

"Good, good!" Corset Lady enthused as I backed up to take my place with the others. She added, "Now it's the moment you've all been waiting for: the fireman's spin."

"The what?" I didn't need to spin. After the flute of champagne, I was already spinning.

I watched the instructor model the move twice then Rain bounced up to the pole and executed a perfect spin, her long hair flowing behind her. I knew I shouldn't be cheering her on. I knew Granny would probably freak out and Mom would give us both a long lecture on how strippers catered to the patriarchy, but darned if she wasn't so graceful. As if to prove my point, each woman who attempted the spin after Rain had very limited success.

"Miss Observer?"

That was my cue. I closed my eyes and willed the room to quit spinning long enough for me to. I thought through all of the steps: how many laps around the pole, where to put my arms, when and how to hoist myself high enough so I had the space and momentum to spin. In my mind I was almost as graceful as my little sister. In reality, I barely lifted myself an inch off the ground and slammed my shin into the pole so hard I saw stars for a few minutes.

"Ow, do you want to try again?" the instructor asked.

"No, no. I think that's enough."

Blessedly, the lesson was over. As the instructor gave the room full of women information on when classes would be held and how much they cost, Rain and I slipped out.

My heart still raced, and I was still sweating when I stopped to lean against one of the Pole Cat's blacked-out windows. "And that's where you're going to work?"

"Just through the summer," Rain said. The pay is really good—especially if I can progress to being an instructor. Then I'll move over to a club to pay for college."

"Must you?"

"I don't know why you are so uptight," she said. "Dancing isn't prostitution, you know."

"I'm not worried about what you'll do. I'm worried about the people in the audience."

She rolled her eyes. "There'll be bouncers."

"How do you know you can trust the bouncers?"

"For crying out loud! Is this like that lecture Granny used to give me about not staying out late, not because she didn't trust me but because she didn't trust other people?"

"Yes!" Well, that, and I didn't want my little sister to be forced into wearing anything she didn't want to wear or doing anything she didn't want to do. My sister Rain was so beautiful and graceful and young, and I didn't want anyone to ever take advantage of her.

"Well, you're going to have to trust me. I've got this."

I chanced a peek at my shin. A huge goose egg glowed purple in the beam of the security light. That was definitely going to need some ice. "That was quite a workout."

"Yeah, it was," she said. "Why don't you wait here and I'll go get the car."

"I like this plan." If I leaned against the window and held myself as still as possible, then the world didn't spin as much. Also, the cool air made me feel much better. The Pole Cat's back studio had been entirely too warm, not to mention the exertion after copious amounts of alcohol. I had to be getting more sober, though, because my shin throbbed something terrible.

"Posey? Is that you?"

I opened my eyes, but it took a minute for the person to come into focus. "John the Baptist! What's a place like you doing in a guy like this?"

He winced. "Don't say that. He ended up without a head, you know."

"Sorry," I said. I'd never intentionally hurt John. He was my favorite.

He took a step closer. "Are you drunk?"

"A little," I conceded. "Okay, a lot. First time."

The wind shifted, picking up strands of his hair in the wind. He'd worn it down and looked more like a dangerous pirate or the rock god he'd almost been than a piano tuner. My eyes wouldn't look away from his full lips.

"Are you okay? Do I need to help you get home?"

"Rain's gone to fetch the car."

"Oh, good. I'll wait with you until she gets back."

More concern for me in five minutes than my husband had shown me in ten years.

He probably acted like the men in those books Rain lent me. He probably *kissed* like the heroes in Rain's books. I burned to find out. After all, I'd had a crush on him forever. What would it be like to kiss a decent man? Before I could stop myself, I raised to my tiptoes and placed my lips on his. He froze in surprise, but then his arms wrapped around me, and he joined the kiss enthusiastically right up until the moment I came to my senses and broke the embrace to lean against the wall with a contented sigh.

"What?" he asked.

"Just always wanted to do that," I said, my fingertips touching my tingling lips.

"Really?"

"Since eighth grade. You really knew how to turn in a paper."

"That's funny." He laughed a little and looked away.

My cheeks burned hot from embarrassment as much as from the alcohol. "Why is that funny?"

His eyes locked with mine. "I've had a crush on you almost as long, but I always thought you were too smart to want to go out with the likes of me."

"Too smart? I'm a freaking idiot."

"No, no you're not." He closed the distance between us, and his right hand cupped my cheek. Oxygen became awfully scarce. This time, *he* kissed *me*. This time, my arms wound around his neck. This time, we went from barely touching lips to tongues and even a bump of the teeth.

"Hey!" Rain called. "What do you think you're doing to my sister?"

Cold air smacked me in the face as John took a step back, taking all of his warmth with him.

"I, uh. She kissed me first."

My little sister looked from him to me and back to him. An ache bloomed behind my left eye, the euphoria of earlier was giving way to something darker, but my heart still hammered at the thought of one perfect kiss with John O'Brien. "Rain, I did kiss him first."

And I would totally do it again.

"Well, I'm taking you home," Rain said. "If you two want to knock boots when you're sober, that's none of my business, but not while you're wasted. Not on my watch."

John took another step back. "I would never take advantage of her. I promise."

Rain held up her hand in a V and pointed at her eyes, then at him, and back again. "C'mon, Posey. We're going home."

I kept looking over my shoulder at John, who stood on the sidewalk with his hands in his pockets, head to one side as he studied me. Rain had to put a hand on my head as she helped me into the passenger seat, and I touched my fingers to my lips because they still tingled.

I tingled all over.

Lust.

Lust was my new favorite.

chapter 14

Gluttony was so not my favorite. Neither was tequila.

I ran to the bathroom and bowed before the porcelain god before lying down to put my too, too warm cheeks on the cool tile.

My head throbbed. I needed to brush my teeth, but that would require standing. Standing was not good, so not good.

"Posey, you need to get out of the bathroom so your grandmother can go."

Was that my mother's voice coming from above? For irrational reasons, I didn't want her to know I was hung over. Sure, she'd no doubt experimented with various mind-altering substances while out in California, but, for whatever crazy reason, I didn't want her know I'd been drinking.

Maybe I was still hoping for a normal mother-daughter relationship.

"Posey!"

With a groan I made myself stand even though my head was heavier than a cinder block. As I brushed past mother and grandmother, Granny said, "Pregnant, are you? Eat some crackers."

No, Granny, and thanks for the reminder.

"Go on to the kitchen, and I'll make you some ginger tea," my mother said before disappearing in the bathroom where she was helping Granny.

What the heck was ginger tea going to do?

I stumbled into the kitchen and lay my head on the table. The sound of water heating up in the kettle told me this mysterious and, hopefully, miraculous, ginger tea was on the way. A cool, damp washcloth appeared out of nowhere.

"No lectures?" I asked before I put the washcloth over my mouth.

"Tempting as it may be, no. You're an adult. Besides, I'm banking on this hangover being its own worst punishment."

She always had been a huge fan of what she called natural consequences.

"At least my little sister likes me again?"

"Yes, and getting drunk to win her over was such a good idea."

"Mom, she was the model designated driver and didn't drink a thing. She even talked about college."

And doing exotic dancing to pay for it, but we could only cross one bridge at a time. Besides, my head wouldn't be able to take the yelling that would occur if I told Mom that. For the most part she was all about making one's own decisions, but she had strong opinions on anything that might perpetuate the patriarchy.

"Well, that's something. I was beginning to fear she was going to skip it."

"Like you did?"

"Well, I wasn't doing my best thinking then. I would never force her to go, but she's so smart and could do so much good. Can't you imagine your sister as an activist? Maybe even a politician?"

"Uh." My first mental image was of Rain spinning around a pole. "Sure."

"Or maybe a lawyer. An activist lawyer!"

My mother, still hoping for an activist in the family.

"Mom, she's afraid you and Santiago don't have the money to pay for college."

"Really?"

Even as I'd said the words, I knew I shouldn't, but now I knew my sister's hatred of high school was her way of looking for an out. If she flunked out of high school, then her parents wouldn't have to pay for her college tuition. They would *make* her pay her way, which is exactly what she wanted to do in the first place. It was all very convoluted, far more convoluted than I could handle that early in the morning with a hangover.

"We need to get enough fluids in you and send you back to bed," Mom said, obviously not willing to talk more about Rain and college.

The kettle whistled causing me to jump again. She gave me a curious look before bustling about making tea for me. She surprised me when she put a saucer over the top of the cup.

"Ginger," she said. "It'll take longer to steep, but it'll be better for your stomach."

I closed my eyes. No need to subject them to sunlight if I had to wait for the tea to steep.

"I certainly hope you've learned something from this experience."

I nodded. "I promise I will never drink again."

She reached across the table and took my hand in hers. "Posey, don't make promises you can't keep. Besides, the problem wasn't so much that you drank but that you drank entirely too much. You know what Emerson said—"

"Moderation in all things."

I ought to know what Emerson said. Next to Amelia Earhart, my mother loved Emerson and Thoreau best. She was especially fond of paraphrasing Emerson to say "Whoso would be a woman, must be a nonconformist." As for Thoreau, she'd sent me off to school each morning for a month with "Go confidently in the direction of your dreams." Then she'd gone back to finding herself and let Granny get me off to school. Granny, on the other hand, said things like, "If you get a whupping at school, you can bet just as sure as God made little green apples that you'll get another one here so behave."

I must've been quite the disappointment since I was neither nonconformist nor dreamer.

I had been very good at avoiding corporal punishment, though.

"I'm glad to see you trying new things," she said. "But I'm worried about you. I know Chad's leaving was a shock, but maybe you should be more gradual in the new things you try."

"I'm not sure who I am anymore."

Mom chuckled, and I heard the saucer being lifted and something being stirred in a cup. "Well, they say the first step is admitting you have a problem."

"I have a problem."

She placed in front of me a cup full of a murky liquid that looked very little like tea. The concoction smelled terrible and tasted worse, but I had to admit my stomach felt better almost immediately after drinking it.

For once I felt lucky to have the once crazy but now mellow mother who believed in home remedies and natural consequences.

"Go take a shower so you can feel human again," she advised. "Then drink some water and go back to bed."

Bed. Bed could be my new favorite.

The doorbell rang twice before I sat up fully awake, even then it was the groggy semiconscious state after a day nap combined with the last bits of a hangover.

"Just a minute!"

Where were my pajama pants? Where were the other people who could just as easily open the door?

The doorbell rang again as I hopped into my pants and donned my bunny slippers. I drew my hair into a scrunchie as I padded down the hall. Halfway to the door I realized I was braless and smelled like a person who'd spent the better part of the day sleeping off a hangover.

Well, Posey, there's a reason for that.

Without checking the peephole, I opened the door to see Miss Georgette. She wasn't pleased.

I was incredibly confused.

"Miss Georgette?"

The older lady pushed into the house leaving the scent of

Giorgio in her wake. Today's knit ensemble consisted of a chee-tah print shirt and black knit pants. Her earrings were black cat faces that made me dizzy when they swayed, so I had to look away. "I have a bone to pick with you, Posey Love!"

She came in and had a seat on the love seat, so I could only ask, "Could I get you something to drink?"

"No, thank you." She sat on the edge, back ramrod straight and her tiny feet pressed together.

After we sat in silence for what felt like an eternity but couldn't have been more than two minutes, she said, "Do you have any-thing to say for yourself?"

"About?"

"About your little adventures last night, that's what! Miss Lot-tie happened to be in El Nopal, and she saw you drinking mar-garitas and doing those shot things. Then my niece had her bachelorette party at that Pole place—you can bet she got an ear-ful, too—and she said you were dancing around poles like some kind of wanton woman and drunk as a skunk to boot."

My face burned. "I can assure you—"

"What were you thinking?"

"I don't know. I—"

"I'll tell you what you were thinking. You weren't thinking. You weren't thinking at all about how I stuck my neck out to give you a reference even though you don't have any classroom expe-rience beyond the student teaching you did ages ago."

"Miss Georgette—"

"You weren't thinking about how schoolteachers have to sign a code of conduct that says they'll be a proper example to their stu-dents both inside and outside the classroom. For heaven's sake were you sleeping when we went over that in class?"

"No, I—"

"As if all of that wasn't bad enough, Mr. Yardley said you and the O'Brien boy were making out on the other side of the Pole Cat."

Her mouth kept moving and words flowed out as they always did, but at the memory of kissing John I felt light-headed enough to pass out. Then I wanted to walk down the hall, crawl under the bed, and then never come out. Oh, God. I had kissed him. I had admitted to him that I'd had a crush on him since eighth grade.

He admitted he had a crush on me.

We kissed, and it was fabulous, and I think I think I may have copped a feel by putting my hand in his back pocket.

"Oh, no, no, no, no," I groaned, burying my face in my hands.

"Oh, but yes you did. I know your life isn't easy right now. Believe me, I do. When I heard that no-good *man* left you and left the church in the lurch, I was so glad I was able to give you a good reference and hopefully get you back on the straight and narrow. Then I started getting the phone calls this morning. Oh, Posey. I am so disappointed in you."

I wanted to be swallowed by the floor, maybe live in the crawl space forever. Sure, there were probably snakes and possums under there, but I wouldn't have to suffer from mortification, now would I?

"I genuinely apologize, Miss Georgette. I will not make the same mistake again. I had never drunk before, and Rain convinced me to drink one margarita, and it all went downhill from there. I am so sorry."

"That's great and—what in heaven's name is this?"

She picked up *that* book, the gray one with a tie on the front.

"Tell me you haven't been reading this filthy trash."

"I can't." I couldn't think of a half-truth to cover my butt this time, and, really, why should I have to?

"I like to consider myself a tolerant woman, but I am the head of a committee that has worked extremely hard to get this smut removed from the public library. So far, Wendy Cope has blocked me at every turn with her carrying on about free speech. I said speech should only be free if it's decent."

I could only nod. I didn't want to be on Wendy Cope's bad side. I also didn't want to point out to Miss Georgette that speech didn't have to be decent to be free.

"Young lady, I know your life has not been easy as of late, and I'm really hoping this is just a phase that you are passing through.

I did not recommend you as an elementary schoolteacher only to have you gallivanting around in sex shops, drinking like a fish, and fornicating out where God and everyone can see you. Any one of those things could keep you from getting this job or could get you fired. You know this, right?"

"Yes, ma'am."

"I'm not one to dismiss the medicinal purposes of the occasional dose of Wild Turkey, but that is not to be done in public, right?"

"Yes, ma'am."

"As to carrying on with one man while you're still married to another, even if he is a low-life, sorry excuse for a human being? You know that's not right, too?"

"Yes, ma'am."

"And for heaven's sake don't dance around any more poles. You're applying to be one of a chosen few who mold our children and thus are held to a higher standard. I won't say anything about these particular incidents, and I trust you not to get into such things again. If you do, then I will call Ms. Varner over at the Ellery Elementary and tell her that I have made a most grievous mistake because you are not the person I thought you were. Is that clear?"

"Yes, ma'am."

Miss Georgette reached across the coffee table to pat my hand and then stood. "I'm glad we have that all straightened out. You're going to be just fine. As long as you don't do anything else stupid."

"Yes, ma'am."

In a daze I walked Miss Georgette to the front door, certain I looked like a deer caught in headlights. Perhaps, a recently hungover deer in headlights.

At least my heart hadn't been blessed.

I closed the front door and fought off the urge to go back to bed because I knew I needed to find something to eat and do a load of laundry so I'd be ready to go to work in the morning. At my lunch break, I'd visit Ben Little, our local attorney. At some point, I'd have to apologize to John for my ridiculous behavior. At least I had that old LP as an excuse to go see him.

"Well that was a load of bullshit."

There Henny stood in the doorway between the living room and the kitchen. "What?"

"All that 'yes, ma'am' business. You're a grownass woman and don't need to be letting anyone tell you what to do."

I brushed past him, casually studying him as I did. Pupils the normal size, no scratching, no edginess. He seemed clean for once. "Actually, she had every right. She gave me a good recommendation, and I hauled off and did a very stupid thing."

"Says who? What right do they have to put in some kind of morality clause? As if drinking or dancing around a pole defines you."

I couldn't help but give my brother the stink eye. He, no doubt, was making excuses for himself just as much as for me.

"Fair or not, it's the way things are." I opened the fridge, searching for something appealing. Celery was the most appealing thing I saw, which said a lot about food selections in La Casa Adams. Didn't Mom know that women in the throes of crisis needed ice cream and cookies and chocolate and potato chips?

"Dude, I'm a loser. I get that, but you're not a loser. Having a drink or two and dancing around a pole don't make you a loser."

"Around here it does." I smeared peanut butter on a few pieces of celery then took a bite. Yep. Still disgusting.

"Well, what does any of that have to do with what kind of teacher you would be?"

"Henny, people don't want a drunken pole dancer to teach their kids."

"Yeah, but you're not a drunken pole dancer. Heck, how do they even know a pole dancer wouldn't make a good teacher?"

I had to smile. My little brother indignant on my behalf was kinda cute. "They don't."

"See? Bullshit. Who comes over to someone's house unannounced to chew them out for something they did one town over?"

"Someone who cares?"

Huh. Did Miss Georgette care about me? Sure, she didn't want to recommend me only to have me be seen publicly drunk and doing sexy dances in a store with blacked out windows, but was that more about me or her?

"Well, I think it's stupid. It's like these people who won't give me a job because I was in the joint for a while. Am I rehabilitated or not?"

More stink eye in his direction. I couldn't help myself. "You managed to get fired by your own mother."

"Yeah, I know," he said. "I got mixed up in things again, but I'm trying to get straight. I swear."

I'd heard that one before.

What had happened to my scrawny little brother? The pasty child with bright red hair who seemed to be without front teeth forever? The scrappy baseball player who once hit a walk off home run to take tiny Yessum County High School to the state championships? He'd been a handsome young man who was a runner-up for Homecoming King.

Then in the spring of his senior year, he'd taken a dirty slide to the ankle in the last game of the season before the playoffs started.

Mom wanted him to sit out the postseason, but the coach was having none of it. Henny was his star player: pitcher, hitter, short-stop. Next thing we knew, Henny said he was fine. We didn't find out until much later that he was taking some of Coach's oxy-codone and lots of it. Sometimes I feared he'd branched out into heroin.

"Maybe you need to move, get away from these people around here," I heard myself say.

"I don't know." He scratched the back of his neck. "I still have to check in with my parole officer, you know."

"Then you can stay and help me get it together," I said. "Goodness knows, I need to get it together."

He stood. "Nah, you've always had it together far more than I have."

"Henny—"

"No. I've got a night shift job at a warehouse. I'm hoping that if I sleep all day, those losers I used to hang out with will leave me alone."

He left the kitchen, and I found myself hoping the same thing.

I also couldn't kick the shame I felt for all those years of thinking myself superior to my little brother who always seemed to be in trouble. He needed help. Now I knew what it was like to need help even if it wasn't for the same problem. Mom had been slow to see the problems the first time. Then she'd attempted to coach Henny on mind over matter. Henny's father, unlike Rain's, couldn't help fund a trip to rehab because he was dead. He'd had too much to drink one night and wrapped his truck around an ancient oak tree between two forks of a lonely country road.

Now I had nothing extra to offer my brother, either.

I lay my head on the table, not wanting to think about hangovers, my brother and his pill problem, or how I'd killed all chances of the first-grade job while also alienating a friend. If I squeezed my eyes tight enough, would it all go away?

At least, I could rest comfortable in the knowledge that tomorrow couldn't possibly be any worse than the day I'd just been through.

chapter 15

First thing on Monday morning I walked to work with my mother. Business at Au Naturel was the busiest I'd seen it. Monday was the day of good intentions; women in yoga wear with rolled up mats filled the store, their high ponytails bobbing as they signed in then climbed the stairs. Meanwhile, at least three women stopped for a tarot session with Julia, suggesting she had been right about how her business was going to pick up.

At lunch I went to see Ben Little and picked up what he called a couple of "divorce worksheets" that would serve as a guideline for how to divide what was left of Chad's and my worldly possessions. The worksheets looked more like packets, and I didn't know how I was going to convince Chad to fill his out. Ben walked me through the entire process, and a dull headache began to bloom as I realized getting a divorce could be easy—but only if Chad cooperated.

Back at my station behind the cash register, I was studying the worksheets to get a handle on how to divorce my husband when the man in question walked through the door.

Today could, apparently, get worse.

"Posey."

I clenched the edge of the counter, glad I had a barrier between him and me. "Chad."

"You weren't answering my calls."

My heart hammered. My knuckles had already gone white, but I said. "I changed my number so I wouldn't get any more of your calls. By the way, I picked this up for you."

"What the—?" He took the packet and ripped it in half. "I thought I told you we would *not* be getting a divorce."

He leaned over the counter, and I leaned back as I always had before. The old Chad would have never done anything that seemed like a fight while we were out in public. No, all arguments were to wait until we got home. Maybe it was finally sinking in to him, that there would be no more arguments at home. Slowly, I straightened my spine. "There is no longer a *we*. It's also not the Middle Ages, so you cannot force me to stay married to you. I will take you to court if I have to."

He closed his eyes and cast a glance at Julia before turning to me with his public smile, a one-thousand-watt beauty that could charm anyone in a five-mile radius. Her eyes were glued on the cards in front of her, but I knew she was listening. Nothing got past her.

"Let's step in the back room so we don't discuss this in front of your mother's customers."

He had a point about that, and the back room didn't have a door—only a curtain of beads—so it wasn't so isolated that I feared his usual treatment. I didn't need anyone from the school to see us arguing. "Okay."

I waited for him to go to the doorway to the side of the stairs, the one currently covered by swaying beads.

"No, ladies first."

My eyes narrowed. His voice had gone back to charming, a trick he often used to keep me off balance. Once I was sure we were out of hearing range, I said, "Chadwick, we are getting a divorce. I told you from the beginning that infidelity was one of my deal breakers. So you might as well—"

He struck quickly, jerking me over to where he sat on a bench. Before I knew quite what was happening, he'd tossed the skirt portion of my dress over my head and was spanking me. "This time you have gone too far, Posey. I am the head of this household, and you will act like it."

He hit me so hard, I cried out. I could both see and feel stars. I scrambled to get away, but my arms got caught in my dress, and he had leaned his upper body over mine, his elbow digging into my back as he administered more licks. "This is for your own good, and—"

Then I was on the floor. Chad thrashed beside me making an almost inhuman sound.

Fighting my dress as if my life depended on it, I managed to get the skirt portion down and to find my feet. Julia stood to the side with her arms crossed, a small device in her hand. "Tasered him."

"Thank you," I said.

"I'm going to call the police, and you need to get a restraining order," she said, taking me by the arm and leading me out into the store. She sat back down at her table and took out her cell phone. I couldn't tear my eyes away from her. What did she know about Tasers and restraining orders? How could she remain so calm?

The good Lord knew I wasn't calm. In a million years I'd never thought he would actually *spank* me. I knew he wanted to, but I didn't think he would.

Maybe I needed a Taser.

Chad started to emerge from the back room, then retreated as a gaggle of yoga students made their way out the door. To my left Julia was talking on the phone to the police, and I was so grateful she'd made the call for me. My hands shook. My posterior stung almost as much as my pride. Thank God I had never procreated with that pitiful excuse for a man.

Once assured the store was empty except for Julia and me, Chad stalked toward the desk, his face flush with anger. Was that a wet spot on the front of his pants? Oh, Julia was going to get a wonderful gift as soon as I had the money to buy her one. Seeing my soon-to-be ex-husband humiliated did me more good than it ought to have done a Christian woman. Good thing the church and I were on a break, wasn't it?

"I can't believe that you would do such a thing!" Chad said, his speech a little slurred as if he were having trouble controlling his lips.

"That I would do such a thing? You *hit* me. You promised to never hit me."

"Well, you needed to be reminded of your place."

"Of course, you also promised to love and cherish me, and we all see how that turned out."

"I will not have you disrespecting me! Go to the corner." His voice broke on the issued order.

"No." I sucked in a ragged breath and looked him square in the eye. "But you should go get new underwear."

He howled in rage.

I willed myself not to flinch. "I'd suggest the back door and never, ever coming near me again."

Sirens outside got louder.

Chad leaned over the desk to growl. "We're not finished."

I forced myself to lean so close that my forehead touched his. "Yes. Yes, we are."

He took off for the back door, no doubt because he wasn't going to have his incontinence documented on a police report.

"Hey, Julia, think you can tell me more about this Taser of yours?"

She smiled widely and walked over, "We can order one right now thanks to the convenience of online shopping."

"Excellent. I'm thinking something not pink."

"Oh, we can do that," she said as she passed over her phone so I could scroll through my options.

If she noticed that I still quaked, she didn't say anything. I practiced keeping my voice level as we chatted about volts and colors and reviews. I was going to fake calm until I made it.

It took forever to tell Len everything that had gone on, and it was embarrassing to admit I had been spanked. Especially after the third time Len asked me if I wanted to take a seat, and I had to say no thank you, a reminder to him that my posterior was still sore. Julia got an earful from him about having the Taser, but, technically, it was legal in the state of Tennessee. Mainly, Len didn't want Julia to go to trial for having assaulted someone. No matter how much they deserved it. My mother, who'd shown up just after Len did, kept muttering about how she'd never even spanked me as a child.

She neglected to mention that Granny had had no such aversion to the practice.

At long last, we were free to go, knowing that the restraining order—or in this case something called a protection order—was in process.

"I can't believe it," my mom kept saying.

"Are you sure you're going to be okay?" I asked Julia. "I don't think he'll come after you, but he's done so many things I wouldn't have predicted as of late."

"Don't worry about me," Julia said. "I can handle myself."

Of that, I had no doubt.

When we arrived home, Rain had ordered a pizza. We sat around the kitchen table eating pizza and drinking soft drinks. Miranda/Mabel had made a frozen dinner for Granny but had put it on an actual plate. Granny didn't eat pizza. She even said the word with disgust, only she pronounced it more like "Pisa," and I thought of the leaning tower every time.

"You know I would've come to get you if you'd asked?" Mom said for the fourth time.

"Yes, Mom." I shifted on my sore bottom. "It's not like he'd ever done this before."

"Abuse comes in other forms. Why didn't you tell me? Or Liza? Or someone?

"I don't know."

"I do," Rain said. "He told you to stay away from us, told you that Granny and Mom didn't care about you and that they loved me more because I was the baby. I heard him one Christmas when he didn't know I was on the other side of the door."

I opened my mouth to contradict her, but in my mind I heard his words. At first, he told me not to bother Granny and Mom because they were too busy with Henny and Rain. Then he pointed out how they'd abandoned me. When I called him on the first, he told me I had to be mistaken.

"Why did I believe him?"

"Because he's a master of gaslighting, that's why."

"What is gaslighting? What are you talking about?"

Rain rolled her eyes and put down her piece of pizza. "It's when a dude does stuff to make you question your sanity. I've watched him argue with you over the stupidest stuff, just argue and argue to prove that he was still the master of the house. Remember that time you told him you didn't like Adam Levine and he badgered you for half an hour as to why? Or that time you told him you didn't like nutmeg, and he suddenly got up to get you a glass of egg nog. When you told him you liked it, he pointed out that it contained nutmeg and, thus, you liked nutmeg."

Rain didn't even know the half of it. Originally, I had pointed out to him that Jesus hadn't been the one to tell wives to submit to their husbands, but he argued the necessity of submission for two solid years, often bringing up the topic unexpectedly and accusing me of not remembering what I'd said or of forgetting particular pieces of scripture. By the time he left to form his own church, he had worn me down to the idea of letting him be the undisputed head of the household. Not long afterward, he sent me to the corner for the first time. He said I was spending too much money on clothing for myself, and he talked about how he was punishing me "for my own good." When I'd refused, he implied he would spank me if I didn't do as he said, so I went rather than cause another argument. He read all of these stats and testimonials about how happy these marriages with discipline were, spouting off about them while I stood looking at the corner of the bedroom where the drywall had cracked. It had been humiliating, but I'd done it. After twenty minutes, he had been so affectionate, like an entirely different man almost. He'd cuddled and hugged until we'd had sex, which I would've refused out of principle except for the fact I was ovulating.

God, I had been so stupid.

Rain had taken another bite of her pizza but put it down and daintily wiped her hands. "See, that part I overheard was actually the second stage where he isolated you from us and from Liza. You second-guessed yourself on everything—like that time we went Christmas shopping and you accidentally picked up flat front pants instead of pleated and broke down crying because you knew he'd tell you that if you really cared about him then you would've picked out the right style."

"I don't even remember that."

"Yeah, how much can you remember from the past ten years?"

"Lots of things. I can tell you—"

But I couldn't find the memories—at least I couldn't find good memories and even bad ones seemed to be suppressed unless something specific triggered them. Whole chunks of my life were . . . gone. Holidays and seasons ran together in such a way that I couldn't tell one Christmas from another or what I'd received for my birthday on any particular year. I could only remember not wanting to make Chad angry or wanting to be pregnant. I could remember we argued all the time the first two years we were married, but then nothing.

The arguing stopped when he started getting his way.

Tears pricked my eyes. "I'm so sorry. I didn't mean to, I promise."

At first, my mother and sister let me cry it out.

"Oh, Posey, please don't cry," my mom finally said. "We're here for you now, aren't we? We never left. And *you* did nothing wrong."

"Pose, it's okay," Rain said. "But I want you to be prepared because he'll keep trying to make you doubt yourself. A piece of paper isn't going to stop him."

I shuddered, still sniffing and struggling to regain control of my breathing. "How are you so young and you know all of this?"

Rain sighed. "Last year I was going out with this senior, and he was doing all of this crazy stuff. My friend, Jenna, pulled me aside because she was worried about me."

She stopped to take another bite of pizza, and I had to marvel at how she could put it away. "She said I was depressed and didn't want to hang out with anyone but my boyfriend anymore, and that just wasn't like me."

"It wasn't," Mom said. "I remember that guy, and you were such a little snot while you were going out with him."

"Thanks, Mom," Rain said with a roll of her eyes. "Anyhow, at first I argued with her, but then I started paying attention. He'd be thoughtful one minute, but the next he'd find some way to guilt trip me into doing something he wanted to do. He accused me of locking his keys in his truck because I hadn't picked them up like he'd told me to. I knew he'd said no such thing, but by the time we got done arguing, he had me confused."

I could empathize with that feeling.

"Then I got suspicious he was cheating on me. He told me if I kept bringing it up, then he *would* cheat on me because I'd deserve it for doubting him. At that point, I was smart enough to talk to Mami."

My brash little sister had lived a taste of my last ten years to the point where she accidentally used her old pet name for our mother, "Mami." The Spanish word sounded almost exactly like the English "Mommy," but not quite. My heart broke for her. I wanted to break the kneecaps of the boy who had done all of this to her. "Then what happened?"

My mother cleared her throat. "I told her she didn't have to put up with any of his mess, and that a response like that meant he probably was cheating on her."

I looked at my rebellious little sister. "And you listened?"

"Mom said if I didn't believe her then to look it up, so I did. I fell down a rabbit hole of research about domestic abuse. I dumped him so hard, he's still seeing stars, and I decided then and there that I wanted to be a lawyer who helped women who got tangled up with men like him."

"Wow." So mature!

Rain's brown eyes sparkled. "I also put a piece of store-bought sushi in the glove compartment of his truck right before I broke up with him."

Maybe not as mature.

Mom lifted an index finger. "That one was *not* my idea. I told her to let karma take its course."

"For one moment in time, I *was* karma. It took him a month to find the sushi, and no one wanted to ride with him for a *while*. He thought one of the other football players did it to him."

For once Mom rolled her eyes.

"C'mon, Mom. You can't mean to tell us you've always done the right thing to make sure karma went your way."

She stood and took her plate to the sink—no paper plates because they were wasteful. With her back to us so we couldn't see her expression, she said, "Oh, I could tell you stories, but I'm not going to. The past is past. I'm living my best life now, and that's what counts."

Was she really? Her voice held more than a hint of sadness.

"I know what you can do to get back at Chad," Rain blurted.

"What?" I asked, even as Mom said, "Girls, no."

"That credit card. I think he owes you a brand new wardrobe," Rain said, as she shook her head affirmatively.

I had to admit I wanted no part of dresses, possibly ever again. And he did owe me underwear that didn't cause a perennial wedgie. Maybe those cowboy boots Rain had suggested. He'd never allowed me to buy things that weren't on the clearance rack, but every item of his clothes had to be just so. Also, I'd bring things home, and he'd make me return half of it because it showed too much cleavage or the skirt was too short or it was the wrong color or . . . whatever reason struck his fancy.

"Maybe just a thing or two," I said.

Rain clapped her hands with glee, while my mother leaned over the sink and hung her head.

Mom turned around, "Posey, you're going to end up in debt!"

My mind traveled back to when we'd obtained the credit card and something the bank teller said. He told Chad to make me a co-signer because then I'd be responsible for the debt. Ever cocky, Chad had said something about being in charge of me. He'd made me an authorized user. And that meant he was on the hook for any debt. "Actually, I'm not."

I thought of the embarrassment of having my soon-to-be-ex-husband lift my skirt and spank me. He needed the equivalent of the experience, and I needed pants.

"Rain, why don't we go to the mall on Saturday when Au Naturel closes early?"

"You're on!"

chapter 16

Wednesday afternoon I got the call from Ellery Elementary that I'd been hoping for.

Now, I sat on a stiff and too-tiny chair outside the principal's office waiting to be interviewed for the first grade supply teacher position.

Ms. Varner herself stepped out into the hall and asked me to come to her office. She wore a tailored suit and wore her dark hair slicked back into a no-nonsense bun. To me, she looked more like a high school administrator than an elementary school principal. I wasn't about to tell her that, though.

"Have a seat, Ms. Love."

Fortunately, she had a couple of adult-sized seats in front of her desk. I sat down.

"I'm going to be honest, I was all set to hire you until I heard about some of your escapades last weekend."

"I, ah, won't let that happen again," I said, willing my blush to subside. It didn't.

"I would hope not. Seems my options are down to you and an older lady who sometimes falls asleep when she's substituting. Last time, a fourth grader drew a mustache on her using permanent marker."

I winced. "I don't plan to fall asleep."

"And you have some classroom experience?"

"It's been a while," I admitted, "but I completed my certification and my student teaching, and I've kept my certificate up to date.

For the next twenty minutes, Ms. Varner quizzed me on IEPs and curriculum standards and integrating technology in the classroom. Much had changed in ten years, but I did well with her scenarios about how I would handle certain disciplinary problems because, well, kids were still kids.

"I need to think on this," Ms. Varner said as she leaned back in her chair. "But I have to make the decision sooner rather than later, so you'll hear back from me one way or another by Friday."

"I, uh, have my portfolio from when I was a student." I pulled out a binder from my college days that contained sample lesson plans and all of my test scores as well as my original certificate.

She did me the courtesy of flipping through it, but, of course, I had no recent experience and was ashamed to see that some of the pages had yellowed in what had once been my pride and joy. She handed it back to me with a thin smile. "I'll be in touch."

And just like that I was dismissed.

Next I had to go to the Public Safety building for a background check. Getting my fingerprints inked took longer than the interview with the principal, and having someone else ink my fingers and press them on the paper made me uneasy even though I knew I hadn't committed any crimes.

Yet.

Yeah, I probably shouldn't go on that shopping spree.

It's not a crime if you're authorized to use the card.

That shoulder devil sure could twist things around.

I'm kinda with her, my shoulder angel said. So much for her integrity.

Even so as I stood outside the Public Safety building with my floral dress flapping against my legs in the brisk March wind, I knew I needed a different wardrobe. Not only did dresses now make me uneasy, but I'd watched the other elementary teachers come and go while I waited for my interview. Unlike when I was in elementary school, they no longer wore dresses and heels. Now, most teachers appeared to wear nice but casual tops and pants, sometimes even jeans. I spotted Lexi Lynne Richards, a kindergarten teacher, wearing tailored jeans and a nice top with her hair in a messy bun. She looked as though she was ready to get down on the floor and finger paint with her kids. Knowing her from First Baptist, I could imagine her doing just that. Or playing tag. Or conducting science experiments that left so much goo she'd have to leave the janitor a tip.

I decided then and there I wanted to be more like Lexi Lynne.

For now, however, it was back to Au Naturel—the store, not the lifestyle.

I entered through the back door, flinching as I walked through the storage room that had so recently been the scene of yet another humiliation. I rolled my shoulders back. One way or another, I would get rid of Chad Love. Hiding my purse in a half-empty box of kale chips because no one would look for it in there, I walked out into the store proper and ran headlong into John O'Brien.

"I was hoping I'd find you here."

"I, uh, I think I owe you an apology for my behavior the other night," I said even though I couldn't take my eyes from his lips.

"And I was hoping you might want to go to dinner sometime."

Was I hearing those lips correctly?

"John, I don't—"

He held up a hand, "Forget I said it. Probably stupid to ask."

He turned to go, but I grabbed his arm. "No, I would love to go to dinner with you, but I need to get through this divorce. I wasn't thinking logically the other night." Okay, so I wasn't thinking at all. I was feeling, nothing but feeling. At the moment, I wanted to kiss him again because I remembered the feel of his lips on mine.

"Weren't thinking? Did you only say those things and kiss me because you were drunk?"

"No, I meant them. My inhibitions were . . . relaxed, though."

His blue eyes met mine. "You're probably right. I need to work out some things before I start a relationship, too."

"So we're not saying never."

"I never say never," he said with twinkling eyes and tempting dimples.

I sucked in a breath. "That's good to know."

"For some reason, I couldn't get you off my mind after that kiss."

He couldn't stop thinking about *me?* "I might've thought about you once or twice."

"I don't believe you," he said, but his smile suggested he was pleased.

I smacked his arm lightly and immediately felt thirteen all over again.

His expression faded into seriousness. "You know where I am if you need anything. Anything at all."

"Thank you." The words came out as a whisper because my throat had closed up at his kindness.

He held up a jar or honey and a pack of organic dog treats. "If you don't mind?"

"Of course!" I jumped to the register and rang up his order. He started to say something else, but decided against it and left with a little wave.

"He's an old soul," Julia said.

"Yeah," I said, not really sure how she knew such a thing.

"Lots of adversity he's overcome," she noted.

"Did you do a reading for him or something?" I asked.

Julia chuckled. "No, but sometimes I can just tell. People like you and him wear your emotions on your sleeves and are easy to read."

"Really?"

She patted my cheek. "Look at you, still wanting to believe after all you've been through. Your nature is to be open and trusting. I'm proud of you."

"I need to be less open and less trusting," I grumbled.

"No, you need to be more discerning, but trusting the right people is always rewarding. Poor John. He doesn't have that many friends because he's not sure whom to trust."

I hated to think of John without friends. He was one of the kindest people I knew. Not many people had been kind to him when he first came back to town, and he must've remembered what it was like to be an outsider. Even after I rejected him, he still offered me anything. Anything at all.

That definitely deserved some brownies and the old record I'd found.

Maybe I'd feel more confident about going to see him after Rain and I went shopping. Maybe.

chapter 17

First thing Friday morning, I got the call I'd been waiting for. Ms. Varner admitted she had reservations, but she needed someone to take over Heather's class and she was going to take a chance on me. I spent that entire day observing the first grade class and talking with the other teachers about lesson plans and schedules, and the whole thing made my head spin. Even so, I left that afternoon with a smile on my face. The ache in my cheeks told me I hadn't been smiling enough the past few years.

For once I was doing something I wanted to do.

My garage sale earnings, while more than I'd hoped for, were still barely enough to make the car payment so I could keep my car. I hadn't worked at Au Naturel long enough to make much of anything, and now I was leaving Mom in the lurch once again. At least Liza had volunteered to take the register on Friday and Saturday since Mom had no complaints if she brought Nathaniel with her.

I went straight from the elementary school to Au Naturel where I found Liza and Julia chatting as if they'd been friends forever. I tamped down a stab of jealousy as Julia bounced Nathaniel on her knee. "Afternoon, ladies."

"Well, if it isn't our new elementary schoolteacher," Liza said.

"Almost. I officially start on Monday." And I was nervicited, as

Rain used to say when she was little. Half nervous and half excited—and 100 percent on edge. Especially since I still looked
over my shoulder for Chad. I'd caught a glimpse of him with
Naomi Rawls at the Piggly-Wiggly, but I'd left without milk
rather than chance running into them.

"Julia here did a reading for me," Liza said with a giggle. "But
you had better not tell my mom."

"I wouldn't dream of it."

"She says Owen and I will have a girl next."

I kept my smile in place. "You aren't rushing into that, are you?"

Liza's eyes went wide. "Oh, hell, no. I do owe your granny a
thank you, though, because her cereal idea has worked like a
charm."

I opened my arms for Nathaniel, and Julia relinquished him. I
bounced him and made nonsense sounds until he smiled. He
looked happy with the cereal solution, too.

"Look at my girls." Mom came down the stairs with a happy
glow. It might have taken her a while, but she'd figured out who
she wanted to be, and she'd made it happen. I marveled at what
she'd done with this store and her studio. It was a place that radiated happiness. She'd built that.

"And my boy," she added as she squeezed Nathaniel's tiny
hand then made a face so silly that he giggled.

We all froze, drinking in the glorious sound of a baby's giggle.

"Has he done that before?" I asked Liza.

"I don't think so."

We spent the rest of the afternoon finding new ways to make
the baby laugh until all of us were tired from crazy antics and the
satisfaction of our own laughter. Remembering my past flirtation
with envy, I tried to fill that hollow spot within with Nathaniel's
laughter.

The next morning, Rain burst through my door at nine and
jumped on my bed, reminding me of the last Christmas I'd spent
in the house. That Christmas would live on in infamy. Rain had
set all of the house clocks to seven thirty and then woke us all up

at four so she could open presents. We all fell asleep before lunch, but Mom let her get away with it because she said the plan and its implementation showed ingenuity and initiative.

This time my little sister wasn't quite as excited, but I did check my phone as well as the alarm clock—just to be sure.

"Posey! Get up! You need a shower, then you know it's going to take us at least thirty minutes to get there and I have to get back in time to go fishing with Papi. I've gone through all of the sale papers and cut out the coupons. I also circled a bunch of outfits I think would look good on you. Then I think we need to go to the school supply store to make sure you have everything you need. Oh! And I have the money from the stuff I sold on eBay for you and—"

"Coffee." Those were the only two syllables I could muster.

"Those crazy angel things—especially that nativity set—sold for almost five hundred dollars."

That number woke me up. "What?"

I looked to the one figurine I'd kept: it was two angels together and made of porcelain unlike the designer collectible angels Chad had told people I wanted. One angel's pair of wings had broken off, but I had glued them on. That angel was me. It made sense that the comforting angel still had her wings intact. She was Liza. How funny that all of those angels I'd never really wanted had been the ones to make me enough money to make sure I'd keep my car.

"Let me speak slowly." Rain dramatically cleared her throat. "You. Now. Have. Five. Hundred. Dollars. As. Soon. As. PayPal. Releases. It."

I threw back the covers and gathered what I needed to take a shower. Maybe I wouldn't even need Chad's credit card.

That resolve didn't last long once Rain explained to me that she didn't have the cash in hand. Also, her enthusiasm washed over me as she steered me from store to store, showing me clothes that better fit my body type. She also talked me into that pair of cowboy boots. Obviously, I needed work clothes. And work shoes. And a new purse. And makeup.

She knew I wouldn't be able to resist the book store or the school supply store. I bought two romance novels of my own, one book on elementary pedagogy and one self-help book about surviving divorce. I bought a book for Mom and a new outfit for Granny's "baby." Once we'd eaten our celebratory cookies, we left for home since Rain had a fishing date with her father. On the way home we rolled down the windows and sang along to songs that had been popular when I was in high school.

The moment we got home and unpacked everything from the trunk, Mom pricked the balloon of my euphoria when she took a look at all of the bags we'd brought home and simply said, "Posey."

Granny boosted me up again, though, as she clapped her hands together and shouted, "Is it Christmas? I love Christmas!"

"Not yet," I said, resolving to let Granny have as many Christmases as she wanted, "but it's coming. Anything in particular you want Santa to bring you?"

"Tom Brokaw."

I couldn't help but laugh out loud.

"What? He's a good-looking man. Also he owes me child support," she said, gesturing down to the baby doll in the little cradle she absently rocked with her foot. I couldn't tell if she was joking or if she really thought she was rocking Tom Brokaw's love child.

"I'll see what I can do, but I don't know how Mr. Brokaw feels about being stuffed inside a bag."

"Well, if you can't bring me handsome Tom, then I'd like some of that fancy Godiva chocolate. I've never tried it."

That I could do.

Rain came through the front door, cheeks pink from the exertion of helping me bring in bags. "I think that's it. Now go start trying them on so Mom and Granny can see the fashion show."

I returned in a knit shirt that showed off what little cleavage I had and the softest, best fitting pair of jeans I had ever owned.

"Ooh la la," Mom said. "Now, who paid for that one?"

"Chad bought it," Rain said before I had a chance to answer her.

Mom's lips formed a thin line. "Posey, I agree with you that he owes you no less, but men like him can't let a slight go. I'd rather have you safe than well-dressed, and it's not wise to provoke a man after you've taken out a restraining order on him."

"I have a Taser on the way, and Julia's going to show me how to use it. If he comes near me again, then he'll be shocked and then arrested," I said. Rain had picked out the perfect pair of jeans. Turns out my hips weren't really that out of proportion so much as the dresses Chad preferred weren't flattering to my body type. The cowboy boots Rain had talked me into were about a hundred times more comfortable than the flats I'd been wearing, too.

"And what if he takes your Taser away and uses it on you before the police can get to you, Posey Lucille?"

"Hey! That's my name," Granny said. "Well, the Lucille part. I don't know about this 'Posey' business. Sounds like a hippie name, if you ask me."

I didn't care for what Mom suggested, but she had a point. So far I hadn't done a very good job of defending myself.

She continued, "It'd be one thing if you were proficient in martial arts or something, but he's bigger than you and now he'll be even more motivated."

I sighed. To keep all of these clothes, far more clothes than I'd ever need, would be greedy. And I was doing it mainly to lord something over my soon-to-be ex-husband. Buying a bunch of stuff wouldn't plug the holes of what had been stolen from me.

Greed.

After my first few run-ins with the Seven Deadly Sins, I'd told myself to quit. Seemed like the sins were following me now.

Greed was *not* my favorite, but this pair of jeans absolutely was. "Fine. I'll return some of it and repay him for the rest."

"You will not!" Rain shouted indignantly.

"Mom's right. He's getting worse by the minute."

"But those jeans make your ass look spectacular, and it's poetic justice considering all that he took from you."

I looked to my mother.

"Those jeans do look fantastic," she said grudgingly. "But I don't trust him. Also? Karma."

"Maybe her karma was preemptive. Maybe this is *his* karma for being such a jerk," Rain said, her arms folded over her chest.

Mom's eyes met mine. "Posey, just be careful."

"Hello?" Santiago called as he opened the door.

"Papi!" Rain cried, jumping up to run to him. He barely had time to step inside before she launched herself at the barrel-chested man who swung her around easily.

"*Mi reina, mija! Mi cielo, mi alma,*" he said hugging her tightly. She made a show of wanting to break up the hug but giggled. They'd played out this scenario at least a hundred times over the years.

Finally he held her at arm's length. "This how you gonna go fishing, *Mija?*"

She tossed her glossy black hair over one shoulder. "Yeah. There a problem?"

"Santi, she loves to smell of fish guts and to smear them all over her nicest clothes."

"Mom!"

"Oh, I see. You want to go to church tomorrow smelling of Eau de Fish, eh?" he added.

"Gosh, don't take her side," Rain said.

"I am always on her side, so you need to change your clothes, don't you think?" he said.

Rain stomped off.

"Your call, but you might want to put that pretty hair in a ponytail," Mom called down the hall.

Santi looked at Mom with a smile on his face, but when she met his eyes they both frowned. If their banter were any indication, my mother and Santiago still had all of the feelings for one another, which explained why my mother hadn't dated a soul since they'd officially broken up about five years ago—not that any of us knew why.

Rain returned in ratty jeans and a long-sleeved shirt with her feet in the green boots she hated and her hair in a ponytail. She had, however, added a new coat of lip gloss. "Let's go."

"Only if you tell me *en español*."

"*Vámanos, Papi!*"

"As long as you haven't forgotten everything Abuelita and I have taught you," he said, the corners of his mouth twitching because he loved to tease his daughter.

"I have a one-hundred average in Spanish Four. Please."

"*Por favor,*" he supplied helpfully. She smacked his arm, and the two left chattering in Spanish, which was, now that I thought about it, how they also discussed our Christmas presents each year. I chuckled. Señor Brokaw would be hard to hide in the conversation even if it were in Spanish. When I looked over to my mother, her smile had faded into longing.

"Mom, are you okay?"

"Hmm, what? Oh, yes. I'm fine."

She didn't look fine. She looked bereft. "Did Santiago ever hurt you?"

She sat up quickly. "No, of course not! Nothing like that. If anything, I think I hurt him."

That was the end of the conversation and also the end of the fashion show since Mom had to go to work soon and Granny didn't care. In fact, now she lay back against the recliner she sat in, snoring lightly. I walked back to my room and laid out all of my new clothes on the bed. It hadn't taken as long to rack up five thousand dollars' worth of merchandise as I had thought it would. Each piece had been selected out of love or necessity. I fingered a teal blouse that I particularly liked. I supposed I could part with it.

Not the jeans, though. One simply did not return a pair of perfectly fitting jeans.

Looking from one treasure to another, I wanted to keep every last thing I'd bought.

For once in my life I had only bought what I wanted without any thought to the price. I'd bought expensive makeup, but I could return it and get something similar at Target now that I'd learned some of the techniques from the makeover Rain had talked me into getting. I put the makeup to the side first. It was something Rain loved far more than I did.

Next I put aside some of the school supplies. I didn't *need* them for a supply position. I'd bought them in the excited mania of knowing I would have a classroom, even if only temporarily. I could return those and buy more if I managed to snag a job the following year.

I sat on the bed and grunted as I yanked and tugged off the cowboy boots. I loved them, but I didn't need them. At least I knew a size and a brand for someday when I had enough money of my own. I gently lay them back in their box, putting the wadded paper back at their toes and tucking them into their tissue paper.

"I'm sorry I ended your fashion show," Mom said from the doorway where she leaned. "I should stay out of your business, let you make your own decisions. I had no idea Chad would ever hurt you, and I'm worried, that's all."

I wanted to tell her that I could handle myself, but past experience suggested otherwise.

As if reading my mind, she said, "I haven't had the best track record with men. What do I know?"

Another of her cryptic references to the past, but just the opening I needed. "Speaking of your track record with men, who is my father?"

She looked away. "I told you I don't want to talk about it."

"Yes, you've been telling me that my whole life, but even Henny knows who his dad was, and that man was horrible."

"Not one of my better decisions," she said with a shaky breath.

"Surely, *my* father can't be any worse than his," I muttered as I slammed clothes into bags, keeping only what I could pay for with my PayPal money. Mom was right. I needed to return what I couldn't afford and do whatever it took to get Chad to leave me alone.

"I don't think he is," she said.

"You don't think? I think I have a right to know."

"You know what? Don't return this stuff just yet," she said.

"What?"

Was she seriously attempting one of her famous subject changes? I was too old to fall for it. I would ask her every day, three times a day, until she told me just to get me to shut up.

She held out one finger as she answered her own phone, listening intently before saying "I don't know how you got this number, but you can forget you ever learned it."

She held the phone away from her ear as an angry male voice spilled out. When he'd talked himself hoarse, she put the phone back to her ear. "No, I will not give you her number, especially not after the stunt you pulled."

I mouthed "Who is it?" and she waved me off.

"Well, it serves you right. I hope she buys more," my mother said. She vibrated with rage.

Chad. Had to be. Mom was about to disconnect the phone, but I motioned for it because I wasn't going to let her fight my battles no matter how much I wanted to.

"What do you want, Chad?"

"What do I want? What do I want? You have the audacity to take my credit card on a shopping spree and then ask me what I want?"

"Well?"

"I want you to return every last thing you bought."

"No." It didn't matter that I'd been meaning to do just that. At the hateful, controlling sound of his voice I rebelled. My audacity? He'd somehow weaseled my mother's private number from someone and was calling her to irritate me.

"You will," he said. "If it's the last thing you do. I told you time and time again not to overspend."

"You are no longer the boss of me. If you hadn't left me and cleaned out our checking account then I wouldn't have needed a new job and the clothes for it."

I looked at my mother. She nodded her understanding.

"I will take you over my knee and make sure you can't sit down for a week," he growled.

"No, you won't," I said calmly, even though my heart beat so loudly that I could feel it in my ears. "I filed a restraining order, and you aren't to come anywhere near me."

And I have a Taser on the way, not that I'm going to let you in on that particular little secret.

He greeted this information with silence, and I started to hang up the phone. I should hang up the phone. Why couldn't I? What made me stay on the line with this man?

Habit. Fear of retribution, possibly, but mainly habit.

I was about to kick the habit when he spoke, this time with attempted charm even if I could still hear an undertone of anger. "Posey, I understand now that those changes were a lot to make, but you only have yourself to blame. If you had done a better job with those mailers to solicit money, then we wouldn't be in this predicament."

"I did exactly what you asked me to do about those mailers!" As the words left my mouth, I knew I'd made a mistake. He meant to confuse the issue. These are the sorts of arguments we got into early in our marriage. He'd blame me for things I had no control over or tell me I hadn't done things I knew I'd done. Eventually, it had been easier to cater to his warped sense of reality.

Gaslighting. That's what Rain had called it. No sense in arguing with him, even if he explained in a calm, patronizing voice why he was right and I was wrong. I had to ignore all that.

"Chad, hush," I said. "Look, I'll return everything if you will do one thing for me."

"What?"

"Fill out that worksheet and take it to Ben and then sign the paperwork we need to get a divorce."

He hung up on me.

"That's it, I'm keeping everything," I announced.

"Damn straight you are!" Mom yelled.

"Did you just cuss?"

"I think I did."

"Why are we yelling?"

"I don't know!"

"I think it's because I feel like a new woman."

Mom smiled. When she spoke, her words were much softer. "Me too."

chapter 18

I watched the sun rise Sunday morning while enjoying a very quiet house. None of the stores were open. Mom and Granny had gone to one church and Rain, to another. Henny had trudged in from his warehouse job and fallen face first on the couch into a deep sleep. Antsy because I was having a hard time adjusting to not having church, I picked up and put down each of my books at least three times. The pedagogy didn't hold my interest. Emotionally, I didn't want to tackle the book on divorce. And the romance? Well, it was about a blond pirate so all I could do was think about John.

I did need to take him that LP, maybe some brownies to apologize for being, well, whatever it was I was being. I'd been a bit too forward while drunk. Then he'd caught me off-guard in Au Naturel. The more I thought about how earnestly he'd asked me about dinner with that forced casualness you use when you're afraid someone's going to say no, I winced. I wished I could've done the whole thing over again. No clue what I'd say, but I wish I could do it again.

Knowing that he was probably still in church, I went to the kitchen to make the brownies. Of course, I was missing three ingredients and had to go to the store. By the time I got back and finished making the brownies, it was one o'clock, and there was no one to talk sense into me. Mom and Granny said they were going to see the drawings at the Chalkfest after church. Henny snored on the couch. Rain always spent Sunday afternoon with her father and *abuelita*.

Three times I picked up the pan of brownies and walked to the car.

Three times I walked back.

What was I thinking? I couldn't drive over to his house and barge in—especially not after turning him down.

He did say he'd be there if I needed anything. Anything at all.

With a deep breath I took the brownies and picked up the LP from the table just inside the door.

The old Busbee farmhouse was farther off the road than I'd remembered, with a driveway consisting of only thin gravel ruts that wound between old trees. I rounded a corner and came into a clearing with a neat little white house. The front of the house had been recently painted and another side was ready for a coat, having had all of the old layers of paint scraped off. A huge black dog bounded out to greet the car—or growl at it, I couldn't tell which yet.

"Rowdy, come back here!"

John O'Brien stepped out on the porch, shirtless and barefoot, and I sucked in a breath.

Posey, you will walk over these brownies and this record, and you will say your piece then you will leave before you do something stupid.

I had to tell myself this because I was thinking about all kinds of stupid things: What did John mean by *anything?* What would it be like to kiss him while sober? How would making love to a kind, giving man feel?

I juggled the brownie pan in one hand and album in the other. John opened the car door for me, and I found myself eye level with his chest. "I, uh, wanted to bring you some brownies and a record that somehow didn't make it into the box you took."

He grinned. "Thank you. Come in, and I'll make some coffee."

I knew I shouldn't, but I wanted to, so I did. The dog walked around me snuffing and wagging his tail. "I didn't know you had a dog."

"I didn't. At least not until last week," John said as he opened the front door for me.

Everywhere I looked I saw plants. He also had Liza's couch, that floral monstrosity that managed to pale in comparison to prayer plants and ferns and spider plants and even African violets. "Whoa."

He blushed a little, and I noticed his shoulders were dusted with freckles. "I read somewhere that taking care of plants was a good way to prove personal responsibility. I might've overdone it."

"No, they look great." I couldn't even keep a cactus alive, but John's house looked like a greenhouse with plants hanging from the ceiling and on a rough bookcase and window sills. I followed him to the kitchen where I found more plants.

"Yeah, I had to get rid of some of them because they were poisonous to ol' Rowdy here. You should've seen the schefflera. It was a tree."

I didn't know a lot about houseplants, but I did remember how Liza would complain about her ferns dying or not being able to get her African violets to bloom. John definitely had a green thumb.

"Oh, and here's the record," I said as he put the brownies down on a counter.

His eyes widened. "Is that . . . ?"

I handed him the album, and he took it with reverence as he turned it over and examined it. "This is an original *Yellow Submarine*."

"Sure," I said with a shrug.

"An original Beatles album, and not just any Beatles, a *Yellow Submarine* album."

Words were coming out of his mouth, but they weren't making a lot of sense. "I guess? I found it and the rest of the records in one of the closets when we moved in."

"I have been looking for one of these forever," he said, shaking his head. "I could kiss you!"

"Why don't you?" The words came out of my mouth as though my shoulder devil had taken control of my vocal cords. Who knew my shoulder devil could make my voice sound so husky?

He put down the album and walked toward me. Part of me wanted to back away, but I held my ground. As my reward, his hands cupped my cheeks tenderly, and he brought his lips to mine. My hands went automatically to his chest then wrapped around his neck, and his hands moved lower to press me against him. *This* was what sex and attraction were supposed to feel like: this feeling that I might pass out or explode, but I didn't know which and didn't really care.

What started out as tender quickly proceeded to hungry, but this time Rain wasn't there to pull us apart.

"Remember when you said you'd do anything for me?" I asked while John kissed along my neck.

"Mm-hmm?"

"Show me what love's really supposed to be like."

He paused to look at me, his brow furrowed in surprise as he reasoned out my words.

My heart had gotten ahead of my head. Now that I'd made the request, I wondered if all sex was the same. Since I'd only had one partner, how would I know? Maybe John would want wigs and clear shoes and bondage. Chad had told me he needed such props because I'd taken all of the joy out of sex with my constant harping for a baby. Then he'd taken all of my joy from sex with his requests that I didn't feel comfortable accommodating. But accommodate him I did. I did as he asked because he was my husband and because all of the literature suggested I needed to keep sex fresh so trying to conceive wouldn't become monotonous.

Not a one of those articles had mentioned what I should do for myself when the going got tough.

"What do you mean?" John asked. Maybe he couldn't imagine a world where a man would take his pleasure and leave a woman wanting. I knew the world he couldn't picture a little too well.

My face flushed at the thought of trying to explain myself. "I want to know you—biblically."

"I get that. But why?"

"I don't know anything anymore. Chad told me—"

"That man knows nothing."

Resolved, John swept me up as if I were a waif and carried me to his bedroom.

He lay me on the mattress and took my hand to kiss it, an old-fashioned sentiment incongruous with what I'd come to know of as sex.

"How beautiful are your feet in sandals," he said as he took my shoes.

"The curves of your thighs are like jewels." He unbuttoned my perfect pair of jeans and slid them down so he could kiss each leg, pausing to remove my socks and tickle one foot as he climbed over me.

"John, what are you doing?" I said, partially to hide my automatic uneasiness at having anyone over me.

"Reciting *Song of Solomon* while I make love to you properly," he said before kissing me to the point I couldn't catch my breath. He pulled me up to a sitting position so he could take my shirt then lay me down so he could kiss my belly button, his long hair tickling the skin around it as he bent over. "Your navel is a rounded goblet."

I giggled at the sensation of his hair on my skin and his lips on my navel. "Are you going to quote the Bible the whole time?"

"You said you wanted to get to know me biblically, right?"

My heart swelled. He'd made me laugh because he could sense how nervous I was. "John?"

His index finger lazily traced circles on top of my bra as if he had all of the time in the world. "Yes?"

"I think we've shared enough Bible verses," I said, arching my back as his finger came to my other breast. "Please make love to me."

Slowly, systematically he touched and kissed and teased until the world melted away and only he and I remained. The bright afternoon sun decadently bathed us until we each sneaked a peek at the Promised Land.

Once we'd been pulled back to earth, he lay on his back beside me. "How fair and pleasant you are, O love, with your delights."

I smacked his arm, and he rewarded me with a blindingly handsome grin. Back in eighth grade I had no frame of reference for making love to the tall, lanky boy with the too long hair. I wanted to take his picture in this perfect light, to capture this moment forever. Nothing kinky, just the way the warm light captured the contours of his face. Since I didn't have my camera, I'd have to hope my memory would do it justice.

I sighed, and he pushed a strand of hair from my face. "You don't regret it, do you?"

"Regret? I could die a happy woman right now."

He kissed me gently with chaste affection rather than heat. "Please don't die on me."

"You're right," I said as I snuggled up to him. "If I die then we won't be able to sing the *Song of Solomon* again."

That evening we sat on his bed, a mattress and box springs on the floor, while we ate brownies and drank milk. "We're going to get brownie crumbs in your sheets," I said.

"Posey, don't ruin the moment."

I giggled. Nothing could ruin the moment.

Rowdy whined from the other side of the door, so unhappy we weren't letting him participate in whatever we were doing on the other side of the door.

"I suppose I should let him out," John said. "Just in case."

He stepped into a pair of boxers.

Lust.

Lust was my absolute favorite.

I sighed and fell back on the mattress, never wanting to leave the moment and certainly never wanting to leave John. Logically, I knew no human being could ever be perfect. Emotionally, I felt John had to be pretty damned close. I didn't care about the dirty clothes and stacks of books on the floor. I could learn to love the greenhouse aesthetic he had going on. Why would I ever *have* to leave this moment?

Posey, you can't stay. You're married to someone else.

"Shoulder angel, you are such a buzzkill."

"What?" John asked as he came back in and slipped down beside me.

"Just talking to myself."

"I, um, I'm sorry about the accommodations," he said, waving a broad hand over the bed. "I haven't found a bed frame that I like."

"As long as it's not four-poster," I muttered.

He studied me but must've decided against asking why I'd make such an outburst since he added, "I was thinking more of an antique sleigh bed, but it's hard to find one that's long enough for me."

"Those are pretty."

"Not as pretty as you," he said, leaning in to kiss me, a light kiss that held neither demands nor obligations. Just a kiss.

"When you say it, I almost believe you."

"You should believe me. I have it on good authority that my eyesight is excellent. Twenty-twenty, doc says." He put the pan of brownies on the floor. Then he took my glass of milk. "Maybe you need more convincing."

"Maybe I do."

"If I were to kiss every square inch of you, do you think that would prove my point?"

My pulse raced again. Outside, the sky had darkened, but the gray light of the room only added to the otherworldliness of what we were doing, as if it were a dream, and we could both wake up tomorrow and go about our lives with a mysterious smile on our faces. "I don't know. I'm awfully hard to convince."

"I think I'm up to the challenge," he said with a grin that allowed me to finally touch each dimple. Then he lay me down and made good on his promise.

chapter 19

Humming, I entered the back door, my cheeks once again aching from a smile I couldn't shake.

"Where have you been?" my mother asked from where she sat at the table.

"I went to take John some brownies and to give him a record that he missed," I said.

I also had the most glorious sex of my entire human experience, not that you need to know that.

"Next time, could you please answer your calls?"

"Of course. I guess I'm just not used to having a phone that actually works," I said, some of my mellow harshed. "What's wrong?"

"Your grandmother wandered off this afternoon. It took us an hour to find her," Mom said. "I could've used your help."

"Mom, I'm sorry. I didn't know."

She ran her fingers through her short blond hair, her elbows resting on the table. Finally, she looked up. "You're right. I'm sorry I snapped at you. It was my fault for turning my back on her for even a second."

I took a seat across from my mother at the table. "What happened?"

"They had a chalk art festival down on Front Street, and your granny wanted a funnel cake. I made her promise to sit on a nearby bench and thought I was keeping an eye on her but, as too often happened with you children, I got distracted. The credit card machine had a problem so they had to run my card twice. Next thing I know, I have a funnel cake, but your granny has wandered off."

I grabbed Mom's hand and squeezed it.

"I don't know how much longer Granny can stay with us," Mom said. "She's completely in her own world now."

I swallowed hard. On a superficial level, I'd known that Granny's dementia had worsened. As long as she asked for Tom Brokaw for Christmas and could still solve Liza's problem of a baby who wouldn't sleep through the night, wasn't she okay to stay with us, though? She'd never learned to drive, so we didn't have to take the keys from her, as Liza had had to do with her grandfather. "Mom, it may be time."

"I know." A tear trickled down my mother's cheek. It was the first tear I'd seen her shed. "But she's just now stopped arguing with me."

"Mom, please."

"Of course she argues with me about what to wear or why couldn't I make a pot roast for once, that's not what I'm talking about. I'm saying she's forgotten how much of a disappointment I was because she's forgotten who I am."

"You're not a disappointment!"

This time she leveled me with a glance. "Posey."

"Okay, fine. Yes, I was disappointed that you didn't do more with me when I was younger. Yes, I was jealous of Henny and especially jealous of Rain because we were finally starting to have a mother-daughter relationship when you hauled off and got pregnant again. And, yes, I find your new devotion to Christianity irritating because I'm questioning a lot of things right now, but you took me in when I had no place to go. You could've said I told you so, but you didn't. You're my mother, and I'm proud of what you've done with the studio and your shop. I'm proud of how you've taken care of Granny this long. I'm proud of how well Rain's turned out

and how you keep trying with Henny. You aren't a disappointment."

Mom smiled. "You're a better daughter than I deserve."

Now would be a good time to ask about your father.

"Want me to make some tea?" I said quickly so I didn't bring
my shoulder devil into the conversation and ruin what had been a
lovely mother-daughter moment thirty-two years in the making.

"Sure."

I filled the kettle with water and put it on to boil. "And
Granny's okay?"

"We found her," Mom said with a sigh. "Said she was off to
find someone even if she had to walk to get there. Len picked
her up on Maple Avenue."

I nodded. If she were walking down Maple Avenue then she
was headed to the highway that would take her to the interstate
that would take her to Nashville and no doubt the commune
where mom had gone once upon a time. Granny hadn't forgotten
about her youngest daughter.

"Her sister Pamela used to live off Maple Avenue."

I didn't think Granny wanted to see her sister, Pamela. I thought
she was searching for her lost daughter, but I didn't say it because
Mom didn't need any more guilt.

Then Rain came in, all excited animation, talking about taking her *abuelita* to feed the ducks and about how many fish she
and Santiago had caught the day before. She touched up her nails
and brought vibrancy and laughter to the kitchen as she told tales
on her father's side of the family.

My phone buzzed in my pocket, but I let it go.

Somehow Chad had found my number.

The next morning I arrived at Ellery Elementary before the
sun came out. After checking the lesson plans that Heather had
sent, I laid out supplies I needed and studied the schedule on
the board. The moment of truth arrived when twenty sets of eyeballs looked on me in wonder. I introduced myself and we listened to the morning announcements. I herded the kids to

reading groups and through their learning centers, took them to recess and lunch, read aloud to them. The one thing I forgot to do, but should've known to do, was to tell them more about me as a person.

The other thing I should've done was make sure I had an extra activity or three because I completed all of the lesson plans with ten minutes to spare. In those ten minutes, the questions started:

"Are you going to be here the rest of the year?"

"Do you have a cat?"

"Where's Ms. Mickens? Has she had her baby yet?"

"Do you have a baby?"

"Do you like brussels sprouts?"

"Can we watch a movie tomorrow?"

I answered all of their questions as best I could until one sly-eyed little boy—Heath, if I remembered correctly—raised his hand and asked, "Do you get drunk every weekend? 'Cuz that's what my mama said."

My face went red. "No. I do not get drunk every weekend. Or really at all."

"That's not what my mama said! Are you calling my mama a liar?"

"No, Heath, but you do need to watch your tone and be more respectful."

"I'm not Heath. I'm Noah."

Great. Calling a student by the wrong name was a sure way to undercut any attempts at discipline.

The bell rang, and my charges, their backpacks long since ready to go, piled out of the door and headed for the buses. I wanted to sit at my desk and bury my head in my hands, but I had to go to the front of the school and monitor kids who were waiting for parent pickup. As luck would have it, Noah was one of the kids in the lobby. He screwed up his face and yelled across the lobby, "I'm going to tell my mama that you said she's a liar."

"What's this all about?" Ms. Varner's low, calm voice made me jump. I turned and quietly explained what had happened, hoping that she would say that she would happily handle the situation for me. Oh, no. She told me that I could walk Noah to the car and confront his mother right then and there. She didn't even wish me luck.

When the secretary called Noah's name, I accompanied him outside. His face had turned a little green. He hadn't expected me to actually come with him. His mother, a pretty brunette with a baby strapped in a car seat in the back, gave me a quizzical look as I gestured for her to pull into the side parking lot so the carpool line could continue.

I leaned over to speak through the passenger side window she'd rolled down. What had I got myself into? I wasn't ready to talk to parents or handle kids who asked me about being a drunk. "Hi, I'm Ms. Love, Noah's teacher for the rest of the year."

She blanched, and I kept a smile on my face to press my advantage. "Noah decided to announce to the entire class that I get drunk on weekends."

"Well, if the shoe fits. Please move. I have an appointment to make."

"That is not all," I said through gritted teeth. "I would appreciate it if you would speak to your son about not announcing such things in the middle of class."

She rolled down the windows, turned off the engine, and slammed the door on her way to speak to me. "Look, did you or did you not get drunk the other night and make out with my cousin?"

"I did get drunk for the first time in my life, and I did kiss John O'Brien, if that's who you're referring to as your cousin. I don't plan to drink ever again. I am more than qualified to teach this class and was enjoying doing so until your son decided to interrupt it by making comments not appropriate for a first-grade class, comments that could easily undermine my authority."

She laughed, a bitter sound, and then continued our conversation in that sotto voce that adults used when they didn't want children to hear. "You're going to quit drinking? I don't care if you drink like a fish as long as you don't do it at school. I want you to quit kissing John. The last thing he needs is to have to deal with a married woman. You do know he's in AA? That they suggested he progress from plants to pets and then, maybe, a relationship with a person? He finally made two years of sobriety, and then you come along? Just the taste of alcohol on your lips could send him spiraling backward. Now imagine if you decide you like drinking. So help me if you drag him back into that hell, I will beat you to within an inch of your life."

"I would never—"

"I know you were over at his house yesterday. Leave him alone." And with that she rounded the car. When she drove off, she sprayed gravel at me.

My God. Could I cause John to relapse? I'd known in the abstract that he was a recovering alcoholic—almost everyone in town did—but I hadn't thought about it yesterday. Of course, it made sense now. All of those plants, a dog, me. What if he was with me only because he hadn't been with anyone else for so long? Or what if I had triggered something in him the other night because I'd been drinking too much?

Posey, you're being paranoid.

Maybe so, but I shouldn't be with him until I officially got rid of Chad. I turned and walked back to the school building. Only a few more car riders remained. Ms. Varner walked to me. "And?"

"I'm not sure that went well," I said.

She cocked an eyebrow. "Then do what you need to do to make it go well in the future."

Once the last kid had left, I walked back to my room and packed up my books and such. My phone buzzed yet again. I took it out of my pocket to see who was calling just in case. Nope. Chad had called for the fifth time that day bringing the total up to ten between the two days. Yesterday, he'd left a voicemail about why filling out paperwork was ridiculous. I'd decided to let him stew until he came around to my way of thinking.

When I returned home, John was there on the porch with a bouquet of flowers. My heart leapt at the sight of him, but I also couldn't get his cousin's nasty words out of my mind. The only thing I could do would be to ask him, so I pasted a smile on my face as I got out of the car and walked for the front door. "Hi."

"Happy first day of school!" he said as he extended the flowers.

I took them with my free hand then smelled the blooms. I could count on one hand the number of times Chad had brought me flowers. At the time I would've echoed his words that flowers were a frivolous waste of money. Now, I could see that the thoughtfulness behind bringing flowers was, at least sometimes, worth the cost. I lowered my nose above the blossoms and inhaled their fresh scent. "Thank you."

He held the door for me and followed me inside.

"Hi, Mrs. Adams," he said to my granny as she crocheted another chevron afghan.

"Hello, young man. Are you here to fix the air conditioning? It's sweltering in here."

Mabel/Miranda sat on the couch and inclined her head to indicate that John should *please* play along.

"Yes, ma'am," John said. "I'll have it fixed for you in a jiffy."

His crooked grin made me smile then he followed me to the kitchen where I put down my bags and lay the flowers by the sink so I could find a vase. He wrapped his arms around me from behind, and I jumped out of my skin before remembering that I was with John, not Chad. He backed off, his hands in the air. "Whoa, now!"

"Sorry," I muttered. How could I explain to him the momentary panic of thinking he was Chad? I couldn't find the words I needed, so I kissed him instead.

"Gosh! Get a room."

At Rain's voice we broke apart even though she'd clearly been passing through. "I guess I should get these flowers into water, huh?"

"Here, let me," he said. "If I bring a gift, I shouldn't make you work to keep it."

Deftly, he found a pair of scissors to snip off the ends. I handed him a vase, and he added the plant food and water before putting the flowers inside.

"John?" I said, once I'd put the flowers on the table. "I spoke to your cousin today."

"Which one?"

I didn't know her name. "Noah's mom."

"Ah. Fiona. Yes." He crammed his hands in his pockets, and I curled mine into fists. I wondered if he was working as hard not to touch me as I was not to touch him.

"She, uh, she threatened to beat me up. Said that she heard about my exploits the other night and that the taste of alcohol on my lips could cause you to relapse."

He laughed out loud. "She is a teetotaler of the first order. Your lips are far more tempting than alcohol."

"Fiona doesn't seem to think so."

"Oh, Posey, don't worry about her," he said, pulling me into a hug. "She's still mad that I won't let her set me up with some friend of hers."

Nestling against John, being able to hear a steady heart beat through his solid chest—that was a place I never wanted to leave. Even so . . .

"I hate to say this, but I think we'd better not see each other until I figure out how to get Chad to grant me a divorce, and we can make it final."

He kissed the top of my head. "You haven't really been married to him in your heart for a long time, have you?"

I thought about how Chad had had sex with me just minutes before walking out the door to be with another woman. For him, it was all about power and control. He could, and would, use my relationship with John against me.

"Not in mind or heart," I admitted. Unfortunately, there was the pesky part about being married to him under the eyes of the law.

John sighed. "I'll do what you ask me to do."

I pulled away and looked up into his eyes. "Really?"

"Of course," he said.

I took both of his rough, strong hands into mine. "Then I want you to wait for me. I'm going to figure this out. The minute I am a free woman, I will be on your doorstep with a bottle of champagne."

He arched an eyebrow, and I winced. "Sparkling cider. It will be sparkling cider."

He kissed each cheek and then my forehead. "Can we at least have coffee from time to time while we wait?"

"I don't know. We might start playing footsie under the table, and who knows where that would lead?"

When he realized I was joking, he tickled me without mercy. I laughed until tears came.

"Seriously. Like, get a room," Rain said, as she reached into the fridge. "Or something."

"One more time?" he whispered into my ear, the feel of it sending delicious shivers down my body.

"I'll meet you at your place in ten," I whispered back.

He made his formal goodbyes, to which Rain rolled her eyes.

Five minutes later, I left the house, speeding down the country roads that would take me back to him. He met me at the door, and we made the most of our evening.

chapter 20

Each day as a first grade teacher went better than the last.

Noah and I found some common ground in a mutual love of dinosaurs. It felt so good to be able to talk about dinosaurs again. He'd been the one to suggest a class project where we put each student's face on the head of a dinosaur for our newest bulletin board. I'd brought in my camera and taken pictures of each of the kids. I'd forgotten about how much I'd loved to read about dinosaurs when I was a kid. Chad's biblical interpretation left no room for the terrible lizards. Personally, I figured there was a lot in the world that I wouldn't understand until I passed through those pearly gates. If anyone could reconcile dinosaurs with Genesis, it would be God.

Having picked up on my first graders' routines, I was better able to guide them through the day. I even joined them in the kickball game at recess, which earned me some goodwill. My phone buzzed off and on all day, but I ignored it.

Having finished afternoon duty and packed up my papers and lesson plans and the set of manipulatives I needed to cut out, I sat behind my desk. Teaching was harder than I'd thought it would be, downright exhausting even.

But I loved it.

Dust motes caught the last beams of hazy afternoon light, and

I drank in the smell of old building and new crayons. I loved my students' smiling faces, their sense of wonder, the joy that lit up a student's eyes when she managed to read a tough passage for the first time. I loved the chaos and the bright colors of the classroom decor, the order of the day as it progressed from one subject to another. For heaven's sake, I loved drinking my chocolate milk from a tiny carton again.

At the knock on my door, I turned to see Chad.

"Go away," I said as I fished my phone out of my purse.

"Now that's no way to talk to your husband," he said from the doorway. He leaned against the door facing casually, his charming tone of voice suggesting he was up to no good.

"My soon-to-be ex-husband, you mean." Satchel strap and purse over shoulder, I stood. I'd already typed in the nine-one-one and had my hand poised over the button. "Also, I have a restraining order so you need to leave. Now."

"Maybe if you'd answer your phone—"

"I didn't answer my phone because I don't want to talk to you. I also didn't give you my number for that same reason."

"Good thing it's not unlisted, then, because we need to talk."

I took a deep breath. The longer I spoke with him, the more likely he would twist things up on me. "I don't need to talk with you about anything. Sign the papers and leave me alone."

"Oh, I don't think we'll be getting that divorce."

"Then you're thinking wrong." I wanted to leave, but he blocked my exit. Somewhere down the hall, the swish of the janitor's dust mop gave me hope. At least one other person was in the building. "You knew that adultery was nonnegotiable for me."

"That why you decided to screw the piano tuner? Or have you been at it behind my back the whole time?" He spat out the words. At first I couldn't understand why he was making life so difficult for us both if he had such ridiculous suspicions, but the epiphany hit me so hard it almost knocked me backward: He enjoyed my pain. If he stayed married to me, he thought he could punish me and hold such things over me for the rest of our lives. In his mind, any offenses he committed were now null and void.

"I wanted to see what it was like to make love with someone who actually cared about me," I said softly. "And, no, I wasn't the first to break our marriage vows."

"What the hell?" he sputtered, taking a step closer.

Remembering my afternoon of delight with John reminded me that not all men were like the asshole in front of me. Knowing that I wasn't insane or asking too much helped me stand tall despite the banging of my heart. "You heard me. Leave now, or I will call the police."

He looked me up and down, taking in the tailored pants and flattering blouse. "Those some of the clothes I bought? You look . . . different. Nice."

"I look like myself, and thanks for the lovely parting gift," I said, glad for the lip gloss I'd applied before afternoon duty. "Now go."

"I'll leave," he said, giving me the crooked naughty boy smile. "But this discussion isn't over, and we're not getting a divorce."

Satisfied he was having the last word, he turned on his heel and walked through the door. He didn't know about the camera in my satchel, the one that only had my students' smiling faces on it now that all of the ugly pictures were on a flash drive my sister had given me. He didn't know about those pictures or how he featured in some of them.

"Oh, Chad?"

"Yes?"

"I'll take you to court if I have to."

"So everyone can find out about how you screwed around on me?" He laughed and then gestured to the classroom around him. "You wouldn't dare risk all of this."

"To get rid of you, I would. Besides, the court would find out how *you* screwed around on me. Oh, and I'm sure I could sway them to my side with the pictures I found."

I did not want to show anyone the pictures in question, but it was the only bluff I had.

"Len Rogers saw me burning wigs and lingerie, too. I'm not sure your reputation could withstand some of the stories I could tell." Somehow I got the words over the lump in my throat. "I know they wouldn't look good in a trial for how you've violated my restraining order."

He blanched. "You agreed to everything we did."

I cocked my head to one side. "Did I? Or did I reluctantly participate because you insisted it was my duty as a wife? I can't remember."

But I could. He'd told me I needed to play along to keep his interest. He dragged me into all sorts of things I hadn't been ready to contemplate. He'd told me it wasn't something we would do all the time, but my repeated requests for sex and constant use of ovulation kits and pregnancy tests were just so unsexy and so draining for him.

God, that should've been yet another clue that he would make a piss-poor father.

Anger infused his face as he pointed at me. "You wouldn't dare."

"I have nothing to lose," I whispered softly.

"You have everything to lose." He practically choked on his anger.

"Not as much as you do. Not anymore. Oh, and when you talk to Ben, add a provision that I keep *everything* I bought with your credit card. That's the least you could do."

He stormed down the hall, and I sank down in my desk chair once more.

Only, it wasn't really my chair nor my desk nor my room nor even my job. He could take everything from me. If we went to court, and I told my story complete with graphic illustrations, I would destroy myself along with him. It was, however, a risk I had to take because I would never go back to him. Never, ever.

Cautiously I moved through the rest of the week, learning more about my students and about my job. I looked over my shoulder constantly until my Taser finally arrived and Julia gave me a tutorial. In spite of my attempts at constant vigilance, however, I settled into the routine, happily exhausted when Friday rolled around. That afternoon, Ben called to let me know that

Chad had finally finished his portion of the paperwork and had agreed to the uncontested divorce. The papers would be ready to sign next week, but he'd let me know after Chad signed them so we wouldn't have to run into each other.

Part of me wanted to celebrate; the other part wondered when the other shoe would drop.

Either way, I was overdue for catching up with Liza and picked up a bag of Oreos on the way to her house. She answered the door with a baby on her hip. The dark circles under her eyes had grown fainter, and she smiled. Then scowled. "Why can't you bring a bottle of wine like a normal human being?"

"Oh, no," I said, almost turning green at the thought. "Alcoholic beverages and I are taking a long hiatus, possibly a permanent one."

She sighed. "You should've gone out with me instead of your sister. She didn't know what she was doing."

I couldn't argue with her. "Still, I think I'll stick with Oreos for the time being."

She traded me the baby for the Oreos, and I followed her to the kitchen where she started the coffee maker. "I hope decaf is all right. I'm trying to avoid caffeine after lunch."

"Probably for the best," I said as I held Nathaniel up and blew raspberries on his little belly until he giggled. "I'm so tired I thought about going home and straight to bed."

"So no babysitting tonight?"

"Not tonight even if he is the cutest little man," I said, repeating that last sentence and continuing with the raspberries because they brought smiles and giggles.

"Oh, stop. You're making me sick."

I cleared my throat. Liza wasn't a fan of baby talk.

"Nathaniel, you have a smidgen of drool there, old chap," I said, reaching out a hand.

Liza rolled her eyes as she gave me the plain cloth diaper draped over her shoulder. "Your British accent is even worse."

Turning my pseudo-nephew around, I held him against my stomach as I bounced him gently. Seeing a colorful plastic key ring, I held that in front of him. He slapped at the keys and chewed on them. "So I, um, have something I need to confess."

"Really?" Liza jumped to her feet as the coffee maker finished percolating. "Do tell."

"I may or may not have slept with John the Baptist." For some reason I looked down at the baby as if he could make note of my transgressions. He gnawed away on his keys.

"Wait. What?" Liza said, the coffee pot poised midair. "I thought I heard you say you did the horizontal tango with John O'Brien. Surely, my sleep-deprived brain has betrayed me."

"Ha. You're downright chipper from newfound sleep, and you heard me just fine."

"And?"

"And wow."

Liza silently made coffee for me. She knew how I liked it, one of the advantages of hanging out with a friend.

"You took all necessary precautions?"

"Of course," I said. "It's not like I can even get pregnant, but John had condoms so—"

"Wait. What?"

"I can't get pregnant, Liza. I've been trying for almost ten years now. A doctor even told me so. You know that."

She studied me, "No, I may be in the HOV lane to senility, but I would've remembered that."

Had I really not told my best friend about my struggles? I told her about trying to get pregnant, but then I took the job as a receptionist. Then she got pregnant and had Nathaniel. My heart sank. Just another way I'd been isolated from the people who actually cared for me. "I'm sorry, Liza. I thought I'd told you."

"You told me you were trying, but you never told me you couldn't. I'm sorry I wasn't more understanding when Nathaniel was born."

I kissed his head, inhaling scent of baby and brushing that soft hair against my lips and cheek. Tears pricked at the corners of my eyes, but I was well accustomed to keeping those particular tears at bay. Finally I choked out my new phrase on the subject, "It is what it is."

Liza opened her mouth, but wisely closed it. If I knew Liza—and I did—then she had been about to launch into a discussion of all the miracles that could happen, all the specialists I could see, and how she would personally find a way to get me pregnant. I half chuckled at the thought of Liza coaching me into pregnancy, probably telling the in vitro people how to do their job. Even worse, she wouldn't hesitate to stand at the side of my bed and dictate the best sex positions and practices to get me pregnant.

"What are you laughing about?"

"You." I hugged Nathaniel, but he got very excited about those keys and jumped up enough to pop my lip against my teeth. I ran my tongue over the injured lip, glad the child hadn't drawn blood. "I know you were thinking of how you were going to get me pregnant if that's what I really wanted."

She shrugged but didn't deny me. "Well, you know me. Always wanting to help."

"Someday you can be a reference when I adopt."

She smiled.

I looked down at Nathaniel. "Oh, and I don't want to get my hopes up until it's a done deal, but Ben says Chad has turned in the paperwork and agreed to the divorce."

Liza sucked in a breath. "Well, I'll cross my fingers and say my prayers."

We sat in silence for a few minutes.

"How 'bout some Oreos?" she said brightly.

She fed the baby and put him down for a nap, and we sipped coffee and ate Oreos the rest of the afternoon. When Owen came in, I tensed. He leaned in to give Liza a kiss on the cheek, and I relaxed, reminding myself that not all marriages were like mine. Hopefully, none of them were.

Owen stood at the sink, washing grease off his hands from where he'd probably been changing oil in both of their cars. He was the model for the strong and silent type, but Liza swore he was a regular Chatty Cathy when no one else was around, doing all sorts of jokes to make her laugh. He looked over his shoulder.

"It's payday. If you'll order a pizza, I'll fetch it along with some beer."

"Deal," Liza said. "Pose, wanna join us?"

I almost said yes, but, by the way Owen was looking at his wife, I had the idea he might like for them to spend the evening together so I told one of those patented half-truths I'd learned from my mother. "I wish I could, but I told Mom I'd eat at home tonight. Both Rain and Henny will be at supper for once."

This was all true, but Mom had also told me I didn't have to be there. She'd hinted that I should get out and visit with Liza or even John.

"Bummer."

"Next time," I said.

"You'd better," she said with a laugh. "I'm going back to work next fall so we only have this summer to get into whatever shenanigans we want to get into. Maybe I'll make you take me to one of those pole dancing lessons."

I groaned. "You heard about that, too?"

"Rain told me when she gave me a coupon."

"Pole dancing?" Owen asked.

If I hadn't had a reason to leave before, I had one now. I had no intention of returning to the Pole Cat. "All right. I'm outta here."

"Don't do anything I wouldn't do," Liza said with a grin.

chapter 21

The next day I went by Ben's office I signed the divorce papers with little fanfare. I ran my fingers over Chad's signature, almost unable to believe he'd finally caved. Everything I wanted was within my grasp. Ms. Varner had complimented me just the day before for the job I'd been doing and had hinted there might be a position opening up in second grade. In two months or so, I'd be able to pursue whatever was between John and me. Could be love or could be lust, but either promised to be fun. I itched to call him at least three times a day, suggesting absence really did make the heart grow fonder.

Each day I loved my charges a little more. Each day I relied less on Heather's lesson plans and created my own. Each day I grew a little more confident, a little less apprehensive that Chad would show up. Days became weeks, and before I knew it a month had passed.

"Would you like to come with me to the Maundy Thursday service tomorrow night?" Mom asked one evening while I washed dishes.

"The what service?"

"Maundy Thursday, the day we celebrate the Last Supper. You know, tomorrow's Good Friday."

Ah. Good Friday. I knew that one even if I had often questioned the descriptor "Good" for the day that Christ died. Maybe it was all a case of perspective. "I've made it this far. I think I'll wait until Sunday."

Maybe I'd buy a new outfit now that I'd made my own money. I still didn't want a dress, though.

"Wanna come to church with me on Sunday?" Mom asked as she sipped herbal tea.

I said nothing, but the picture in my mind was First Baptist, the place where I'd been baptized. The place that had welcomed me long before I met Chad. They might not welcome me with open arms after all that Chad had said and done or if Fiona had blabbed about John and me, but First Baptist was the church of my heart so I had to try. "Oh, I'm not going back to your church. I'm going to mine."

"To Love Ministries?"

"No. I'm going back to First Baptist," I said, surprising myself with the conviction in my own voice. "They are my church family, and I should've never left them."

"But I am your actual family."

"My going to a different church doesn't change that fact."

"I guess you're right."

I wondered if she ever thought about how she'd tried to keep me from First Baptist when I was little. Did she blame them for Chad? She shouldn't. As hard as it was to separate him from the scriptures he'd used as a weapon against me, I could almost do it because I'd been there first.

"We can be a family at dinner after the service," I said. "I didn't feel comfortable at your church."

I dried my hands and draped the dish towel over the few dishes in the drainer then turned around to see her studying me with her head cocked to one side. "That was a very brave thing for you to say."

"Why do you say that?"

"In the past, you would've deflected my idea rather than answer me straight on or you would've come along with me but sulked all the way. I guess those self-help books are working, huh?"

"Yeah," I said softly. "I guess they are. Rain helped me the most by putting a name to what I'd been feeling for so long."

"I'd like to borrow some of the books when you're done with them."

"Mom, I think you've got it together now."

She chuckled. "You'd be surprised. Well, I'm going to miss you tomorrow and on Sunday, but maybe I can talk Mabel into helping me take your granny to church."

Oh. I hadn't thought about that. Mom could use my help since Granny got a little weaker every day. She'd really burrowed into her own world after her trip down Maple Avenue. "I guess I could help you so Mabel could go to her own church."

Mom stood and put a hand on my shoulder. "Now, now. Don't renege on those nice boundaries you set. We'll work it out."

As she left, Rain passed her, lugging her backpack and dropping it on the ground in a huff.

"I hear you haven't missed a day of school since that last migraine you had," I said with a smile.

"Ugh. I don't see what the point of all this is. My college applications have already gone through. No one's going to take a look at my spring semester grades."

Maybe not, but after I'd told Mom and Santi about how Rain secretly feared they wouldn't be able to pay for her college, they'd subtly reassured her on that point. Santi had even promised her a newer car if she could make it through the spring semester with no absences and all As. If he'd known about the Pole Cat, I'm sure that would've been a part of the deal, too, but Rain let everyone keep believing she was still working at the mall. Which was kinda true. It was a strip mall. With an establishment that helped women learn to strip.

"What are you up to?"

"This research paper I have to do. Most everything is winding down, but my English teacher is nuts. She made us write down all of the quotes we want to use as supporting evidence on notecards like it was nineteen eighty or something. Everyone else uses computers, but, no, not her. Then she told me my quotes didn't support my argument, which is total crap." Rain punctuated her sentence by dropping a library book from her backpack on the table. "And we have to use at least one *real* book even though everything we could possibly need is on the Internet."

"I'm sorry for your struggle," I said, attempting to hold back a smile.

Rain took two packs of Twizzlers from her backpack and reached into the fridge for a two liter of Mountain Dew, a substance Mom only grudgingly permitted in the house. "The struggle is damn real, and I'd appreciate it if you wouldn't patronize me."

I held up both hands in surrender. "Okay, okay."

Rain looked over her shoulder. "And don't tell Mom I cussed."

"Wouldn't dream of it. I can, however, take a look at your index cards, if you would like."

"Would you?" Her eyes widened with hope and her mouth unsnarled from disgust. How could I say no?

The next morning I deeply regretted the amount of Twizzlers and Mountain Dew I'd consumed while helping Rain with her research project. My digestive system was no longer that of a teenager as demonstrated by my nausea. At least I never threw up. I could happily go the rest of my life without ever seeing either of those foods again.

By dressing quickly and skipping breakfast in favor of peanut butter and crackers, I still managed to make it to school on time. When the kids asked me why I looked a little green, I told them the truth: I had eaten too much junk food the night before. I could be their cautionary tale. Of course, that meant a five-minute discussion about what "cautionary tale" meant, in which they thought they were getting me off track. Nah. I had a few extra minutes to spare. Even so, I'd already learned it was best to sometimes let my students think they were getting the best of me. All the better to surprise them with my upper hand later in the day.

As I shielded my eyes from the sun to watch them on the playground at recess, I realized I would miss them. I'd grown to love the students in my charge—even Noah. Maybe especially Noah since I'd had to work so hard to win him over. Each morning he brought me a new dinosaur fact as our own special bond.

That evening I took a trip to Jefferson to get a new Easter outfit. I tried on a few dresses, but I still couldn't bring myself to buy one. Not only did they remind me of Chad, but I was tired of having my thighs rub together when I walked and summer would do me no favors in that area. Granny would've pointed out that I *could* wear pantyhose, but I'd given up hosiery in anticipation of the world's demise at Y2K. The world kept spinning, but I hadn't picked up hose ever again.

Nope. I wanted pants, and, by golly, I was going to have some pants.

I hung up the dresses and went over to the racks that held suits. It couldn't hurt to have a professional suit for future interviews. Ms. Varner seemed pleased with my work, but one could never be too sure in such situations. I passed up pastel pinks and purples. Mint green was *so* not my color. I held out a white pantsuit—it had such a nice cut, but white made my butt look bigger and was just an invitation for a period mishap.

My face drained of all color there in the middle of a department store with only thirty minutes before closing. When was the last time I'd had a period?

It had been over a month. A month and two weeks, to be exact.

I let the suit go as if it had singed me, and walked back to my car a zombie.

What if my first pregnancy test really had been a false positive?

What if I'd somehow managed to get pregnant with John even though we used condoms?

What if I had some kind of dread disease?

Ridiculous. You know the main reasons for a missing period are pregnancy, menopause, and extreme weight loss—two of those most certainly don't apply to you.

Once home, I walked back to my bedroom and dug through the closet until I found the box of pregnancy tests I'd bought over a month ago. I had one left.

As much as I wanted to know, I also didn't want to know. I told myself I'd go to bed and try in the morning, but I couldn't sleep. Even so, the part of me who'd studied fertility so obsessively couldn't take the test until first thing in the morning to maximize the accuracy. I drank water and herbal tea and worried, happy I could at least keep Granny company for a few hours while she watched old episodes of *Murder, She Wrote*.

At some point after three, we both fell asleep, more than one mystery unsolved.

chapter 22

I jerked awake at the sound of my alarm going off in the other room. To say I felt terrible was the understatement of the century.

With trembling fingers I removed the last pregnancy test from the box and barricaded myself in the bathroom, the rest of the house still asleep. This time, I glued my eyes to the pregnancy test the minute I finished washing my hands. Watched pots never boiled, and watched pregnancy tests never came up positive—these were two things I knew.

What I couldn't know is what I would do if I were somehow pregnant. Having mixed feelings for the first time ever made my head spin. On the one hand, having a child was what I wanted most in the world. On the other, I was almost divorced, had a new job that was didn't take kindly to pregnancy out of wedlock and was less than secure. Then there was John.

Oh, God. What would he say?

Despite the faulty math, the baby almost certainly had to be Chad's because John and I used protection. I mean, sure there was a statistical possibility of failure, but wasn't it more likely that Chad was the father? Would a pregnancy derail the divorce? Make him double down on making things work between the two of us?

No child of mine will grow up in a house with that man.

Just the thought of having to share custody of a child with Chad made me want to hurl. At least John was a kind, decent human being.

You think that now, my recently dormant shoulder devil said. *Wait and see if a pregnancy doesn't change his tune.*

Before my very eyes, a second line emerged in the blank area next to the line that was already there. The line grew darker and darker, and I swallowed hard.

I'm going to be a mother.

I sank against the opposite wall of the bathroom, wanting to cry, but not knowing if the tears would be joy or sadness or confusion or d) all of the above.

"Posey? That you in there? Your Granny needs the restroom."

"Just a minute!" I scrambled to my feet and wrapped the test in toilet paper to conceal it, washing my hands one more. Odd how I didn't feel different. I'd always thought being pregnant would immediately make me feel something. Other than a mild foretaste of nausea, I felt . . . nothing.

"You okay?" Mom asked as I exited the restroom.

"Just ate too much yesterday," I said, willing myself to meet her eyes but unable to do so for very long. Why should I feel ashamed about being pregnant? She didn't marry a single one of the men with whom she had babies.

You're embarrassed because you once swore you would never do what she did.

That could be. Even so, I needed to think about things, get the doctor to confirm it, maybe. At the very least, I needed to talk with Chad and John and figure out how to proceed.

Oh, God, what would I do about insurance? I was about to be off Chad's plan. John probably didn't have insurance. What if this pregnancy meant I didn't get the job at the school? That full-time gig could be my only hope for insurance, and there was no way I could afford to pay out of pocket for having a baby.

I closed the bedroom door behind me and looked longingly at

the bed. How I wanted to burrow up under those blankets and never come out, but I needed to go to work and do a fabulous job in the hopes of earning a full-time position.

Guess you're even more of a cautionary tale than you thought.

Chad didn't answer when I tried to call him at lunch, nor when I called him after school.

I thought about calling John, but I couldn't bring myself to dial the numbers until I spoke with Chad.

Finally, as I was getting out of the car at home, fumbling with all of my school bags, Chad answered.

"Posey, what a surprise," he said drily.

I slammed the car door and headed to the porch where I dropped all of my bags, choosing to sit on the porch swing rather than to take my business into the house. "Chad, I'm pregnant."

Silence.

"It has to be yours," I said in a shaky voice, "John and I used protection."

"It's not mine, you whore."

I winced at the word but forged ahead. "But it has to be."

"It's not."

"How do you know?"

He laughed, an ugly bark that held no humor. "Because I had a vasectomy back in oh-one."

Surely I'd misheard.

There had to be some kind of mistake.

"You what?"

"You heard me. I had a vasectomy before we even married. I knew I didn't want to have kids, and I wasn't about to use rubbers. You refused to go on the pill, always carrying on about children. It was easy to hide the operation since you insisted on being a virgin for our wedding night."

My turn to sit in silence.

My memory banks struggled to reach back to the time before we married. In my mind I'd attributed the promise of kids and white picket fences to him. He had joked about getting a dog, but he'd never been enthusiastic about the children discussion. How had I not seen it? How had he so thoroughly fooled me?

"But what about the doctor who told me I couldn't have kids?"

Chad snorted. "I paid him to tell you that."

My fists clenched so tightly that fingernails dug into my flesh. How could any human being be so evil?

"Our whole marriage was a lie."

He sighed. "It was fun while it lasted."

"Fun?" Fury snapped somewhere behind my eyes. "Fun? You call lying to me and letting me cling to the hopeless notion I'd one day be a mother fun? Of all the awful things you did to me— and there were plenty of them—that is the most despicable, and I hope you rot in hell."

I threw my phone over the railing, my nostrils flaring and my heart trying to beat its way out of my chest. I paced the front porch.

Never before had I contemplated injuring another human being, but I wanted to skewer my soon-to-be ex-husband. I wanted to knee him in the groin repeatedly. I hadn't lost ten years of my life; he had *stolen* them.

You've got to calm down for the sake of the baby.

Sitting down on the porch swing, I closed my eyes and forced myself to think about my breaths, making each inhale and exhale even. My mind conjured a blond baby with blue eyes, one who looked a lot like John O'Brien. I could live with that.

But what would John say? What if he demanded that I—no, I wouldn't. Everyone in the entire godforsaken town could point and laugh and bless my heart for the rest of my life, but I, like Madonna, was going to keep my baby.

Maybe I should go to the doctor first and confirm my pregnancy before I told John. He wasn't Chad, but the previous conversation had rattled me. How could I have been so stupid as to stay married to such a sadistic bastard for so long? If I'd married Chad, then how could I know if John was truly good or just a wolf in sheep's clothing? Chad had seemed nice, too, right up until the point when he wasn't.

Back then, Mom was still struggling. She'd just opened Au Naturel and was dealing with backlash over the name. Some of the churches in town were arguing that yoga wasn't Christian and trying to shut her down. She was also arguing with the elementary school because Rain's teacher had told her dinosaurs didn't exist. Meanwhile, Henny had a learner's permit, but he thought he could drive around town without supervision. Granny and Mom weren't speaking. I remember the night I told her I was getting engaged to Chad. She'd come in late after working from seven in the morning until nine at night.

"Mom, I'm engaged."

"Why? To whom?"

Great. My Mom didn't even know the man I was dating.

"I've been dating Chad. He's asked me to marry him."

Mom flopped into one of the kitchen chairs. "Is he that short guy you brought for Thanksgiving?"

"Yes."

"He's too old for you. And you need to live more on your own before you jump into marriage."

My blood boiled. "Excuse you? I did not come to ask your approval. We are going to get married, and I'm going to get out of this circus of a house where, hopefully, I'll be able to conduct my life without angry calls from Creationists or the police bringing my brother home from an illegal joy ride or women leaving flyers on the front porch about how your business is anti-Christian and too racy for Main Street."

"Posey, I am trying to provide for this family as best I can. You will notice that your Granny isn't working anymore."

"Then I guess I'll be one less mouth to feed."

I'd flounced off, and we hadn't spoken at all until the wedding, at which point we had to forge an uneasy truce. Chad had offered to pay for everything since Mom and I weren't speaking during the planning. At the time I'd thought he was being generous. Looking back, I can see he paid the bills so he could influence all of the decisions from what I wore to where we honeymooned. In those months before the wedding, though, he'd said repeatedly, "Don't worry, Posey. I'll take care of everything."

I didn't yet realize that he really meant that he would dictate everything.

You wanted security and normalcy. He promised you that, and you made the mistake of believing him.

Security. That was one of the things Julia had mentioned a lifetime ago when she'd read those tarot cards. She'd warned me about my dark side and about indulgences. She'd predicted I would get pregnant. She foretold a sweet and ardent lover.

She told you that nothing was impossible with God.

I didn't have to go to the doctor before I spoke with John. I knew the pregnancy test was accurate because Chad's vasectomy explained every negative test up until this point. All of this time I'd thought there was something wrong with me, but my biggest fault was previously being a poor judge of character.

Everything made sense except for how I became pregnant if John and I were using protection. I mean, condoms were supposed to be 98 percent effective.

Well, if anyone could be in the 2 percent, it would be you.

How many times had I prayed for a child? For almost ten years, each morning had begun with that prayer and each evening had ended with its refrain. I had prayed and prayed and prayed for a child.

God had to be having a huge chuckle right now—especially since I'd been arrogant enough to give up church.

I picked up my things and placed them inside the door, telling Mom not to wait on me for supper. Instead, I drove my car to John's house.

chapter 23

Sick with dread, I shook as I rang the doorbell to John's farm-house. Somewhere within Rowdy barked and barked to the point I was beginning to think John wasn't home. Then he answered the door, shirtless with his hair still wet from the shower. His eyes lit up and he smiled. "Posey!"

My first instinct was to kiss him and to initiate the very act that had gotten me in trouble in the first place. Fortunately, I came to my senses.

"Hey," I said as I brushed past him, trying to ignore how his smile melted into a frown.

"I was afraid I wouldn't get to see you for another month at least," he said, pulling me into an embrace. He leaned in to kiss me, and I almost let him.

"We gotta talk."

"Uh-oh. Those are three words no man ever wants to hear."

"I'm pregnant."

His face blanched. "Okay. What do I need to do?"

I stared at him. Such a different response from Chad. His immediate responsibility and willingness to roll up his sleeves caused tears to prick my eyes. He was an infinitely better choice for my baby's father. If only I hadn't been so selfish and had waited so we could do things properly. Now we'd both be ostracized, and our baby would be made fun of just the way I was.

By this point sobs racked my body, and he put his arms around me and led me to the couch. "Hey, now. Everything's going to be okay. We'll have this baby—you are having the baby, right?"

I cut him a dirty look through my tears. As if I would ever abort a baby—especially after wanting for so long to get pregnant.

"Thank God," he said. "I mean, I'll support you no matter what, but—"

"Just shut up and hold me."

He did. He stroked my hair and murmured comforting things until my sobs finally slowed down to great hiccupping gasps.

"You're going to be okay," he said, holding me at arm's length. "We're going to be okay."

"I don't even understand how," I wailed. "We used protection."

He squeezed my shoulders before going back to his bedroom and returning with a frown and the condom box. Only one condom remained. I took it from the box and turned it over to see a two thousand nine expiration date. "These have expired."

"Yeah," he said, running his hand over his mouth. "These were old when I went into rehab, and I haven't slept with anyone in over two years."

"One of them must have torn," I said.

"I'm so stupid," he said as he paced. "I didn't mean to put you in this position."

"John, I asked you to," I said softly. "And I still can't regret it."

He treated me to a dimpled smile, but his eyes couldn't quite meet mine. "I'm glad for that."

"Okay," I said. "We'll figure this out. I need to go to the doctor next week, but I can't see how I'm not pregnant."

He knelt beside the couch where I sat and took my hand. My mouth went dry even as a part of me screamed, *no, no, no.*

"Posey, will you marry me?"

At the thought of getting married again, I couldn't breathe. Sweat poured off me, and I trembled.

"I know this baby is unexpected, but we're good together, don't you think?"

Oh, what a glowing declaration of love. I wanted to tell him so, but I couldn't form the words.

"As soon as your divorce is final, then we can go to the courthouse. You can move in here—I have plenty of room—and I'll get you a pretty ring just as soon as I can afford one."

I clutched at the air, but he was too busy problem solving to see how his proposal had induced panic.

"I'll have to get a better job, though," he said with a frown. "High time I did something meaningful with my life anyway. I mean, other than this baby, of course."

I jumped from the sofa, jerking my hand from his. I bent over, gulping for air. I couldn't. I wouldn't. I would not have another man dictating my life to me, no matter how much easier it would be, no matter that the man in question was one of the good ones.

"Posey?" he patted me on the back.

The world spun around me.

"I'm going to help you sit on the couch. You're going to put your head between your knees. We're going to make it through this."

He gently eased me back on the couch, bending me over. But we? He already assumed there would be a we? Logically, I knew he was only trying to help. Emotionally, I wanted to run screaming from the room because I kept hearing Chad's voice instead of his. I hadn't thought about it in a long time, but my first marriage proposal had been "Of course we're going to get married. I'm thinking June."

No, no, no. I would not jump from the frying pan into the fire.

But I did have to think about the life inside me.

Slowly but surely, air came back to me.

"You scared me half to death," he said once my breathing had returned to normal.

I nodded because I didn't trust myself with words just yet.

"When you've got your breath, then tell me when your divorce will be final, and we can make plans to get married. I'll take care of you. I promise."

He would take care of me? Bile rose in my throat. "No."

"No? Posey, don't be ridiculous. We made a baby. Of course, I'm going to marry you."

It didn't matter that his tone was almost playful. In my head I heard Chad's snide version of "Posey, don't be ridiculous."

I jumped to my feet and he did, too, towering over me in a way that suddenly felt menacing instead of protective. I poked his chest with my finger. "I didn't mean to get pregnant yet, but I am not going to leave one marriage and hop right into another."

"Be reasonable—"

Another one of Chad's favorite admonitions.

"Be reasonable? A reasonable person would've known if his condoms were expired and wouldn't have assured me that everything would be okay when he didn't know if it would be or not. A reasonable person would stop for five seconds and ask me what I want to do instead of barreling ahead with a proposal while I was hyperventilating!"

My breath wanted to leave me again. I willed it to stay even.

"Hey!" He held up both hands. "It takes two to tango."

"Yeah, yeah. The dance was lovely, but maybe that's all I wanted from you."

Punching him in the gut wouldn't have been more effective than my words, and I regretted them almost as soon as I said them, but I continued as if driven by another part of me. "I am done being controlled and bossed around."

"Posey, take a few breaths and—"

"I just took about a thousand breaths, and here you are asking about my divorce so you can plan my next wedding after the world's least romantic proposal. No. I can do this myself."

I snatched up my purse and headed for the door. He grabbed for my arm, and I reflexively hit at him. He let go, stepping back with wide eyes.

I made a run for it.

"It's my baby, too!" he shouted from the door.

"Good. You can help pay for it!"

I plopped down into the car too hard and slammed the door before reversing entirely too quickly and almost hitting a tree.

John came running out into the yard barefoot, shouting about how I needed to think about the baby.

That made me even madder. I'd been thinking about babies for over ten years. My husband had intentionally kept babies from me. Now that I'd managed to conceive it was due to the carelessness of another man, who, apparently, also wanted to run my life. I wouldn't have it. No, I would not.

I tore out on to the main road, tires squealing and the scent of burning rubber invading the car.

The whole thing wasn't fair.

If only I'd gotten over my shyness and talked to John in high school, maybe admitted my crush. Maybe I could've married him in the first place. Maybe he wouldn't have been an alcoholic, and we would've had four lovely towheaded children by now. If only I'd figured out Chad was an asshole from the outset, I could've saved myself from wasting ten years and then making a lifetime of bad choices in just a few weeks.

Now John O'Brien thought that getting his sperm inside me meant he could boss me around. Well, he had another thing coming. He could just see if I ever fixed him any damned brownies ever again. In fact, I didn't even need his money. I'd figure out how to raise this child on my own. Heck, my mother raised three children, two of them without any assistance from their fathers, and she still hadn't married the third father.

And how was growing up without a father, Posey?

The soft, still voice of my shoulder angel caused my foot to ease off the accelerator.

I would need John's help.

It was only fair because the child was half his, and he, unlike Chad, would be a good father. So I didn't want to marry him. He hadn't deserved my anger or what I said about only wanting him for sex or money. It wasn't his fault Chad had been such an awful husband. Unlike Chad, he hadn't even doubted me, taking responsibility immediately. He certainly hadn't called me a whore.

Unbidden, I remembered our first afternoon together, warm hazy sunlight bathing us in a glow. I had marveled at his strong arms, the pattern of freckles on his shoulder, then I'd closed my eyes and surrendered to the magic that he and I could make.

I'd thought that moment was perfect.

I almost turned around to apologize to John then and there, but I couldn't quite make that U-turn. I needed to calm down, get my wits about me, make sure I actually was pregnant. Everything could wait until tomorrow.

Well, everything except talking to Liza.

This time I rapped lightly on Liza's door, not wanting to wake up the baby. After my third attempt I rang the doorbell. Beyond the door I could hear the baby's wail followed by Liza's muttering as she stomped to the back of the house and then to the front door. "For the love. Could you text me to let me know you're at the door?"

"Oh, yeah." I had forgotten that my new smart phone had that feature. I'd also forgotten that my new smart phone was somewhere in the azaleas, hopefully still functional and without a cracked screen. "I'll remember next time, promise."

Baby on her hip, she stepped back and made a grand gesture for me to enter. She didn't look as chipper as the last time I'd seen her. She kinda looked green.

"You okay?" I asked as she closed the door.

"Yeah. I'm exhausted. Little man is teething so even the cereal isn't getting him through the night. Owen's working double shifts, too. It's a regular party at Liza's House."

How would she feel about a baby shower? I supposed we'd find out soon enough.

"It's too late for tea. Wanna beer?"

My stomach lurched. "Oh, no thank you."

"Try out this couch that this nice friend of mine gave me. There's a blanket since I know you don't like to sit on the leather."

I took her up on the offer even though I was wearing pants and wouldn't have to renew my antagonistic relationship with the sofa. She sat in Owen's recliner and lifted her shirt to feed the baby. "It was only about thirty minutes until he was due to wake up and eat. I shouldn't be mad at you."

Now that I was sitting, all of my anger had left me leaving only fatigue in its wake.

"To what do I owe the pleasure?" Liza finally asked.

"Yeah, ah. Hmm. I have news for you."

"You and John are getting married?"

Why did everyone want me and John to get married? At the mention of the word my wind pipe constricted, but I coaxed it back into its normal breathing functions. "Not exactly. I'm, well, I'm pregnant."

"What? How?"

"When a man and a woman love each other and get really, really close—"

"Quit stalling, smartass. Spill."

So I told her about Chad's ultimate betrayal, and she cussed him so fiercely, little Nathaniel broke off her breast for a minute to give her a dirty look. She burped him, put him on the other side, and continued her tirade. "I can't believe anyone would be so low-down mean, but I guess you dodged a bullet there. Now you don't have to look at him every holiday and weekend."

True. "John asked me to marry him."

"And?"

I told her about John's reaction, his less than romantic proposal that occurred as I was sitting on her former couch of stones and malevolence while having a panic attack.

She rolled her eyes. "Men. Owen's always telling me he deals in solutions—not sympathy."

"But, Liza, what am I going to do? I don't want to go straight from one marriage to another, but you remember how awful some people were to me because Mom was unmarried."

"Posey, it's a different world. More babies are being born out of wedlock than in. I know it doesn't seem like that in such a small town, but better to take your time and get things right, you know. Besides, John will actually show up for Donuts with Dad."

That would be a big difference. I hadn't known who my father was—still didn't—but my child would. Despite being angry with his high-handedness, the idea cheered me. I could see John doing all sorts of things Chad would've never done: playing board games on the floor, teaching our kid to play the piano, playing catch in the backyard.

"You're right."

"Of course, I'm right. I'm always right."

"Very humble about it, too," I said, even though I did feel better.

"Humility is for chumps," she said as she stood to take a now sleeping Nathaniel down the hall.

When she returned she slumped into the recliner. "That's it. We're having frozen pizza tonight. Turning knobs and removing cellophane is all I have in me."

"I'm worried about you. You didn't seem this tired a few weeks ago."

Liza lay back, her eyes closed. "I think my iron is low again."

"Well, go check it out."

"Yeah, yeah."

I had another question weighing me down, but I wasn't sure I wanted to hear the answer. Liza would tell me straight up if I would be considered too much of a slut to continue teaching. The whole idea was so ridiculous. I'd slept with two men my entire life. I'd taken precautions. Yet here I was, living proof that prayer worked really, really well and in really, really unexpected ways. I took a deep breath and started to speak, but chickened out. Before I could muster the courage for a second try at the question, Liza lightly snored.

Never in my days had I known Liza to fall asleep in a chair. At one of her slumber parties she'd gone into a fifteen-minute diatribe about how she needed to be horizontal in order to sleep. Of course, part of her speech was a ploy to get the couch instead of the floor.

"Liza?"

She jerked awake. "What? Huh?"

"You fell asleep."

"So weird." She wiped the back of her hand against her mouth. "I didn't drool, did I?"

"You were only out for a minute. Want me to leave?"

"No, no. I'm awake."

She did not look awake.

"Do you think I even have a chance at the second-grade job that's coming open next year?"

She yawned. "I don't see why not."

"You know. I'm pregnant."

"Yeah, yeah. One of the women I teach with has had two kids and isn't married yet. I don't see—wait, the principal over there is Varner, isn't it?"

I nodded.

Liza whistled. "She's tough, runs a tight ship. Hmmm. I don't know because they use that morality clause as justification for all sorts of things. I really don't know. I mean, I think they'd be idiots not to hire you, but I'm not in charge. Put in your application over in Jefferson, too. It's not that much of a drive."

At least thirty minutes one way, so not ideal, either.

"Think I should go apologize to John?"

"What on earth for?" She scooted to the edge of the recliner and yawned again.

"The things I said."

"No. Go home. Get a good night's sleep for both of us. I beg of you."

chapter 24

Little did I know my best intentions of getting a good night's sleep would be interrupted by a call at two o'clock in the morning. I nicked my thumb on the screen that had, indeed, cracked when I had thrown my phone. I answered with a groggy, "Hello?"

"Posey?"

I sat up trying to figure out who was calling. Finally, I gave up. "Who is this?"

"What d'ya mean who's this? It's John."

Oh, thank God. We could make things better between us. I really should've driven over to his house after Liza, but I hadn't been up to another fight. "Thank goodness. I'm so sorry for the awful things I said. I didn't really mean them. You gotta understand—"

"No. *You* gotta understand some things."

His voice didn't sound right at all.

"John, what's the matter?"

"Nothing's a matter. I feel great. But you. You gotta let me make things right."

He was drunk. After our argument, the man who'd been sober for two years had gotten drunk. I'd caused this.

No. He made the decision. He's letting you down like every other man you've ever known and quite a few women.

"How much have you had to drink?"

I could hear the slosh of liquid.

"Over half the bottle. Really hit the spot, lemme tell you."

As mad as I might be I didn't want the man to drink himself to death. "How big's the bottle?"

"Oh, I got the *big* one." He paused to drink.

"Pose, I'm serious. We gotta do this."

Yet another unromantic proposal?

"John O'Brien, I'm not having this discussion with you while you are three sheets to the wind."

"Look, here . . ."

I waited, but he never finished that sentence. Instead I heard rustling and a thwump then Rowdy barking emphatically.

With visions of my formerly sweet and ardent lover lying dead on the carpet, I jumped out of bed and slid my feet into flip-flops, glad I'd worn a T-shirt and shorts to bed. No time for a bra, so I'd have to hope no one pulled me over and that he'd simply passed out rather than requiring an ambulance. I grabbed my keys from the dresser and ran for it.

When I got to John's house I could see through a window on the front porch that John lay face down on the floor, but the front door was locked. I walked around the house to try the backdoor, but it was locked, too. I tried calling him, but the phone buzzed and even jerked at his side, but he didn't respond.

God. What if I've killed him?

In hindsight, he had been so upset. What had I expected? Of course, he would want to take responsibility. That's who he was, and I had shot him down. I'd said such awful things to him.

By the couch sat an almost empty bottle of Jack Daniels, almost hidden under the fronds of one of his ferns. I bit down on my fist, and my unhelpful brain reminded me that Jimi Hendrix had met his end due partially to too much booze.

I had to think. I walked around the house again, this time looking for a window I could reach. At the back of the house, in the breakfast room, I found a window that wasn't quite closed.

Thank goodness the house was old and the windows were huge and without screens. Once I managed to move the window up enough to get my fingers underneath the sash, I could push it up and step inside. Rowdy met me, his tail banging against the kitchen chairs. He gave one short woof as if to say, "What took you so long?"

I ran to the living room and tried to rouse John. By putting my face close to his, I could tell he was still breathing, but he wouldn't wake up. I ran for wet washcloths. "John O'Brien, if you do not wake up right this instant, I am going to call nine-one-one."

When the washcloths didn't work, I smacked his face as hard as I dared, and his eyelashes fluttered.

I sucked in a deep breath and slapped his other cheek harder.

"Gah, what the hell?"

"John, did you hear me?"

He blinked. "Posey? Zat you? You came over."

"It's me. I'm going to call nine-one-one now."

"No!" His eyes widened. "No."

He tried to sit up. It didn't work.

"You're sick. You could have alcohol poisoning."

"Could, but don't." This time he managed to sit up, but his upper body still moved in tiny circles as if he were spinning with the room.

I picked up my phone. How the heck did he know how sick he was?

It took two tries, but he finally managed to put a hand on mine. "Please. Jus' stay."

We sat on the floor, our backs against the couch of rocks and hatred. I closed my eyes to get rid of the memory of his one-knee proposal in that very spot. What had he been thinking? What had I been thinking? I should've turned around and apologized, told him that I very much meant the part about not rushing into marriage, but that it wasn't all his fault and that I would like for him to be a part of the child's life, not just a money and sperm donor.

Somehow, someway, I fell asleep with my head on his shoulder and my tailbone aching from the hard floor.

My phone woke me up with buzzing just as the pink light of dawn invaded the room. For a split second, I panicked. I'd stayed at a boy's house and hadn't told Mom. Then the rest of my faculties came to me, reminding me that I was no longer sixteen and that, technically, I'd done far worse than just stay out all night.

"Hey, Mom."

"Posey Lucille Adams, where are you?"

"John's house. Long story."

"Well, I need you to get back here right now. Your granny's gone missing."

"Be there in ten."

When I jumped to my feet, I knocked John over. He moaned then scrambled for his feet. I gave him a hand because I had a feeling he was heading to the restroom. I was correct.

Tapping my foot outside the bathroom door, I waited. I couldn't leave him like this, but I also needed to hurry home.

Finally, he emerged, his eyes half shut, the heel of his right hand pressing into the corresponding eye socket.

"John O'Brien, I have to go find my granny, but I will be back and you will be sober. Is that clear?"

"Are you bossing me?"

"Yes, yes, I am. So help me, you scared me to death, and that's not good for me or the baby. You nurse that hangover because I am coming back later to yell at you."

He stood a little straighter. " 'Kay."

"I'm serious."

"I know," he whispered.

I pivoted but at the last minute turned around to place a kiss on his cheek. On my way out the door, I picked up what remained of the Jack.

Chaos was in full swing by the time I made it back to the house, my heart once again in my throat. I had to park a block away due to all of the traffic, and the front door was wide open when I got there.

"I don't know how long she's been gone," my mother was saying. "I don't know how she got out, but I think I have a good idea."

The dead bolt.

Under Mom's supervision, Santiago had installed a second dead bolt at the top of the door. Not only was it out of Granny's reach, but she wouldn't think to look up there. I'd been in such a hurry that I hadn't taken the time to relock it from the outside. "I forgot the dead bolt."

"When did you leave?" Mom asked with narrowed eyes. The why was unspoken. For now.

"About two in the morning," I said.

"She's been outside for almost four hours? In this chill?"

"Mom, I'm sorry. I can—"

"You're going to be sorry if we find her dead in a ditch, I'll tell you that."

I took a step backward. It was unlike my mother to be so . . . menacing.

"Where are Henny and Rain?" I murmured.

"They're out looking, and that's where I'm going now. Len needed to know how long she'd been gone to set up the area to canvas. I hope your phone's charged because you're staying here."

"Staying here?"

Mom was already putting on her jacket. "Yes, here. In case she somehow slips past all of us and comes home."

Just like that I was left alone in the house, helpless again. Since I couldn't help John and I couldn't help Granny, I put a protective hand over my belly. How could I have been so stupid as to forget the deadbolt? I knew Granny had started wandering. I knew she didn't sleep well at night.

While pacing the kitchen, I caught a glimpse of the calendar in the early light. Maundy Thursday had given way to Good Friday. How had time traveled so fast to get me to Easter? Had I even missed church?

No, but everything that had happened was my punishment for not going to church, wasn't it?

Posey, don't be ridiculous.

I squeezed my eyes tightly against images of Granny lying cold in a ditch or of John keeled over from alcohol poisoning.

"Alondrita?"

My head jerked to the back door where Santiago stood.

"She's not here."

He rubbed his hand over his mouth and unshaven jaw. "She was so upset in her voicemail. Have you found Lucille?"

"No. Mom's out looking for her."

"Do you know where?"

I shook my head.

"Don't worry. I'll find her," he said over his shoulder as he rushed out the back door.

If I'd thought Santiago was over my mother, his appearance had proven me wrong. Not only did worry lines crease his face, but he'd also called her "Alondrita." He'd once told me the nickname meant "little lark." I hadn't heard him use the endearment since they'd broken up.

Then there was the fact my mother had obviously called him before she called me.

My phone rang bringing me back to the search for Granny.

"Where are you?" Henny asked.

"The kitchen."

"Where's Mom?"

"I don't know."

He sighed deeply then told me all of the places he'd been. "Any idea where I should look next?"

"Henny, I don't know what the plan is. I'm the one who forgot the dead bolt, and Mom left me here to stew. No one told me anything about—"

"Just where would you go. I need to do something."

I opened my mouth to say I didn't have a clue but then I remembered the other time Mom had lost Granny. "Try Maple Avenue."

"That's in the opposite direction of where everyone thinks she would've gone."

"Just do it, please."

"On it."

Mom had thought Granny had gone down Maple Avenue earlier because she wanted to see her sister, Pamela. I still thought
Granny was headed toward the interstate and the daughter she'd
once lost to the hippies. I'd been so wrong about so many other
things, though, that now I had nothing left to do but pace and
pray.

chapter 25

Twenty minutes later, my pacing and praying blessedly came to an end.

Henny found Granny walking down Maple Avenue just as I'd predicted. They'd missed her on their first pass because she had taken a diagonal pattern through backyards then forgotten where she was going. She headed in the opposite direction for a while before recommitting to her task. If I'd hoped Mom would forgive me quickly since I'd helped find Granny, then I was mistaken. To make matters worse, my brother was doubling down on his conviction that Granny was more than Mom could handle.

"Mom, I'm serious," he said.

Face in her hands, she shook her head. "I won't do it. I can't afford it, and it's not right."

"Posey, can you help me talk some sense into Mom? It's time for Granny to go to a memory care place, don't you think?"

"I don't care what she thinks," Mom snapped. "If she hadn't been sneaking out in the middle of the night and leaving the door unlocked, then we wouldn't be having this conversation right now."

I took a step backward, eyes wide. Mom had never spoken to me like that before.

She, however, now touched her lips as if making sure they

were still there. "I can't believe I said that. I think my mother said something very similar to me once."

She didn't apologize, though. Never one to apologize, my mother.

"At the risk of sounding like my mother once again, 'What the hell were you doing running around at two in the morning?' "

I wanted to go back to what *she* had once been doing running around at two in the morning, but I knew that conversation wasn't happening. "Long story."

"Pull up a chair," she said drily.

"Mom, chill," Henny said. "Posey's a grown woman. I'm sure she had a very good reason for what she did."

The moment of truth had arrived.

Over the years, I'd thought about all of the ways I would announce my pregnancy. I'd bake cookies in the shape of bottles. I'd bring a balloon with a stork on it. Maybe I'd give her one of those memory books to fill out or a shirt that said World's Best Grandmother. In the end I had to settle for, "Mom, I'm pregnant."

"Whoa." Henny took off his cap and scratched his head. "I did not see that coming. Congrats?"

At the same time my mother said, "I can't believe you. I thought I raised you better than that."

Her fingers traveled back to her lips as though measuring them once again for treason.

So I turned to my little brother—my sober younger brother, my favorite sibling for the moment—and pointedly ignored her. "Thanks, Henny. Or I guess I should say Uncle Henny."

He grinned. "I like it."

We might be ignoring our mother, but we could feel her glare.

"Know what? I need to sleep before I go into work 'cuz I've got a mid shift, and I bet there's woman talk about to happen," Henny said, waving his pale hand in a circular motion to convey the feminine mystique. "I'll, uh, leave you two and go take a nap. Pose, can I crash in your room?"

"Sure." No way I'd make my defender sleep on the couch.

The minute we heard the bedroom door click, my mother turned on me. "I thought I told you everything you needed to know about sex so you would never find yourself in this situation. For heaven's sake, I used to hand you condoms when you were in high school."

"Which I didn't need at the time," I said. "Look, Mom—"

"I never wanted you to be subjected to the same mistakes I made. I tried so hard to keep you from this—"

"Mom."

"Seriously, accidentally pregnant after all this time?"

"It wasn't an accident," I said through gritted teeth. As I said the words I believed them. Sure I would've preferred the horse before the cart and the white picket fence route, but I had asked and a baby had been given unto me.

"But now?"

"Death, taxes, and childbirth. There's never a convenient time for any of them," I murmured, echoing *Gone With the Wind*, a book I'd read against my mother's wishes. She'd said it reinforced inaccurate racial stereotypes (it did), but Granny claimed it was the best Southern novel ever written (arguable). At the time, anything my mother had been against was something I wanted to be for.

"What?"

"Nothing."

"Posey, why? I wanted better for you than to follow in my footsteps."

So I told her the whole story. How Chad had tricked me, how John had been wonderful right up until the moment he started making pragmatic marriage proposals, and how I'd gone over to his house when he'd called me while in a drunken stupor.

"Okay. I guess I can see how you might've been distracted," Mom conceded.

"D'ya think?"

She got up to make tea, turning her back on me. I knew I'd never get an apology from her. I didn't know why I'd felt the need to be a smart aleck other than the fact I'd had a rough past few hours, very little sleep, and now felt the full effects of the nausea that was the hallmark of early pregnancy. If I were being truthful with myself, a bit of nausea had been with me for a while, but now that I knew, I couldn't ignore it.

"So, are you going to marry John?"

She couldn't be serious. She couldn't even pretend to be that nonchalant, could she? "No."

"Why?" Her question was more curiosity than indictment.

"Do you really have to ask that question? I'm not about to go from one bossy man to another. I'm not going to be domineered again. That was miserable."

"But John—"

"But John nothing! He practically demanded that I marry him. You raised all three of us, and we turned out just fine, thank you very much."

She laughed bitterly. "My oldest married an abusive asshole, my middle child is a recovering drug addict, and my youngest squanders her potential through chronic absenteeism. Tell me again what a good job I've done."

Had she just owned a part in our problems? That had to be a first.

The kettle whistled, and she busied herself with tea bags and pouring water. "If I'd been a better mother, I would've found a father figure for you, someone who would be a better example. Unfortunately, your and Henny's fathers weren't good candidates."

I sucked in a breath. That was the most she'd said about my father in years. We all knew about Henny's sorry father. The only mystery there was what had possessed Mom to sleep with him in the first place. But my father? Talking about him had always been verboten.

"What was wrong with my father?" I asked, trying to keep my tone nonchalant.

She chuckled. "So many things wrong with that situation. Let's just say intentional communities weren't as idyllic as I had hoped."

"Mom, I might need to know more about who he is and his health history for the baby."

"I had you just fine, now didn't I?"

Well, it had been worth a shot. I thought of another father, one who'd been so worried and who obviously still cared for my mother. "What about Santiago?"

"What about him?"

Thinking of how they'd bantered over Rain's fishing garb and then his worried face earlier that morning, I said, "I think he still has feelings for you."

"Oh, that ship's sailed. He asked me to marry him five times, you know." She put the cups on the table and then took a seat herself. "I always told myself I'd marry him if he asked me a sixth time, but I think five was his limit."

Ah, our pact from reading Amelia Earhart. Maybe we should've considered how her marriage, much less her last flight, wasn't successful before we took any kind of advice from her.

She smiled bitterly at our inside joke. There for a few idyllic months after Henny and before Rain, Mom and I had reconnected. Every night she would read a bedtime story to Henny. I watched the pair with ragged jealousy since she'd been too busy "finding herself" to read bedtime stories to me when I'd been his age. One night, she tucked Henny in and sat down on the couch with a book of her own. I found myself shyly crossing the room and asking, "Could we read a book together?"

And so, at eleven years old, I snuggled up against my mother and she read to me from her book about Amelia Earhart. The book, which was meant for adults, was a little dry at times but still interesting because I didn't hear that many stories of adventurous women at school. I learned of how the aviatrix drank no alcohol because her father had been a drunk, how she advocated for women's rights, and, of course, how she set records as a female pilot. I even applauded how she made George Putnam ask her to marry him six times before she said yes. For at least three years, my life's ambition was to be like Amelia Earhart.

Of course, Mom had put the book down before we finished.

She was easily distracted and predisposed to quitting the story before we got to the unhappy ending of Earhart's mysterious disappearance. I was in high school when I checked the same book out of the public library. The once new book was by then dogeared and stained from frequent use. Not only did I learn more about Earhart's last flight, but I also discovered that Amelia's marriage hadn't been the fairy-tale happy ending I'd always supposed. She'd only agreed to the marriage tentatively, and her marriage to Putnam had been strained by the time she took her last flight. He pushed her into appearances and clothing lines and other things she didn't want to do. No, I didn't care for George Putnam much, either.

But Santiago was a far better man than George Putnam had ever dreamed of being.

"Go tell him that," I said.

She shook her head. "He doesn't even care about me that way. Not anymore."

"You won't know unless you talk to him. He even referred to you as Alondrita this morning."

She nodded as she fished her tea bag from the cup. "You just learn from my mistakes. If you don't want to marry John right this minute, that doesn't mean you might not want to marry him later. Most things in life aren't all or nothing."

"Mom."

She shrugged. "You've always seen the world as black-and-white, but it's not. My one consolation about your marrying Chad was that you seemed so confident that you were doing exactly as you wanted. If I'd known what kind of jerk he was, I would've intervened in an instant."

"And I would've married him anyway," I said softly.

She nodded. "That's the tightrope a mother walks—especially a mother like me."

"Oh, good. No one mentioned a tightrope. That was *not* in the manual."

She laughed. "There is no manual. Read all the books you want, but you won't find all of the answers."

We sat in silence sipping our tea.

"You gonna put me in a home when I'm your granny's age?" she asked.

"Not unless you bite."

She laughed, as I'd hoped she would. "I did a good job with you in spite of myself, Posey Adams. Or I guess your granny did."

"You both did," I said.

We sipped our tea, and I considered getting some cookies from the pantry, but the pantry was bare and my newly temperamental stomach wasn't completely on board with the idea. I really wanted SpaghettiOs, and I hadn't craved those since I was five.

Mom was right about one thing: I needed to let John know that I did care about him, that I hadn't used him for sex, that I wanted him to be a father to our child rather than just provide financial support. He deserved that. I also had a hole in my heart where our friendship had been. I missed him. I'd grown enough to know that I could live without him—in fact, I should take the time to learn to live without him—but that didn't mean I *wanted* to.

"I'm going to check on John now." I stood and leaned over my chair. "I'm so sorry about forgetting the dead bolt and causing all of the trouble, though."

"I'm sorry I yelled at you. I should've known you would never be intentionally careless. If I'd installed the alarm system when they first diagnosed dementia, none of this would've happened."

I stared at my mother. Had she just apologized to me? She never apologized.

"So you're not mad at me anymore? For anything?"

"I told you once before. I can't afford to toss rocks at your glass house, now can I? We'll raise this baby right."

"Oh, *we* will, now will we, Granny?"

She shuddered. "I am *not* a Granny."

I grinned, revenge now in my sights. "Now you're going to be a Granny for sure."

She smiled. "Yeah. I guess I am. It'll be nice to have a little one again, especially one I don't have to get up in the middle of the night to feed."

I made a note to make sure she attended at least one midnight feeding.

As I left the kitchen, I paused to kiss her cheek. Sunlight from the kitchen window picked up every fine wrinkle, reminding me my mother couldn't cheat her mortality forever. Before I could let my mind wander to what we would do someday when I was her age and she was possibly senile enough to ask for Tom Brokaw for Christmas, I grabbed my keys from the hook beside the door and drove off to see if I could patch things up with John.

chapter 26

When John opened the door, I didn't have the heart to yell at him as I'd promised. We stood there surveying each other for a few minutes before he finally asked me in. Rowdy trotted into the living room and waited for his obligatory behind the ears scratch before curling up in the corner of the room.

"So."

"So."

"Thank you for looking out for me last night. And for not calling the police," he said as we both took a seat on the couch.

"I couldn't leave you like that. You really scared me."

He leaned forward on his knees, burying his head in his hands. "I wouldn't have blamed you if you had."

"Hey." I shoved his shoulder. "I didn't mean what I said yesterday. It was a really emotional day."

He looked up but I couldn't read the emotion in his eyes. Resolve? "So you will marry me."

"No. That I meant."

"Nice to know I'm nothing but a good lay to you."

That cut me to the quick. "I swear I don't know if I want to smack you or kiss you."

"Can't beat me up any more than I've been beating up myself."

"Look, I'm not saying never." *Unless you keep up this morose hangdog stuff.* "But I can't say yes right now. I've gotta figure out who I am before I marry anyone else, if I can ever marry anyone else."

"Why?"

So I told him about Chad, about the vasectomy, about his idea of wifely behavior, about how I wasn't sure I even knew who I was.

"I thought I had it together," he said. "Then I messed up."

"John," I said. "I feel terrible. I should've come back to apologize right then."

He held out his hand. "I shouldn't have assumed you needed me to solve all of your problems—our problems—especially not while you were having a panic attack. I was trying to make things right."

I scooted closer to him. Clean from the shower, he smelled delectable. I wanted him, and it wasn't like I had to worry about pregnancy. After that talk with Mom, I even thought there might be hope for us someday. Just not today. "So we're good."

"We're good," he said, but he didn't make a move to meet me halfway for a kiss. Instead he stared straight ahead to the door.

Something about being the one to make the first move petrified me. But he said we were good. What could it hurt?

He turned to look at me, and I leaned in for the kiss. At the last minute, he turned, leaving me with nothing but cheek. I backed into my corner of the couch, stung by the rejection. My face burned. Maybe he didn't want me anymore because I was pregnant.

"Posey," he said even though he looked like he was addressing the front door across the room. "I will happily marry you if you want because it's the right thing to do, but I can't do whatever we've been doing, always wondering if we're going to make it or not."

"You're not making any sense."

"I called my sponsor last night."

"And?"

"He reminded me I have to make sobriety my priority."

"And?"

"And being with you puts me at risk."

I stood and began to pace once more. "Oh, but marrying me is okay?"

"Well, yeah. That's what you're supposed to do if you get a girl pregnant."

"Sure. If it's nineteen-fifty." My hands clenched into fists. I muttered, "And Mom thinks I'm the one who deals in black-and-white."

"What did you say?" Now he stood.

"A wise woman told me earlier today that I shouldn't deal in absolutes, yet here I am dealing with yours. Marriage or nothing? That's crazy, John."

He ran a hand through his hair. "I can't risk having a drink every time we get into a fight."

"Then don't have a drink every time we have a fight!"

He laughed, a hoarse humorless sound. "A good way to make sure I don't have a drink is to make sure we don't have fights."

"But you make no sense. You would marry me because that would make everyone in town happy even though we don't know for sure if getting married would make *us* happy, but you won't continue our relationship to see how or if we fit together? That's insane, you can see that, can't you?"

"Insane or not, that's how it has to be. I'm confident that you and I can work together to be good parents even if we don't marry. I'll start looking for a job that pays better, maybe go to a two-year school and get a degree in something."

"Don't do that," I said, barely getting the words over the lump in my throat. I imagined John working a nine to five job with stiff clothes, short hair, and dull eyes. I mourned the loss of his long hair, and he hadn't even cut it yet.

"I've been hiding from responsibility most of my life. I've even used recovery as an excuse to keep fiddling with pianos and church bands, neither of which pays enough to help you raise a child. It's time for me to grow up."

Tears pricked my eyes. I should've never made that quip

about how he could help pay for our baby. It was crass and unnecessary. "My mother raised me alone, and I can raise this child. I mean, I'd like your help, and I want you to be a part of our child's life. But I don't need your money. I don't need to be rescued."

"I have a bad habit of trying to rescue people," he said.

"Maybe I was the good lay for you," I murmured.

He faced me, cupping my face so he could thumb away each of my hot tears. "No. I don't think I've ever wanted anyone or anything as much as I wanted you."

Wanted. Past tense.

Buck up, Buttercup. You aren't going to get hung up on another man.

"So this is it for us as a couple," I said, willing my tears to be the silent, calm kind—at least until I could make it to the car.

"I don't know. Probably. I can't be a good father if I'm not sober. Maybe we're too broken to be together."

"But everyone is broken in one way or another."

"Not as broken as you or me."

I nodded. He was right, and I hated him for it. I hadn't known how much hope I'd held out for our eventual reconciliation until it'd been taken away. Maybe that could be my memoir title: *Figuring Out What I Want Only After It's Been Wrested Away: The Posey Love Story.*

No, the Posey Adams story.

"I have to go now," I said. Too many emotions, too many scars, too many changes. Who cared that it was broad daylight? I was going home to take a nap.

For a second he looked as though he might ask me to stay, but instead he stood and walked me to the door. Rowdy came to say goodbye, and I gave him an extra pet because something told me it would be quite some time before we met again.

On the way home, I stopped for those SpaghettiOs. The dictatorial kidney bean within demanded meatballs. I had to question his—or her—judgment. Even so, the baby was the boss at the moment so SpaghettiOs with processed meatballs it was. I grabbed a two-liter of ginger ale and tried my best not to be conspicuous. Unfortunately, Miss Georgette almost ran into me as I rounded the corner with my eyes drawn to the Hostess Cakes.

"Why, Posey! I've heard such good things from Ms. Varner. She says you have settled in so well."

"I've been enjoying those kids, too. Thank you for nudging me in that direction, Miss Georgette."

She drew me into a fleshy, Giorgio-drenched hug. "I know it's been a tough few weeks, but I am so proud of you for getting your life together and walking around with such a glow."

My smile wavered. She wouldn't be as proud once she figured out the source of my glow.

"Thank you," I murmured.

"Well, I hate to cut this chat short, but I have to get some sherbet and 7UP to make the punch for the Ladies' Ministry meeting. We're getting the church all spiffed up for tomorrow."

I froze. "At Love Ministries?"

"Oh, honey, no. I went back over to First Baptist. Hope I'll see you there tomorrow."

Agape, I watched her shuffle toward the ice cream aisle. She'd waltzed right into First Baptist and was already a part of the Ladies' Ministry again? Could it possibly be that easy for me?

I took my purchases to the register. If the teen cashier smacking her gum had any inkling about my secret, she said nothing to indicate it. I had at least a few more weeks before anyone would notice. Right?

After a well-deserved nap, I heated up the SpaghettiOs and ate half of them before my stomach decided no more. I had the oddest craving for Long John Silver's fish and chicken, but I was not about to drive to Jefferson to scratch that particular itch. I pushed the not quite empty bowl to the center of the table and leaned on my hand.

So.

This was pregnancy.

My mother burst through the back door and pulled a chair

over to the refrigerator before I could even say hello. She climbed on the chair and stood on her tiptoes to open a cabinet above the fridge, taking out a stack of placemats and reaching behind a cookie jar to bring out a bottle of something. She didn't even bother to replace the mats or close the cabinet before jumping down and opening a drawer to take out a souvenir shot glass.

She downed two shots and pulled the chair to the table to have a seat.

"Mom?"

She poured a third shot and tossed it back.

"Mom."

What was with all the drinking?

When she reached for the bottle a fourth time, I grabbed her wrist. "Mother. What are you doing?"

"For the second time in my life, I am drinking myself into a stupor."

"Want to talk about it?"

"No!" She buried her face into her hands and sighed heavily, finally looking up at me. "My talk with Santi did not go well."

"What a coincidence! My talk with John didn't go well, either, so I drowned my sorrow in SpaghettiOs."

Mom looked at the bowl at the center of the table and scowled at its many offenses: processing, sodium, meat. "That's disgusting."

"I know. It wasn't my request."

She chuckled. "When I was pregnant with you, I wanted strawberries, always strawberries. I think it's because your father—"

She clamped her mouth shut.

"I'm over thirty now. Don't you think you can finally tell me who my father is?"

She reached for the bottle of whiskey again, and I let her because I would willingly let her have a hangover if it meant she would finally tell me where I really came from. At this point, it had to be something awful like my father was Satan himself. I'd worry she'd been one of Manson's girls, but he'd gone to prison before I could've been conceived.

Conjugal visit?

I shuddered. "Mom, you have to tell me. Please."

She tossed back her fourth shot and closed her eyes. "There. There's the warmth I was looking for."

I glared at her, unwilling to break eye contact until she told me. "The truth is . . . I don't know who your father is."

Oh.

My mother had a reputation for being loose, but I had never expected this from her. She might be unconventional, but she was also quite meticulous. Had she done drugs? Had she been drugged?

"You can't say something like that and not tell me more. Please, Mom."

"Oh, I can."

"I am asking you, no, begging you, to tell me," I said.

She shook her head no. "You're like Mama: too judgy."

I threw my hands up. "I don't think I can afford to be judgy now!"

"True." She stared beyond me, thinking of another time or another person, no doubt under the effects of the whisky she'd drunk.

Finally, she took in a ragged breath. "You know I went to California and managed to hook up with the only hippies in creation who, of course, wanted to create an intentional community in Tennessee, right?"

"Let's say that I do."

"I almost left them then and there. To finally make it all the way to California only to be dragged back out to the boondocks, well, that was like a slap in the face. But I was in love. Or, at least I thought I was, so I followed a man back to Tennessee. An older man."

Ah. That explained part of her reaction on the night I told her about my engagement.

I wanted to ask if that man was my father, but I didn't. I waited for her to continue. At this point the whiskey had taken effect, and she slurred her words enough to give a hint of her original Tennessee accent, something she usually worked to hide.

"Only problem is, that man I loved didn't love me enough, or he said he loved me but he also loved another girl. I was young and stupid, and I joined what they called a 'four marriage.'"

"A what?"

"Four marriage. A marriage with four people."

I tried to keep from staring at her, but I couldn't seem to keep horror out of my expression. "That's a thing?"

"In our community it was rare, but some people insisted these marriages would work." She reached for the bottle, but I took it and put it on the other side of the table out of her reach.

"So my father is one of two men?" As I said the words I realized there were even more possibilities. "Or three?"

"One of two. Either Jamie or Roger."

"Mom!"

She pointed her finger at me, "See? That judgment in your voice? That is why I never told you."

She was right, and I was sitting at the table with my own baby out of wedlock. Well, I was wed, but the baby hadn't been conceived in lock. At least my mother had been married in some shape or form when she'd managed to get knocked up with me. "You're right. I have no room to judge, and I'm sorry. Where are Jamie and Roger? These days we can do a DNA test and figure this out."

Mom shrugged. "I don't know."

"You have heard of this magical place called Facebook, right?"

She grimaced and waved away the idea. Lark Adams didn't care much for technology.

She was also clamming up again, and I couldn't let that happen. "Can you at least tell me what happened?"

She sighed. "Okay. Fine. I had the hots for Jamie. Jamie had the hots for Allison. She held a torch for Roger, and Roger? Well, he wasn't all that particular. At first everything was going well. Jamie and I, who are still legally married in the eyes of the state of California, lived together and grew fruits and vegetables that we'd sell at the local farmer's market. I was learning how to grow strawberries from another lady in the community and thinking about leaving long enough to take the courses to become a midwife. Then one day Jamie came home and told me he wanted to expand our marital bond to include Allison and Roger."

I nodded because I didn't trust myself to say anything that wasn't judgy.

"I didn't want to, of course. I wanted to keep Jamie all to myself, but he wore me down on the idea and eventually we entered the foursome."

My mother was kinda like a sister wife. I can't believe my mother was a sister wife.

"The first week, things went great. Jamie was super attentive to me. Allison and I shared chores and cooking supper. Then we'd play cards and sing songs, often laughing late into the night. I kept trying to prepare myself for the day when we would switch partners. One night, as we headed to bed, Jamie took my hand and put it in Roger's. Then he escorted Allison down the hall to our bedroom."

I had that awful feeling in the pit of my stomach. My mother couldn't have been more than eighteen and far from home. The man she loved, a guy she was still legally married to, was handing her off to another man.

"It wasn't that Roger was bad looking," she finally said. "I just, well, I still didn't *know* him."

Tensing up, I leaned across the table not wanting the story to go in the direction I was afraid that it was going.

She smiled. "But he was sweet and kind and, frankly, better in bed than Jamie."

She paused in the moment, even blushing a bit. I felt like a voyeur to my mother's memories, understanding perfectly why she hadn't wanted to tell me this story. Had she told me any time before, my prudish side would've condemned her. Now, I had no room to talk.

She looked at the shot glass, twirling it between her fingers and finally sighed deeply. "We lasted another week. Jamie ran off with Allison, and Roger ran off to find them. Turns out everyone loved Allison. Even people around town gave me dirty looks because I was 'that little beanpole who ran off Allison.'"

No wonder Mom'd never been keen on remarrying. The one time she tried marriage she'd been abandoned by not just one person, but three. I harbored an irrational dislike of this Allison person on my mother's behalf.

"I waited, thinking surely someone would come back for me, but two months went by with no word. By then I was pregnant. I had morning sickness so bad that I had trouble pulling my weight with community chores. So I packed up and came home with my tail between my legs."

A little over a month ago, I'd come home with my tail between my legs, too. Now I knew why she'd welcomed me: My mother wasn't one to admit her mistakes, but she had enough compassion that she didn't want anyone else to suffer as she had. No doubt Granny had really let her have it when she first came home.

"So Jamie or Roger, huh?"

She shrugged. "Since you were premature, it was really hard to say. You look a little more like Roger, I think, but who knows. At this point I've forgotten their features. Both of them are faceless memories from a time I'd rather forget."

"Jamie, Roger, Allison, and Lark," I mused. "Those don't sound like hippie names."

Mom laughed. "By accident, I already had the perfect hippie name, but they all changed theirs—or tried to. Jamie preferred to be called Moonwalker and Roger went by Hawk." She giggled, the liquor well in effect, well enough that she swayed in her seat and I wondered if she'd even eaten supper.

"What about Allison?"

She snorted. "You mean Divine Rainbow?"

"Ugh."

"Yeah."

I squeezed my mother's hand. "Thank you for telling me."

"You're only the second person I've told."

"Well, I promise I won't name this child Moonwalker, Hawk, or Divine Rainbow," I said.

"You better not!"

"And for what it's worth, I think they all left the best part of their marriage behind."

"Thank you. I think."

"You going to tell me what happened with Santiago?"

"Remember how you're the *second* person I've told?"

I found it hard to believe that Santiago would be *that* mad at Mom for something that had happened so long ago, but what did I know?

"You don't need any more whiskey. Drink some water instead."

"Ah, the daughter becomes the mother," she said.

"Yes. I have it on good authority that you need water, aspirin, and to go to sleep."

"Santi always takes Alka-Seltzer when he imbibes too much," she murmured.

"Do what you have to do, but go to bed, and I'll make you ginger tea in the morning."

She stood, swaying a little as she went for the medicine cabinet to get Alka-Seltzer. She filled a cup with water and dropped two tablets in then turned and pointed in my general direction. "You're supposed to go to church tomorrow. End of Lent."

"Maybe," I said.

She drank her Alka-Setlzer and staggered off to bed, but I heard her checking the locks on her way.

chapter 27

I tried to sleep, really I did.

Instead, I found myself wrapped in an afghan and sitting on the porch swing when the sun came up.

Going to church was a completely different proposition than when I'd started Lent. Sooner or later, everyone would notice that I was pregnant. They might assume the father was Chad. Professional gossips like Miss Georgette might consult calendars and oracles and come up with a different conclusion. I didn't really care other than the fact it might keep me from getting a job at Ellery Elementary, a job I desperately needed for the insurance just as much as the livelihood.

Has going to church ever made me a better person?

At some point when I was younger I think it had. As a teenager, I'd gone on mission trips and worked in soup kitchens. I discovered my vocation at the after-school tutoring program where I volunteered. In college, the church had led me to Chad—there was a strike against it. I'd also gone on mission trips to other countries and made friends there, a plus.

I smiled at the memory of Guatemalan children who'd sung me a song after I'd taught them Sunday School in my broken Spanish. I'd always come away with far more than I'd given when I went on a mission trip, whether local or abroad.

Come to think of it, Chad had put a stop to those when we married, too.

Only, I couldn't think of anything Biblical without hearing Chad's voice. After five years of his preaching, he'd spoken on just about everything.

Except *Song of Solomon*.

I couldn't help but smile at John's version of getting to know me biblically. My navel as a goblet? Please.

That thing was probably going to stick out at some point. At least, Mom's belly button had been an outie while she was pregnant with Rain.

Maybe if I could get back to basics?

Love God with all I had and love my neighbor as myself?

Eh, as long as Chad moved far, far away I could possibly handle that.

Did I want my child to be raised in the church or not?

Well, this was an easier question: My gut said yes despite any misgivings for myself. I couldn't imagine a life that didn't involve putting my little girl or boy in Sunday School and preschool and Vacation Bible School.

Well, maybe not the last day of Vacation Bible School.

So, I'm going.

My shoulder angel beamed, glad with the decision I'd made. Unfortunately, my shoulder devil wasn't quite ready to give up the fight.

What if you have a daughter and she runs into a man like Chad at church?

My blood ran cold. Of course, church was far from the only place a woman could find a bad man, but, when it happened, the betrayal ran much deeper. I'd tell my daughter to be patient. I'd tell her to never pin her hopes on what a partner could do *for* her. I'd tell her that anyone who didn't respect her wishes wasn't worth her time.

If Chad was a product of the church, then so was John. People were people no matter where you went.

Face it, Posey, there's no right or wrong answer.

I would go to church and see what I thought, see if the Spirit moved me. Nothing required me to ever go back, but I would see my crazy, sarcastic Lenten promise through.

As I walked through the front door, I heard the distinctive sounds of hangover coming from the bathroom. I went straight to the kitchen to put on the kettle. I kinda wanted coffee, but that wasn't happening. I chose decaf tea instead and went ahead and took out the box of ginger tea, too. By the time Mom staggered into the kitchen, her ginger tea had been steeping for at least five minutes, and I was working on my tea and staring at a bowl of Cheerios since they contained half my RDA of iron.

"What are you doing?" Mom asked.

"I'm trying to talk myself into eating these Cheerios."

"They are round like those SpaghettiOs you like so much," she said as she drew an icepack from the freezer and put it over her eye.

"Yes, but, thanks to morning sickness, they taste like cardboard. Ginger tea's almost done steeping."

"Today you're my favorite child," she murmured, her eyes closed.

"Well. There's a first time for everything!"

"No, I rotate all three of you—it's a very complicated process."

When the timer dinged, I got up and fixed her tea for her.

"Bless you," she said. "I remember so clearly now why I haven't had anything to drink in years. My aura is . . . not good."

Down the hall Granny yelled, but I couldn't understand what she said.

"Could you please help your grandmother?" Mom asked.

So I did. I helped Granny change her underwear since I hadn't been quick enough in getting her to the bathroom. Still panting, I led her to the recliner. By this time I knew where the *Price is Right* DVDs lived and what to fix her for breakfast. I spooned the oatmeal to her mouth which she opened just as a baby would keeping her eyes glued on the television all the while.

Ever since her recent escape, Granny had been even more withdrawn. Now her body seemed to be in a race to deteriorate as quickly as her mind already had.

Finally, I took the oatmeal bowl to the sink. Mom had progressed to coffee, and was no longer holding an arm over her eyes.

"Mom?"

"Yes, favorite child?"

"It's time."

She craned her neck to check on Granny in the recliner. "I know. But not today."

Old habits died hard.

I parked my Toyota in the spot that I used to prefer, the one under the elm tree at the corner of the lot. As a teenager, I'd been in the habit of parking in that spot, and I took it as a sign now that "my spot" was still available this late in the morning. From behind the wheel I watched people walk into the church in their Sunday best. I wanted to wait until the last minute, maybe sneak in while no one was looking. Already the number of people had slowed to a trickle since most had arrived earlier for Sunday School.

I'd decided that Sunday School would be too much. Where did I even go? Would I go to the Young Married Class? To the Singles Class? Did they have a class for future divorcées who were pregnant with another man's baby? No, Sunday School posed too many questions about my place in this world and promised more stares and awkward conversations than answers.

Or I was stalling.

I hadn't been to First Baptist in forever and had left in the midst of a contentious dispute. Everyone there would have the right to dislike me for some of the things Chad said. Heck, for some of things I said. Why was it so hard to walk into the building that had been a second home to me in my teen years?

Because it reminds you of Chad now.

True, Chad had joined First Baptist only three months after we started dating. It was hard to sift through the memories I had from before we were together, but I had to try. My baptism would forever be etched in my memory. Most of the ones from my childhood were of cookies and Kool-Aid passed out during

Vacation Bible School. Then I was old enough to help with VBS. Then I was married. I couldn't remember those years. It was as though my brain no longer wanted to acknowledge anything that had happened when I was with Chad.

Enough.

Time to leave the sanctity of my car for the more uncertain sanctuary.

As I entered the door, the music began, and I congratulated myself on timing; people couldn't stop me to ask questions if the service had already started. The sun blazed through the plain windows, and I studied the sanctuary, panicking for just a moment because I'd headed to the right but someone was sitting in the spot where I used to sit. Seeing an empty seat on the end of a row to the back left, I quickly changed course and made it there just in time for the opening hymn.

I reached for a hymnal but came away empty. Large screens hung from the ceiling on both the left and the right of the altar at the front of the church. Panic hit me once again, but then they announced "Christ Arose," and I relaxed into the familiar. The congregation and I dug deep into the chorus—"Up from the grave he arose with a mighty triumph o'er his foes!" The swell of music and the strength of many voices soothed my soul even if my voice cracked from disuse.

I'd come home.

First Baptist had a new preacher, at least three times removed from the one who'd dunked me so many years before. At first I took Brother Mark for quiet and well-mannered, but, no, he'd started his sermon softly so he'd have room for a grand crescendo. As he reached the end, he reminded his lambs that Jesus Christ had died for each and every one of us and that he was indeed risen. Anyone who believed would be born new, their sins washed away.

Yeah. My sins. I carried an eternal reminder of one of my sins, but I couldn't be sorry. I'd wanted a child. God had given me a child. I put my hand on my stomach. If my child hadn't been born in love, at least he or she had been born of a mutual admiration and affection far deeper than that I'd shared with my husband. The Lord truly worked in mysterious ways. He could make a positive out of a negative. I chuckled a little to myself. I'd covered five of the Seven Deadly Sins in spite of myself. All except wrath and pride.

Except for how you lost your temper with John and caused him to fall off the wagon.

My eyes widened in the sad and shameful realization I'd fallen prey to wrath, too, when I told John he'd been nothing more than a good lay and then when I told him he could help pay for our child.

Wrath was the worst.

I had to face it. I'd committed all of the sins but pride.

"Just remember that pride goeth before a fall," the preacher said, that one snippet of his sermon reverberating through my mind as though God was speaking specifically to me. Now my blood ran cold, but my cheeks grew warm.

Pride had been my first sin, my last sin, and a part of every one in between.

All those years, I'd heard God's word, but I hadn't listened. If I were honest with myself, a million little things had happened to let me know that my marriage wasn't working. By then, though, I'd become obsessed with preserving the front of a picture-perfect marriage and achieving motherhood. I tried weird diets, acupuncture, and countless books; I allowed my husband to talk me into acts I wasn't proud of. I had thought I could create a baby out of sheer force of will.

My husband's free will thwarted my efforts.

Foolishly I had thought I could outsmart God, that if I did all of the right things he would be forced to reward my efforts with what I wanted.

But that's not how God worked. His ways were not my ways.

Yet my stubborn refusal to worship him had still led me to the one thing I'd always wanted.

You were so arrogant to think you could last one week without God, much less the entirety of Lent.

Stomping around like a petulant toddler, I'd given God the silent treatment. Even now, I couldn't pick up where I once left off and pretend that all was well. I'd have to study and pray and forgive—mainly myself.

Pride was the absolute worst.

"But, beloved, hear the good news: Repent and you will be forgiven."

I lost my breath, mentally clawing for purchase just as I had done so many years before in the water when that fire and brimstone preacher had dunked me.

I could do this.

I would do this.

I would hold my head up high and own my mistakes in order to move forward.

Newly resolved, I looked up to see John with his guitar at the front of the church. Somehow I'd missed the fact that he would be leading the benediction. I couldn't look away from him, but he didn't seem to notice me. The light shone through the window in one of those perfect beams that made one think of God punching a hole in the clouds so he could highlight those he loved most.

Subtle, God.

He sang "Just as I am" with such earnestness that I felt ashamed all over again for causing him to falter. He'd been right when he'd mentioned how it took two to tango, and I'd been his partner only to be mean to him when he'd been trying to do right in the only way he knew how. My heart ached for him, and I couldn't sing for the lump in my throat. He deserved happiness. He deserved someone who wouldn't cause him to relapse, who wouldn't make him give up the jobs he loved just to find ones that made more money.

The minute church ended, the desire to run away had me asking pardon as I tried to go backward while the rest of the congregation moved forward to take pictures among the lilies. If I'd thought I'd be able to slip out of the church as quietly as I'd slipped in, I was mistaken.

"Posey Love! Where do you think you're going!"

Liza.

I turned around into her reassuring hug. Owen stood behind her, cradling a sleeping Nathaniel.

"Nice going. I was trying to make a slick getaway," I whispered into her ear.

She held me at arm's length. "No way are you coming back into this church and not getting a hug from me. Happy Easter, you!"

The hugs kept coming. My old fourth-grade teacher welcomed me back. John's mother hugged me—obviously she didn't know about the baby yet. Amanda Kildare hugged me so tightly I lost my breath for a moment.

Other ladies who'd once attended Chad's morning Bible study embraced me tightly. Older gentlemen who knew my granny either shook my hand or drew me into a hug. Then everyone parted the aisle for Brother Lewis. He leaned heavily on his cane, but he came forward slowly, saying nothing, but wrapping his arms around me. All of these people had welcomed me back and wished me a Happy Easter. No one asked about Chad. No one asked why I was there. It was simply a given that I had come home.

I smelled Miss Georgette before I saw her, but she still surprised me when she tackled me from behind. "Oh, I am so glad to see you here this morning. So proud that you're going to church again. I just knew you'd find your way. You are such a shining star, and it's so good to know that that man hasn't held you down after all. You'll have to join us in the Ladies' Ministry. We're getting ready for GAs, you know. Then there'll be Vacation Bible School to plan and—"

"Miss Georgette, there's something—"

"I was talking to Ms. Varner the other day, and she told me you'd adjusted so well to your class that she was considering you for an opening next year." She paused to pinch one cheek lightly. "I am just so proud of you for getting your life together so quickly. Not everyone can do that, you know? So many people wallow in their sorrows and—"

"I'm pregnant."

I hadn't meant to utter the words, but I couldn't take her adulation any longer. As I'd feared, her face fell. Under other circumstances I might've enjoyed rendering Miss Georgette speechless. Finally she found her words, shrieking, "You're what?"

Only a handful of people remained in the sanctuary, but each and every one of them looked our way, including John, who'd been putting his guitar back in its case. Knowing Miss Georgette, she would spread the word to everyone else later in the day. Or maybe, since she treated gossip like her job, she took the Sabbath off. Who knew?

"I'm pregnant. With child."

"Are you and Chad getting back together?"

"No."

"Oh, thank goodness." Relief gave way to curiosity. "But surely you don't want that sweet baby to be born illegitimate."

I could think of nothing more legitimate than to keep my baby and my person away from Chadwick Love. I'd briefly considered letting her think that Chad was the father to avoid this conversation or the one that would come next, but not admitting the truth would mean living a lie, and I was done with those.

"Chad is not the father," I said.

"Not the father!" Her wail echoed off the glass windows. "What has gotten into you?"

John skirted an arrangement of lilies and started making his way down the aisle.

"Nothing has gotten into me." Except sperm. That happened. "I won't treat this baby like a mistake. I'm only telling you so, if you see my child as a mistake, you can stop being proud of me."

"Stop being proud of you?"

For a second I feared her shriek might shatter windows. Heads swiveled in our direction again. John had almost reached us.

"I messed up. I admit it. I am not perfect," I said at a whisper, trying to not make our conversation anymore public than it already was.

She paused, her mouth opening and closing like a catfish pulled from a pond. "Well, who *is* the father?"

"I am."

Miss Georgette's eyes bulged from her head. I leaned back into John, and he wrapped a protective arm around me. I had to admit it felt nice for someone to have my back. I felt 100 percent better knowing that he stood with me against Miss Georgette's shock and admonition.

She shook her head, the giant cross earrings she wore swinging in condemnation. Then she turned to me. "So. You're the reason this sweet boy fell off the wagon. Well. Bless his heart."

Bless *his* heart?

All my life I had gone to great lengths to keep my heart from being blessed. Even so, I would grit my teeth and bear it. No way, however, was anyone going to pity John O'Brien. Sure, he'd had the misfortune to hook up with me, but he deserved better than a passive-aggressive insult to his intelligence for doing so.

"Know what? Bless *your* heart. Bless it for being in the middle of everyone else's business."

I slapped away John's arm, turned on my heel, and walked out of the church with my head held high.

chapter 28

I slammed the door on my way back into the house, which wasn't very Eastery of me, but the drive from First Baptist to the house hadn't been long enough to cool me down. In the process, two pictures fell off the wall and a decorative mirror to boot.

Great. As if I needed seven years of bad luck after the previous ten.

"Posey Lucille, what do you think you are doing?" my mother said from the doorway where she stood with an apron around her waist and a spatula in one hand.

"I'm sorry, Mom," I said, as I picked up the two pictures first—glass cracked but not shattered—and then went to work on picking up the mirror pieces.

"Seriously, I think you were sixteen the last time you slammed a door."

I paused. "I just wanted to go back to church, to see if I could still fit in there. The service was lovely. The Lord spoke to me. People kept hugging me and welcoming me back. Then Miss Georgette walked up."

"Uh-oh," Rain said. She now stood behind Mom wearing an oven mitt in the shape of a T-Rex head.

"She started carrying on about how proud she was of me, and I couldn't take it anymore. I told her."

"Told her what?" Rain asked suspiciously.

And I'd somehow not told my little sister my news in the craziness of the past few days.

"You, girl. Metamucil," Granny said from the chair where she sat watching Bob Barker once again.

"I'll get it," Mom said. "Hand me the mitt so I can check on the rolls, too."

Rain relinquished her T-Rex and crossed her arms over her chest.

"Baby sister, you're going to be an aunt," I said.

"Really?" she shrieked and crossed the living room to give me a hug. I had to wave her off because I still held the mirror shards. Then she followed me to the kitchen and tried to squeeze the life out of me once I'd gotten rid of the sharp pieces. Just as quickly she stepped back. "Wait a second, why am I the last to know?"

"You were at Santiago's house. I didn't mean to tell Miss Georgette before you."

"Did Mom know?"

"Yes."

"Henny?"

I sighed. "Yes. You were at work the day Granny went walkabout. It's been a busy, stressful two days. I've barely kept my head above water."

"Oh, fine. You're forgiven. This is what you've always wanted, isn't it? It isn't Chad's, is it? Oh, John. Is he treating you right? If he isn't then I will kick his ass, and you can tell him I said that—"

"Language, Rain," my mother said. She'd probably tried peyote and knew which mushrooms were which, but she wasn't keen on curse words. A mystery wrapped inside an enigma, my mother.

"John is treating me just fine." He'd even come to my rescue only to have me throw off his arm. I shouldn't have done that.

"Then what happened at church?"

I told them what happened ending with how I'd been the blesser of hearts for once.

"Bad. Ass!" Rain said, her hand over her mouth in shocked delight.

"Being pregnant has made you sassy," said Mom.

"I hope so," I said.

"Probably another girl," she said.

A girl? Huh.

"Where's Henny?" Rain asked, nodding at the empty place at the table.

"I don't know. I don't remember if he came home last night or not," Mom said. "I thought he said he'd be here, that he had a day off before he had to go back to the night shift."

Our eyes locked, but I wasn't about to tell grandmother or sister that Mom couldn't remember because she'd been into the sauce.

"I'm right here," Henny said with a yawn. "I wasn't about to miss Easter Dinner, although I may fall asleep in the middle of it."

I studied my brother once again. Tired, but he still looked clean.

"Deviled eggs, yes!" he said.

"Ham?" Granny asked.

"Mother, you know we don't have meat in this household," Mom said. "It's cruel to animals and not good for you, either."

"Cruel? No ham," she muttered before stopping to stare off into space. Rain started to feed her mashed potatoes just as I'd fed her oatmeal the day before, and I made a note to get some ham and shred it very, very fine and sneak it into her grits.

Henny was on his third deviled egg, and I was glad Mom was vegetarian rather than vegan because her mashed potatoes tasted of butter and love. I filled up on those and green beans and biscuits, making a note that my baby-to-be tolerated—even enjoyed—each of those things.

I paused. "No one move."

I ran back to the bedroom and found my old digital camera, rushing back to the kitchen. Sure enough, if I put it on the counter and set the timer, then I'd be able to get a picture of all of us. I bent over to double check the angle. "Henny move just a little to the left so I can see Rain. Mom, turn around."

I didn't bother with Granny. She would do as she wanted to do. I set the timer then rushed back to my seat, putting a smile on my face just before the flash.

"There. I wanted to capture this moment for always. When was the last time we were all in a picture together?"

"I don't know, but it's been too long," Mom said.

Rain helped Granny back to the living room while I started the dishes. I'd hardly cleared the table when the doorbell rang. Mom went to get it but soon returned. "John wants to see you."

I snorted. "Tell him I'm busy."

"I'll do the dishes. You go talk to the father of your child. He's on the porch."

With a heavy sigh I dried my hands and walked out, making sure not to slam the front door this time since I couldn't afford to replace the picture frames I'd already broken much less anything new.

"Hey."

He wore scuffed cowboy boots, distressed denim, and a dress shirt with rolled up sleeves. He'd let his hair down. I tamped down a sigh of longing. I thought John O'Brien had given me the one gift I'd always wanted, but it seemed I wanted more. "Hey."

He patted a spot beside him on the porch swing, but I stood. Finally, he said, "I was worried about you."

"Worried about me?"

"You took off like a bat out of Hades. I didn't know what to think."

"I had to get out of there. I'd had a great morning and then Miss Georgette started with the judging. After all, I'm the reason 'that sweet boy fell off the wagon.'"

He winced. "Please have a seat."

I sat, but our weight wasn't quite distributed so the swing didn't move evenly, my side always a little ahead or behind his.

"Sometimes I wish we could start over," he finally said.

"How's that?" I asked.

"Well, maybe if we'd rediscovered each other at a time when you weren't trying to divorce Chad and I wasn't in recovery, maybe we could've made a go of this."

"And if frogs had wings they wouldn't bump their butts when they jumped," I murmured, echoing one of Granny's favorite expressions.

"What?"

"Nothing. Besides, we're too broken for each other, remember?"

The swing went still. He turned and kissed me. Desire shot through my body in an instant, but he soon broke off the kiss. "Is this love or lust?"

"Yes."

"What?"

I stood up and paced on the far side of the porch. "I don't know, John. There's definitely lust. Or is it love? Would I know what love is if it were to hit me upside the head?"

He exhaled deeply. "I shouldn't have come."

"Why did you?"

"I told you. I was worried about you."

"That sounds more like love than lust," I said, my hands on my hips.

"There was some lust in there, too."

I thought of how I'd rationalized sleeping with him the day before. I wouldn't get any more pregnant so what did we have to lose? We had a lot to lose. We had to maintain a civil relationship so our child would have two parents even if we didn't end up living in the same house. "Look, John, your sponsor's right. Your first priority is to stay sober."

"What about you? What is your first priority?"

"To make sure our baby is born healthy," I said. Even as I said the words, the "our" surprised me. Knowing how to properly be pregnant—no caffeine, no alcohol, no deli meats, take a walk every day, drink plenty of water, etc.—was almost second nature to me after all of the years of research I'd done. All of that time, though, I'd thought in terms of "my" baby. But with John everything was different. Or maybe it could've been if our situation were.

He nodded, his hands balled in fists as he stood. "And you'll tell me if you need me?"

"Of course."

"Can I—" He hesitated but eventually found the words, "Can I be there when you get the ultrasounds and things like that?"

"I hadn't thought you'd want to go, but yes."

He frowned, hurt that I'd thought he wouldn't want to be there, and some light seeped into the cracks of my own brokenness.

"What about Lamaze?"

Someone had been doing Internet research. "I don't think so. Mom can go with me."

"Thank God."

I stared him down. He wasn't about to be my Lamaze partner, but he didn't have to be so excited about it.

"I mean, I wasn't ready for this—"

"Stop while you're ahead."

He ran a hand through his hair in frustration. "I don't know what I'm doing here. I can raise plants and tune pianos, but I don't know how to be a father."

"I wish I knew how to instruct you, but I never had one."

"Mine's gone."

"Then we're in a pickle, aren't we? Let's start with ultrasounds and keeping you sober." My tone of voice came out sharper than I'd intended. I shouldn't resent John for focusing on his sobriety, but I did.

"I'm thinking I should go," he said.

"Probably a good idea."

"But you'll call me?"

"Of course."

He walked down the flagstone path and under the lattice arch that led to the sidewalk. A part of me wanted to shout for him to come back, but I didn't—probably remnants of that pride that had gotten me into so much trouble. Besides, I had to figure out how to do things on my own, a tricky proposition since I was on the cusp of being in charge of another human being.

Odd that on a day of rebirth I felt as though so many things had died.

chapter 29

Tuesday morning before the sun rose, I sat at my borrowed desk putting together sub plans. Later that day, I had my appointment with the doctor that would confirm my pregnancy, something that simply had to be true based on my current desire for nothing more than Saltines and Sprite.

"A word, Ms. Love?"

Ms. Varner leaned against the door frame casually.

"Of course, come in. I mean, it's your school so, of course, you can come in, but you know what I mean."

Her heels clicked against the floor as she walked across the room and took a seat in the chair in front of the computer, rolling it around so she could face me. "Why haven't you submitted an application for next year?"

My heart sped up with hope. "I thought, well, surely you *know* that I'm pregnant. Miss Georgette said—"

"Miss Georgette is retired," Ms. Varner said crisply. "I value her opinion, but she comes from a time when the pool of possible candidates was far deeper than it is now."

"So I'm not automatically out of a job because I'm pregnant?"

"Ms. Love, if Yessum County were to fire every teacher who got unexpectedly pregnant, we'd fire at least two teachers a year."

Hope swelled again.

"I really do love this job, and I could use the insurance."

Ms. Varner stood. "Then I'd suggest you turn in an application."

"I will," I said.

She nodded and walked back out.

My heart beat so loudly I felt it in my ears, but I couldn't wipe the smile from my face. All was not lost.

It took over an hour to prod me, poke me, question me about my life history, and confirm my pregnancy. Then the doctor weighed me down with a packet full of instructions, coupons, and classes. Even so, I beamed as I walked out the door. This was it. I was going to have a baby. Maybe it wasn't the perfect circumstances, but, then again, maybe I needed less than perfect circumstances to offset years of reading up on pregnancy and thinking I would be able to control every aspect of motherhood. Goodness knew I didn't suffer from that misconception now.

Even better, I liked Dr. Kim and her nurse, Clarice. Liza had suggested her own OB since I obviously couldn't go back to the doctor I'd been seeing. It might've been worth it to see the look on his face when I turned up pregnant after he told me I couldn't conceive, but I doubted it. I still intended to write a very sharply worded letter to the state medical board.

I did not, however, expect to see Liza herself in the parking lot. She strapped Nathaniel's seat into position then closed the van door and slumped against it.

"Liza?"

She immediately stood up, but I couldn't miss the tears rolling down her cheeks.

"What's wrong?"

She sniffed. "I can't tell you. It wouldn't be nice to tell you."

"Tell me you don't have cancer or some kind of disease. Liza Marie, I swear—"

"I'm pregnant."

She collapsed into my arms, and I patted her back, stunned. "Already?"

"Yes," she said miserably. "I can't have another baby. I'm not doing a good job with this one."

"Okay, you're going to sit in this van and roll down the windows. I'm going to sit with you until you're calm enough to drive."

We sat in the car, and she rolled down the windows. Her van was fancy enough that she could even roll down the side window a little. It wasn't that hot of a day, but we still had a baby in the car.

"I have to go. He's going to wake up and I'm going to have to feed him and I only have one diaper left and no more clean outfits and—"

"Liza, you have to breathe. You have to calm down first."

She took in jagged breaths and released them too quickly. Finally, those breaths began to even out. "You must think I'm horrible. You've wanted babies all this time and here I am complaining about another one. I am awful. I should be grateful."

"You get to feel however you want to feel. I can completely understand why you're so upset. We just got the big man to sleep through the night and here you are looking to do it again?"

"Doc said he may have stopped sleeping through the night because the pregnancy's keeping me from producing as much milk and that I should look into weaning him to formula."

"So?"

"So, you know babies are supposed to have breast milk! I can't give him formula."

"Liza, your mother gave *you* formula," I said.

"Exactly. Just look how neurotic I turned out." She banged her head on the steering wheel, which made the horn go off. The baby cried, but went back to sleep.

"Honey, that's the hormones talking. At least we'll be pregnant together."

"That's not good! That's bad, very bad. We'll burn the whole town down when the grocery store runs out of Rocky Road, and it will be because we're both pregnant at the same time!"

"I'll drive to Jefferson for Rocky Road. We'll eat it together while we watch *Tangled*."

"I do have a crush on Flynn Rider."

"Don't we all, Liza. Don't we all."

"I guess I could text you to see if you're awake in the dark of night when I can't sleep," she grumbled.

"Of course, you can. I'll have to answer because I owe you for all the times I woke up this baby."

Just when I thought I had her calmed down, she exclaimed, "Oh, God. I hadn't even thought about school. I'm going to have to find another supply teacher. Do you know how hard it is to find someone who can teach chemistry around here?"

"It will be okay. Promise."

"I'm not going to make it."

"Of course you are. Have you told Owen?"

"No," she moaned. "But when I do, I'm going to tell him it's all your fault."

"My fault?"

"Yes, I got pregnant that night you watched the baby. We didn't end up going out. I ordered Chinese, and he brought beer. But he forgot the condoms."

"So, you're really saying it's his fault."

She sighed. "Technically, but I have to live with him. It's much easier to throw you under the bus."

There. That was more like the Liza I knew and loved.

"Are you going to be okay to drive home now?"

"Yeah, and I'm not going to tell him it's your fault."

"So kind of you," I said as I opened the passenger side door. "Cheer up, bestie. It's going to be a tandem pregnancy."

"I'm not going to ride one of those damned bikes for two with you, if that's what you're thinking."

I grinned. I'd been after Liza to try one of those bicycles with me since fifth grade. I got out of her van and shut the door but then leaned against it.

"Dammit, I can't drink for another eight months," Liza muttered. "And today of all days I could really use a drink."

"Getting drunk is so overrated," I said.

"Can't go pole dancing now, either."

"Thank goodness for that."

"You are no fun." Liza jabbed her key into the ignition. "You're going to be one of those pregnant mothers who actually makes the oatmeal raisin cookies with freaking applesauce and then tries to convince herself that her cravings are satisfied."

"And you are one grumpy pregnant lady. You aren't getting any of my healthy cookies."

"Oh, screw you," Liza said as she started the car.

"Glad to help you transition from tears to anger," I said. "Let me know when you're ready to commiserate and eat some Oreos."

Liza paused, then looked at me. "Posey Adams, there's no one I'd rather be tandemly pregnant with."

"Back atcha, Liza Hagood."

She peeled out of the parking lot, and I waved even though I knew I'd see her soon. She might still be working through her stages of disbelief, but I was happy to be pregnant with Liza, too. Hagood and Adams, together again. I chuckled at how we'd defaulted to our maiden names. Maybe she and I would raise two more girls who'd be best friends and roam the halls of Yessum County High together as we once had. If I did have a girl, though, her lesson on those who gaslight would immediately precede our chat about the birds and the bees.

chapter 30

"Mabel?" Granny asked. That May afternoon we all sat in the garden of Meadowlark Village, an assisted-living and memory care facility in Jefferson. I preferred the garden to the interior of the building. No matter how hard the staff worked, no amount of air freshener could overcome the smell of disinfectant, sickness, and age. I didn't want to leave my grandmother there, but she now spent almost all of her time in another world. No more requests for Tom Brokaw or Godiva chocolates, although she'd eaten some of the latter just the day before. She didn't even clamor for pot roast or a "nice ham" anymore, but I'd finely shredded some ham in her grits just that morning anyway.

"Mabel doesn't work for us anymore," Mom said.

"Hmph."

As recently as a month ago, Granny would've gone on a diatribe about how that no-good Mabel had never worked for anyone. Miranda, the nurse, however, had worked very hard to help us keep Granny home. As her reward, Granny had bitten her the week before, further confirmation we could no longer put off the inevitable.

"She says she'll come visit you," Mom said.

Granny looked away, her attention drawn to the tidy garden with its bird feeder and butterfly weed.

A nurse walked the short distance between the patio and the garden. "It's time."

"I don't know if I can," my mom said, all choked up.

"If you make a big production of leaving then she may become agitated. Besides, you're not actually saying goodbye," the nurse said as she stepped behind Granny's wheelchair and put her hands on the handles. Leaning over to talk to Granny she said, "Let's take a look at the grounds, shall we?"

Mom watched as her mother was pushed away, and we started walking back to the facility. Rain looked over her shoulder twice. Henny had crammed his hands in his pockets. I put an arm around Mom's shoulders, and we disappeared into Meadowlark Village, walking past a commons area where some folks watched baseball and others played dominoes. We said nothing until we got out into the parking lot.

"That was awful," Mom said before collapsing into tears.

Rain hugged her first, "It'll be okay, Mami."

"You're doing the right thing," Henny said as he took a turn. "You've been running yourself ragged trying to take care of her, and now it's just too much. She'll be fine. Promise."

"And what do you have to say, Posey?"

"Nothing." I hugged her instead.

"I've got to go to work," Rain said, giving me a wink that no one else could see. She had worked her way up to an instructor position. They were even talking about flying her to studios in other cities to train other instructors. She'd declined any appointments other than summer ones because she was headed to college in the fall.

"Me, too," Henny said with a sigh. He'd managed to work his way to shifts that started at seven and went until three in the morning. He assured me this was an improvement, but I couldn't see how.

My siblings each hugged Mom once more before heading to their respective cars.

"You gonna leave me, too?"

I winced. "Actually, Liza invited me over for an adult slumber party," I said. "We're going to watch bad movies and do each other's nails."

"Then I guess I'll go it alone."

I hadn't thought about that. Mom, alone in the big house all by herself? "Rain will be back by midnight."

"I plan to be asleep by then. Maybe I'll catch up on my reading."

She didn't say much on the way home or when I dropped her off. Before I started for Liza's house, though, I took a minute to make a phone call.

"Hello, Santiago?"

"You did not call him," Liza said.

"Totally did. Told him she was depressed and that he might want to check on her," I said as I carefully applied a nail polish called "Trophy Wife" to Liza's toes.

"What if the two of them get into another fight?"

"Won't be a problem. Her car's in the shop, and I hid the whiskey." I put the cap back on the polish and leaned backward to stretch my back muscles.

"Remind me never to piss you off," Liza muttered as she wiggled her toes, now painted a metallic teal.

"Wise words, I'm a new woman."

Liza cocked her head to the side. "I think you've been a new woman ever since you told Miss Georgette off. I hate that I missed it."

"If I'd known how exhilarating it would be to bless some hearts, I would've gotten into that business a long time ago." I sat back on the couch and pulled up the footrest. I might've hated the leather, but I missed the footrest. Mom's ottoman had a way of wandering off when I tried to put my feet up. "She still carrying on about that?"

"To anyone who will listen, but everyone who's spoken to me is disappointed that you haven't come back to church since Easter."

"Look, I'll get there eventually, but I have a lot of memories to overcome."

"That and you might run into John."

"Whatever."

Liza took an Oreo and passed me the package. "If you're over the age of thirty, you don't get to use the word *whatever* unless it's ironically."

"Whatever." I took an Oreo and passed the package back to her.

"And when are you legally a free woman?"

"What is this? Twenty questions? I thought we were supposed to be doing girl stuff like, I don't know, painting my nails. Last time you *forgot*."

"Gotta let my toenails dry first," she said. "Believe me, you're going to appreciate this arrangement in a few months when you won't be able to even see your toes, much less paint them. Court date?"

"June second."

"Want me to come?"

"Nope. Ben says I don't even have to go, but I will to make sure a certain someone doesn't show off his jackass tendencies."

"That's fair."

Down the hall, a pitiful cry crescendoed into a wail. "Could you? My toes are still wet."

I doubted they were, but I didn't mind getting the baby.

"Gonna get that job you wanted?" asked Liza when I came back with a freshly changed but still fretting baby boy. She lifted her shirt enough to nurse the child.

"I don't know," I said as I looked away. I'd seen Liza's nipples so many times I felt confident I'd be able to pick them out in a lineup. I didn't think I could be so blasé about nursing, but we were all about to find out.

"Well, New Posey needs to get crackin' and ask that principal if she's going to have a job."

"New Posey *wants* to watch a mindless movie and then fall asleep."

"Solid plan," Liza said with a yawn.

She was going to fall asleep before she did my nails yet again. I wondered how she would feel about little Sharpie-drawn mustaches on hers.

chapter 31

On the last day of school, I teared up while my students and I sang "See Ya Later, Alligator." At the last bell, I let them leave with a sentiment that could only be described as bittersweet. They'd done so well, and I'd enjoyed being a part of their lives. I touched the clover necklace that Maricela had made for me during recess. It was itchy and starting to droop, but she'd worked so hard on it that I wasn't about to take it off until she'd left for the day. Out of impulse, I took out my camera and took a selfie of myself wearing the necklace before finally letting it go.

I picked up the drawing of a T-Rex that Noah had drawn for me. I'd be putting it on the fridge for everyone in the family to see. His mother still scowled every time I ran into her at the grocery store, but I didn't let that bother me. Her son had given me a hug on the way out the door, and that was the part that mattered—this after I'd teased him by saying I thought the velociraptor was an even more fierce dinosaur than the T-Rex. He'd stuck his tongue out at me on the way out the door, but then he'd grinned.

I packed up my sparse belongings, including the items I'd bought with my own money. I still didn't know if I would get the job for the next year.

Which was ridiculous.

I needed to know one way or another so I could make arrangements, know whether or not to accept a position in another county if it were offered to me.

Once I had both purse and bag over my shoulder, I walked down the hall to see Ms. Varner. Since I was a supply teacher, I didn't have to stay for the next two days to pack up. This was my last day, and I wasn't going to leave without knowing where I stood. Maybe Old Posey would've slunk home and waited for someone to call her, but Liza was right: New Posey needed answers.

I pushed past the secretary and rapped on Ms. Varner's desk. "I'm here to turn in my key."

"You can hand that off to the secretary," the principal said without even looking up. How did she get her hair to stay slicked back into a bun? I would've had enough wispies for a whole new head of hair.

"I also wanted to know about the second grade position for next year."

Ms. Varner looked up, her stern expression enough to make even adults quail. "What about it?"

I took a deep breath. "I know that you probably have a lot of people who are qualified for and interested in the job, but I want it and need it more than they do. If you hire me, you won't regret it."

She leaned back in her chair and smiled. "There. That's what I've been looking for."

"What?"

"Confidence. As it turns out I had already requested approval to offer you the job and was only waiting on the Board to meet. So I assume I'll be seeing you in the fall?"

"Really?" I took a step forward to hug her, but she held out a palm to stop me.

"Oh, don't spoil it now. Heather said to tell you not to worry about the classroom. She's coming in tomorrow to take everything down and make sure all of the records are in order. You are officially off for the summer, but your homework is to find a supply teacher just as capable as you are to take your place while you're on maternity leave."

"Yes, ma'am."

She waved me out of the room, and I clutched my heart. New Posey could get things done.

New Posey's exuberance lasted all of two minutes.

There, leaning against my car was Chadwick Love. A jolt of panic stopped me dead in my tracks. I tamped it down and reached in my purse for my phone. My fingers closed over the Taser, but I could only use it as a last resort because nothing would please him more than taking it to use against me. Instead I dialed nine-one-one as I walked across the parking lot, hoping that I looked as though I were talking to Liza.

"Posey," he grinned as if we were old pals and nothing had ever gone wrong between us.

"Chad." I dropped my phone into my purse even as the dispatcher called for me. I hoped nothing jostled the buttons enough to disconnect the call.

"I'm gonna need to move in with you this afternoon."

"No."

He frowned. "I need a place to stay, as you well know."

"Stay with your other woman. Also, you're in violation of my restraining order yet again, not that it surprises me that you think certain rules don't apply to you."

He scratched the back of his head, looking sheepish for once. "I, uh, can't stay with Naomi. She kicked me out."

"Good. Now move away from my car so I can go home."

"I don't understand why you're so mad about all of this. We had some good times, too, didn't we?"

"Off the top of my head I can't think of any. All I can think of is the time you assaulted me." I reached into my purse, and he flinched. Obviously he remembered the Taser, too.

Old Posey would've caved. She would've given him the benefit of the doubt.

New Posey saw all of his tricks and his uneven charm for what they were. "Move."

He leaned back against the car and cross his arms over his chest. "I don't think I will."

In the distance, sirens blared, getting louder as they approached. I smiled.

He grabbed my arm, his fingers digging into flesh hard enough to make me gasp. "You didn't."

"I did. Now let me go."

He dug his fingers in harder, and I rammed my knee into his groin as hard as I possibly could. He let go of my arm and crumpled to the parking lot, one of the most satisfying scenes of my life to date. "Stop coming after me. I'm not the girl you used to push around anymore."

chapter 32

On June second, I stepped outside the courthouse a free woman. Shielding my eyes against the blinding sun, I half expected John O'Brien to show up with a Justice of the Peace.

He didn't.

Next I looked over my shoulder to see if Chad had shown up.

He hadn't.

The corners of my mouth turned up into a smile of their own accord, and I began to hum. Never mind the fact I couldn't carry a tune in a bucket, a song in my heart bubbled up to the surface, and I was glad I'd chosen to walk because the warm weather perfectly matched my mood. Putting a hand on my belly that was just beginning to protrude, I took the stairs carefully and started walking the three blocks back to First Baptist.

As it turned out, the Lord had a sense of humor that extended well beyond pregnant seahorse daddies or platypuses. Once I'd overcome the euphoria of knowing that I would be a teacher in the fall, I'd realized I would need a job for the summer months because supply pay ended on my last day and my new job wouldn't start paying until the end of August at the earliest. Since I didn't relish the idea of fighting teenagers for a fast food position, I tried Au Natural (my mother had finally hired Julia to be a jill-of-all-trades), the library (no dice), the dollar store (overqualified), and the grocery store (also overqualified). Where was a position available? First Baptist where their receptionist was out on maternity leave.

Truthfully, I hyperventilated out in the car on my first day because I couldn't stand the thought of another church reception desk or of facing people who might judge me. Once I'd reminded New Posey that she didn't have to put up with anyone's crap and that my erstwhile husband wasn't allowed within several feet of her, I'd gone inside and found laughter. Brother Mark, the new preacher, told the worst dad jokes but his secretary, Gigi, laughed anyway. Her laugh was so infectious that anyone nearby had to join her. So I'd been shown my new post with a smile.

Gigi showed me the ropes for the first day. One of the first things she told me was that I could read a book or surf Pinterest if I got bored just as long as I took care of answering the phones and any other tasks that needed to get done. From there we'd settled into an easy routine. Speaking of routines, it was Thursday and that meant Mrs. Morris would come by with Snickerdoodles. I picked up my pace because I did *not* want to miss those.

"Back from lunch?" Brother Mark asked when I took my seat behind the desk.

"Yes, I am."

No matter that I hadn't actually eaten lunch but had gone to court instead. Soon he would head out to visit church members in the hospital, and I would heat up leftovers for a lunch at my desk. With any luck, a Snickerdoodle would be my dessert.

"I know I've said it before," Brother Mark said, "But the Lord really blessed us when he sent you here. You know just what to do to keep everything running smoothly."

"Thank you," I said, warmed from the inside at such praise and glad that something good, no matter how tiny, had come out of my five miserable years doing the job elsewhere.

"Say, why do chicken coops only have two doors?" he asked, his hand already on the door handle.

"I don't know."

" 'Cuz otherwise they'd be chicken sedans!"

I had to groan, but one office over Gigi's high-pitched giggle rang out, and I couldn't help but grin. "Send my love to Mr. Fox, please."

"Will do," Brother Mark said as he walked out the door. Mr. Fox had been my seventh-grade English teacher and was in the hospital after having suffered a heart attack. At least everyone thought he was going to recover.

I heated up my meal and ate quickly, finishing up just in time for Mrs. Morris to come through. The older lady limped in; she'd had hip replacement surgery but had refused to finish her physical therapy. "Hey, Mama, I brought you some cookies."

She placed a container on my desk. Ah, Cool Whip bowls, the Tupperware of the South.

"Mrs. Morris, you are absolutely the best."

"Oh, no. This is all a devious plot to get you to name the baby Celeste after me."

I took a Snickerdoodle from its container and almost forgot to reply out of sugary euphoria, which, I was sure, was all a part of her plan to bring another Celeste into the world. "We don't even know if it's a boy or a girl yet!"

The "we" made me falter. John called to check on me once a week, but his calls were always short. We didn't plan to actually see each other until the August appointment when I'd have the ultrasound that told us if we'd be having a boy or a girl. Well, if *I* would be having a boy or girl. Best to remember I was going through many parts of this process alone.

"Celeste!" she shouted before hobbling down the hall to the Ladies' Ministry meeting.

"That would be an awkward name for a boy," I shouted down the hall.

I heard her uneven return, then she poked her head around the corner long enough to say, "Worked for Sue in that old song Johnny Cash sang."

Eh, the actual boy named Sue might disagree.

Miss Georgette pulled on the door that she ought to push. She gave me only a curt nod on her way to join the Ladies' Ministry. Abigail Bolton waved hello on her way in, and finally Amanda Kildare appeared. She, too, had come back to the fold. The former Homecoming Queen and I had a new ritual. She slapped a paranormal romance on my desk. I drew a historical from my purse underneath, and we swapped.

"I still think we should start a book club," she said.

"Maybe," I answered. "You keep those women on track. We gotta close early today."

"You know I will," she said, brandishing her new book with a grin. "I've got an appointment with a new book and a bubble bath."

Thirty minutes later, I could catch bits and pieces of the meeting down the hall. I ignored them as best I could, though, while I searched Pinterest for classroom ideas and drank decaf tea. When the door opened, I looked up sharply because I hadn't been expecting anyone. I certainly hadn't expected to see John. From the way he'd stopped dead in his tracks, I could be reasonably certain he hadn't expected to see me, either.

"What are you doing here?" he asked.

"Working here while Tammy settles in with her baby. What are *you* doing here?"

"The piano needs tuning," he said. "Actually several of them do."

"If I'd known you were coming, I would've made your brownies. Tammy didn't leave me a note on the calendar, though."

"Must've slipped her mind." He walked in the direction of the sanctuary but stopped. "It's a shame. I did love those brownies."

Did. Past tense.

"I could share my Snickerdoodles with you?"

"No, thanks," he said before disappearing into the sanctuary.

I tried to concentrate on Pinterest, but it wasn't working. I tried reading the romance Amanda had slipped me, but I couldn't concentrate. Edgy, I walked to Gigi's little office. "Got any copies I can run? Mailers? Anything?"

"We're all caught up, dear," she said. "And I'm about to head out the door for a wedding shower. Here's a check for John, and Vic'll lock up so you can go as soon as the ladies finish their meeting."

With nothing else to do, I went back to my seat. Voices traveled up the hall from the ladies' meeting. Tones wafted in from the sanctuary.

John hadn't mentioned if he'd really started going back to school to get a new degree or if he'd started looking for a new job. I was glad to see him still tuning pianos, his hair still long and his jeans still ripped. I only wished I hadn't wiped the smile from his face.

That wasn't all your fault.

No, but the two of us now were so different from those first few afternoons we'd spent together.

I snort-giggled at the memory of how he'd eased my apprehensions that first day by quoting *Song of Solomon.*

"Are you laughing at me?" Miss Georgette stood at the door.

I wasn't about to tell her I was laughing at the memory of "your navel is a goblet."

"No, ma'am. I wouldn't dare."

She harrumphed as she fumbled with the handle yet again. All I could think was . . .

Bless her heart.

The other ladies filed out, and I considered another Snickerdoodle. I had the container in my hands when the atonal pings of tuning stopped and John started playing a song. I sat as still as I possibly could, trying to discern what he played.

I finally managed to pick out the chorus, which I remembered as "He's the Lily of the Valley, the Bright and Morning Star . . ."

I didn't recognize it at first because he was playing the song as a dirge. There was something about that line, though, that I couldn't quite put my finger on so I did what any self-respecting eavesdropping receptionist would do: I Googled it.

Oh.

Rose of Sharon, Lily of the Valley.

Those names came from *Song of Solomon.*

Old Posey would probably take this moment to cry for what could've been.

New Posey could see the merit in such a course of action, but she read through all of *Song of Solomon* instead until she found a few verses she liked. In the end, I wrote "by night on my bed I sought him whom my soul loveth: I sought him, but I found him not" and slipped the note into the envelope that contained John's check. Either he still felt as I did, or he didn't. At this point I knew I *could* live without him, but that didn't mean I wanted to.

On his way out I handed him the envelope. "Thank you very much for keeping our pianos melodic."

"My pleasure. So, are you doing okay?"

"I'm fine, really. Probably going to kick the last of this morning sickness soon."

"That's good, that's good," he said, but his voice felt distant.

"Got my divorce today," I blurted, inwardly chastising myself for tipping my hand.

"Congratulations." His eyes met mine briefly, but he was obviously uncomfortable. I half wanted to take the envelope back, but he mumbled his goodbye and retreated before I could think of a way to get it back. He'd probably played "Lily of the Valley" for any of a hundred different reasons, not the least of which was that it was a good Baptist hymn. I was a fool who read too much into things.

It reminded me of when Julia complimented me for being open and trusting.

She also told you those were good qualities, that you only needed to be more discerning.

Pretty sure giving a guy quotes from *Song of Solomon* was less than discerning.

What was done was done.

I picked up my purse and headed for home.

"The house is so quiet without Granny," Mom said.

"We're going to lose Rain to college soon, too."

"She's never here anyway," Mom said as she placed a serving

of vegetarian lasagna on my plate next to a salad made with let-
tuce from her backyard garden. "Then you're going to run off
and leave me all alone."

"Mom!"

"At least I'll still have Henny," she said in a loud voice.

"Huh? What?" my brother said from the living room where
he'd fallen asleep in the recliner.

"Supper," I called.

"Any meat in the lasagna this time?"

I passed him a plate. "You know the answer to that. Also, if I
have to eat salad, then you do, too."

I didn't mind the salad, but I had as a child. It'd been fun to
make my younger brother eat his salad because I was eating mine.
Took him almost a year to eat dressing, which meant a year's worth
of watching him make faces while he ate his salad dry.

"Pass the ranch," he said just as the doorbell rang. I tossed him
the bottle and went to get the door.

There stood John O'Brien with a bottle of sparkling cider. "As
the apple tree among the trees of the wood, so is my beloved?"

I leaned against the doorway with a smile.

"I know, I know," he said. "I was looking for something about
apples because you once said the minute you were a free woman
you'd be on my doorstep with a bottle of sparkling cider. I hate
the stuff, but I'll drink it if it means we can try this again."

"Well, it's really hard to say no to the Lily of the Valley."

He hung his head. "You heard that, huh?"

"Yeah," I said as I took a step closer. "Brushing up on your
Song of Solomon?"

"Duh, they have this whole section about how your hair is like
a flock of goats."

"Thank you?"

"And your breasts are like twin roes, and—"

"Just kiss me," I said.

He drew me into his arms, and we fit together even before his
lips met mine.

"I've missed you," he said, once we both came up for air. We took a seat on the porch swing, and this time we managed to get it to move back and forth evenly—probably because we were sitting so closely together.

"I've missed you, too."

"Does this mean—"

"If you are about to make one of your patently unromantic marriage proposals, stop right there. I'm not saying never, but not until we figure some things out."

"If I ever propose to you again, it's going to be so romantic, you're not going to know what hit you," he said. "At this point, it's a challenge."

"In that case, I'm sorry. What were you saying?"

"Well, I was going to invite you to come live with me so I could help you take care of our baby when he's born."

"One, you don't know that we're going to have a son. Second, I don't think so."

He put a hand on my belly. "It'd be easier to continue knowing each other biblically if we were living in sin."

I laughed out loud. "I've already had enough of sins, deadly, original, or otherwise."

"What if I told you the dog misses you."

"Mmmm, I do like that dog."

"What if I told you that *I* missed you?"

"I'd say, let's see how we feel in three months."

"You're on."

His lips touched mine, and I almost couldn't breathe from happiness. I had everything I could ever want or need in that moment on that porch swing, and if anyone had a problem with how I'd arrived at such blessings?

Well.

Bless her heart.

Mrs. Morris's Snickerdoodles*

You will need . . .

1½ cups sugar
½ cup butter, softened
1 teaspoon vanilla
2 eggs
2¾ cups of all-purpose flour
1 teaspoon cream of tartar
½ teaspoon baking soda
¼ teaspoon salt
2 tablespoons powdered sugar
2 teaspoons cinnamon

1. Preheat the oven to 300 degrees.
2. In a large bowl, combine the first 4 ingredients (sugar, butter, vanilla, eggs).
3. Stir in flour, cream of tartar, baking soda, and salt.
4. Blend well.
5. Shape into 1-inch balls. (An ice-cream scoop can make this process *much* easier.)
6. Combine sugar and cinnamon, then roll each ball in the sugar and cinnamon mixture. Coat thoroughly.
7. Place 2 inches apart on an ungreased cookie sheet.
8. Bake at 300 degrees for 15 minutes or until edges are set. Immediately remove from the cookie sheet.

Notes: Depending on your oven, baking the cookies at 350 for 10 minutes might be a better option. You may also want to put the dough in the freezer for just a few minutes before you start rolling it into balls. You can also put the cookie balls in the freezer on a cookie sheet for a few minutes and then store them frozen until you're ready to bake them. I've heard this is good for portion control, and, remember, one of the messages of this book is all things in moderation.

*Okay, this recipe doesn't really belong to Mrs. Morris. Thanks to Leslie L. McKee for sharing her recipe, and to Jeanne Myers and Lynne Ernst for adding some detail. For this book, I contribute the following: SpaghettiOs (open the can and heat up—if you dare) and Thin Mint Brownie Mix (open box, follow instructions).

BLESS HER HEART

Sally Kilpatrick

ABOUT THIS GUIDE

The suggested questions are included to
enhance your group's reading of
Sally Kilpatrick's *Bless Her Heart*.

DISCUSSION QUESTIONS

1. Posey decides to give up church for Lent and to sample being bad rather than good. Can you sympathize with her choice? Do you think you would've made the same decisions?

2. *Song of Solomon* starts as a joke between John and Posey but becomes more important throughout the story. Is that a book of the Bible you've read? Do you think that Christianity stifles sexuality or reveres it? Or both?

3. In what way do you think being married to a self-proclaimed pastor blurred the lines between religion and marriage for Posey?

4. If Posey's family and friends noticed that Chad was isolating her from them, what responsibility—if any—did they have to intervene on her behalf? Should they have? If so, how do you think Posey would've reacted to such an intervention?

5. Do you know someone like Chad? If you were Liza, what would you have told Posey? Or would you have been quiet for fear of losing the friendship?

6. Novels, especially romance novels, influence Posey throughout the story. Have you ever read a book that profoundly affected your life or how you view the world?

7. Have you read *that* book? What did you think? Do you think what a person reads should influence his or her job prospects?

8. Have you ever had a tarot reading? If not, would you?

9. When Posey has a yard sale, John tells her that the records she was about to sell for fifty cents each are worth a lot more. What's the biggest steal you've found at a yard sale?

10. Which character did you empathize with most and why? Is that character your favorite? Why or why not?

11. Do you think that John and Posey could've had their happily ever after earlier if they'd gotten together sooner or do you think each one of them had to live through the bad times to appreciate the good?

12. Not knowing her father haunts Posey. Do you think that not knowing him influences some of her decisions for good or for ill?

13. Have you lived your life sheltered like Posey or more adventurously like Rain? Do you think either way of life is right or wrong? Why?

14. It takes Chad's leaving to wake Posey up, but what are some incidents that show she's empowering herself? Did you find her sympathetic or did you lose patience with her?

15. Miss Georgette sparks Posey's return to teaching, a job she loves, but she also shames Posey at the end. What do you think about Miss Georgette and her meddling? Is she good, bad, both, neither?

16. At both the beginning and the end of the story Posey is sitting at a receptionist desk in a church. What's different? Is anything the same?